Death by Culture Shock
a novel

by Kyle S. Colgan

Cover & Interior design by Vinnie Corbo
Cover Artwork by Hafsa Khan (HafandHaf)
Author photo by Lianne Remen

Published by Volossal Publishing
www.volossal.com

Publisher's Note

Death by Culture Shock is a work of fiction. Names of characters, places, and incidents are products of the author's imagination or are used fictitiously. Any resemblance to actual events, locales, or persons, living or dead, is entirely coincidental.

To Fariha, without whom this book would not exist.

"Dreams are the facts from which we must proceed."
        - Carl Jung

"...at the entrance to death's public domain...every plagiarized fear, every beautiful guess...the devil is not sending his best...that an angel is whatever reminds you of one."
        - Father John Misty

I

Death of an Old Man

On some Wednesday in March of the previous year, Kajal's father, Hussein, died from a sudden cardiac arrest. He had returned from the hospital from an elective surgery to remove a bag that had been attached to his gallbladder for the previous five months, due to an infection that had hospitalized him. Lying in the hospital bed, he complained of the pain. The infection had affected his brain making him take on the persona of an infantile boy. It disturbed Kajal to see her father like this but it didn't stop her from visiting him every chance she could. Always making sure he was eating. Talking to him in a gentle tone of voice. She would bring her boyfriend, Dale, with her for support and Hussein spoke to them, crying while reflecting on the Beatles, life in the 60's and Central Park.

Hussein's doctors had given him opioid-induced hallucinogens for the pain and he had visions of his mother coming to visit him. He kept this a secret from the nurses, who shushed him any time he spoke. No one believed him when he told them. His mother wore a lightly covered veil and smelled of goat salan. She stood beside his bed and touched his forearm gently to comfort him when he was alone. And when Kajal and Dale would visit Hussein, his mother watched from the corner of her son's room to give them all space; not wanting to distract her son from his daughter. Knowing the moments where they could engage in this form were diminishing as time went on.

During their visits, Hussein would share his food with Dale and Kajal; never losing his sense of hospitality. To give Kajal time with her father, Dale would sit in silence, looking at the boats cruising past the hospital in the East River from the room's window, while Kajal sat next to her father, her hand on his wrist, speaking to him quietly in Urdu.

On the day he died, Hussein was brought home by his son Ayad, Kajal's younger brother. Ayad picked up his father after learning he refused to stay another night after many months of already being in the hospital. After the infection had healed, Hussein was more of himself. He was more clear headed. He could defend himself. This was the last surgery of many, and Hussein was sick of sleeping in hospital beds and just wanted to be home. Afraid one more night in the hospital would lead to another night and another after that. He told the nurses who barely understood his English these words exactly. The surgeon wanted him to stay because of his age and pre-existing conditions. If anything happened to him, the staff could take care of him. But Hussein fought the surgeon, stayed stubborn, and demanded they call his son.

Kajal's mother, Ruksanna, got the call from her husband's nurse stating that her husband was being difficult and wanted someone to pick him up. Ruksaana didn't think twice. She woke her son, who was in bed sleeping the afternoon away and told him to go pick up his father in the hospital only three blocks away. Ayad arrived home with his father two hours later.

Hussein wanted to rest when he got back. Their cat was happy to see him and he weaved in and out between its master's legs, purring, gently rubbing its lower back against its father's left pant leg, asking for food.

Hussein continued to his bedroom, ignoring the cat. Holding both his hands out towards the walls for balance.

His fingers grazed the chipped paint as he wobbled down the hallway with caution. Hussein entered his bedroom. He was tired from the surgery and wanted to sleep. Sleeping in rooms unfamiliar to him had become commonplace at this stage of his life. During his stay at the hospital, he grew lonely and would complain to the nurses about how much he missed being at home with his wife and children. Though, some time had passed since everyone lived under the same roof. On nights when no one would visit him, he feared his family was getting used to his absence, a thought he kept from them.

Ruksanna offered to make him chai or a snack to eat. He declined his wife's offer and said he just wanted to lay down. Other than the fatigue from the surgery, he felt normal health-wise. He took off his hat and shoes, and lifted the blanket slightly to move in between the sheets. He was comfortable in his bed, tired when lying down but felt peace from being inside his home.

He closed his eyes with the sunlight still coming in through the bedroom window and eventually, drifted off to sleep.

He had dreamt twice that day.

At the hospital, the anesthesiologist put a mask over his face and touched his arm gently, like his mother's apparition would, and asked him to tell her about his childhood, lately his favorite subject.

He looked up at the ceiling of the surgery room and admired, with a child's gaze, a painting of a sprawling bouquet of rainbow-colored flowers that extended from one side of the room to the next. He told the anesthesiologist everything she wanted to hear and quickly fell asleep, continuing his monologue in his dreams, seeing faces he hadn't seen since he was a boy.

The second dream came while sleeping at home in his bedroom. The dream was about a young boy who had tried to bring an elderly man back home to his house for dinner. Hussein's perspective was that of the older man. The boy pulled him with one hand towards his house, not too far in the distance. But however hard the boy tried, the old man wouldn't budge and stayed in his position like a statue cemented into the ground.

Confused by the boy's persistence, the older man believed the boy to be up to no good. He watched the boy pull his arm with an inquisitive look but could not help but smile at him. There was an innocence to the boy that the old man found charming, reminding the old man of himself when he was young.

He took his eyes off the boy briefly to look at the house in the distance, not too far up the road. From where he was standing, he couldn't see inside the house but could smell the essence of goat salan and roti cooking from inside the kitchen; his favorite meal, a meal his mother used to cook for him to perfection, stewed in freshly ground spices.

The old man grew hungry from the smell of the salan, and his mouth started to salivate as his legs grew weak at the knees. It had been a while since the old man had last eaten. Almost forgetting the boy's presence, he pointed his nostrils out and smelled the air as the pungent odor of salan wafted past his nostrils, weakening him more.

The old man noticed a window open on the front side of the house. From where he stood, he could see only a dark interior and a countertop gently lit by sunlight, which broke in through the window's heavy curtains.

Before light would penetrate his cornea for the last time, this was what Hussein had been dreaming about.

The young boy tugged on the old man's arm with great strength, taking the old man away from his thoughts. The old man looked down at the boy again. Starving and weak now, the old man tried to talk but he could not speak. No words would come out of his mouth.

Fearful now, the old man did not give into the boy. Not right away. He wanted to eat the goat salan he smelled from the kitchen but knew he did not want to enter the house. There was something about the house the old man did not trust. His intuition telling him not to move forward. But the boy was persistent and continued to pull him.

A whimper came out of the old man's mouth then. A woman with a loosely draped veil over her head came outside through the house's main entrance and saw the two of them just short a hundred meters from her front door. The old man heard the front door open, looked up from the boy, and noticed the beautiful woman standing on the house's threshold for the first time; the young boy's mother. The old man recognized something in her soft, polite face but could not remember where he knew her from.

The woman smiled at the old man from her front door, her face apologetic for her son's behavior. She called the boy over to her, yelling at the boy to not be foolish and leave the old man alone and to come inside to eat. The boy did as his mother told him to, and he let go of the old man's hand. The old man lost his balance as the boy let go, and he stumbled forward, realizing how attached to the boy he had grown. The boy ran past his mother, disappearing inside his home. The old man had the impulse to call the boy back, but stopped before making a fool of himself and stood still, making eye contact with the boy's mother.

It was just the old man and the woman now. Both said nothing for a moment. The two politely stared at each other as if in a contest nobody was trying to win. She asked him if he wanted something to eat. If he was hungry. He tried to answer her, but he could not speak. He shook his head yes instead. The woman invited him to come into her home when he was ready, and without waiting for a response, she stepped back inside her house and left the door ajar.

The old man was relieved to be alone with his thoughts but he struggled with why he could not speak; the anxiety not leaving him. The old man looked behind him for a moment and saw a beautiful, wide desert pasture. Halfway from setting, the sun burned in the center of his view. The sky above him was a dark red color that changed a shade lighter the further it got from the sun until it appeared the color white, and the old man could see different strands of the projected white light through the cumulus clouds from where he was standing.

A sense of calm had come over the old man. There was no fear inside of him now nor confusion. And when he turned back around towards the house, hungry, he took his first... step...forward.

On the old man's first step, Hussein woke up in his bedroom, unable to talk, looking for the boy and his mother, trying to take in air.

Ayad had been in his bedroom, smoking a joint he'd given to himself for doing as his mother told him to successfully. He lit an incense stick to cover the smell and turned on his fan to catch any extra smoke he hadn't already blown out the window. Through the buzz of his fan, he heard his father's heavy wheezing.

Ayad entered his father's bedroom, and saw Hussein holding his neck with both hands, gasping for air, unable to talk. Hussein's eyes looked up toward his son for help. Ayad had feared it was the smoke from his joint that had caused the state his father was in. He should have known better. He had just come back from the hospital. Ayad tried unsuccessfully to get his father to stand up. His father couldn't stand. Hussein stopped responding to him altogether. Stopped looking at him. The old man had stopped breathing with his son.

Hussein's eyes stayed open, lost, still looking for the boy and his mother wanting to eat, but he ceased making any sounds at all.

Ayad heard the sounds of his oldest sister's sobs coming from behind him on their mother's phone speaker. Ayad dialed 911 and received instructions from an EMT assistant on how to give his father proper CPR. He kneeled on the bed, hovering over his father's body, listening to this voice coming from his phone, handing over all his trust to it.

Ayad pressed down onto his father's chest. He put his lips to his father's for the last time. He blew air into his lungs, hoping to bring life back into him, coming up for a break and then down, again, with both his hands onto his father's chest.

The EMT arrived minutes later. Ruksaana let them in. They attempted CPR on Hussein. Ayad watched as his father was handled by strangers and felt helpless standing in their periphery. The men rushed his father on a stretcher and exited his home. An oxygen mask had been placed on Hussein's face, but they were too late. As they rushed down the stairwell and exited the building, he was already gone.

Ayad followed the men out of the apartment. He was on autopilot. His mother's voice behind him. The EMT hadn't updated him on his father's condition, so he felt hopeful that things could turn around in his father's favor. What other choice did he have?

The EMT took Hussein's body to the hospital three blocks away and was pronounced dead by a doctor who told Ayad the news as he sat alone in the ER waiting room waiting for his family to arrive.

It would be a few days after Dale and Kajal arrived at the hospital, that Kajal would receive an email, while making arrangements to bury her father, that congratulated her on being accepted into Columbia University. Like her father would have wanted her to, she would attend the University for grad school to get her Master's degree.

As Dale had feared, they would have to move out of their apartment in Brooklyn to live with Kajal's mother and brother in Harlem. Due to Kajal's father's passing, Dale's feelings on where they should live felt irrelevant, even to him. So he kept quiet, trying to act as a support to his partner of over a decade.

On the last evening in their Brooklyn apartment, Dale and Kajal slow danced to jazz music in their living room, Bill Evan's *Piece Peace,* and drank red wine out of coffee mugs. They ordered Thai food like they did on their first night in the apartment, sat on the floor while eating, and reflected on the three years they lived together.

However, independently, in the quiet spaces of their minds, both contemplated how each would survive the coming two years.

II

November (A Year Later)

K ajal left class and walked to the library. A Strand tote bag hanging over her shoulder, her stomach craving a snack. She intended to study before heading home to the apartment she lived in, now, with Dale, her mother and wayward brother.

Outside, it was a warm November day, unlike the brisk November weather she remembered from her childhood. When walking to the library, the cool, warm air hit her, the sun's light dehydrating her skin as she walked on the lawn through the clusters of students who laid on their backs on top of blankets, eating their own charcuterie of sliced meat and cheeses, reading novels, taking full advantage of the fortunate warm weather; as if winter was nowhere in sight.

Before she entered the library, Kajal stopped at a nearby cafe for a coffee, but her card declined, so she settled on a complimentary cup of water and walked down the ridged stone pathway to the library.

The library was more relaxed than it usually was on a Friday. A well-known politician was giving a speech in an auditorium 100 yards away, vying for the Democratic seat in the upcoming election. She wanted to attend the event but hadn't RSVP'd on time.

Kajal showed the security guard her student ID and walked through the aluminum metal detectors. She passed an empty receptionist desk and found a secluded spot by a window in the corner on the east side of the library. She put her headphones in, turned on a song by Cigarettes After Sex, and pulled out a large textbook from her tote bag that displayed, in white letters, a quote by John Waters and sat down.

After two hours or so had passed, Kajal stood up from her desk and stretched her legs. She had grown stiff sitting in the library for the time she had and could use a walk. She left the library and went out to the campus grounds to join the other students who were sunbathing, playing frisbee, and reading books. Walking the campus was a ritual Kajal did alone when she missed her father, which she did on this particular evening. It was the main factor as to why she wasn't feeling very social today. There were reminders of him everywhere around the school. There was no particular reason why today was especially difficult for Kajal. The grief inside her ebbed and flowed each day, but still, it was hard to fathom that she and her father once walked this campus together, and now she walked it alone, a student, without him.

Kajal passed a garden where she knew a magnolia tree to be. There was a photo taken of her in front of this tree years ago, with her father. The photo was of him holding her, standing in front of the tree, both of them smiling at the camera. Who took the photo Kajal didn't remember. She didn't remember the day well but could relive the moment in the photo, in front of the tree, whenever she wanted to. She remembered the joy she felt being held in her father's arms and how she felt when he smiled at her and kissed her on the cheek, when he said I love you to her, before putting her down. The feeling she kept from this memory was something Kajal feared to lose as time went on.

On the walk back to the library, Kajal bumped into her friend Kareena, whom she met on the first day of the first semester. Kareena was born in Calcutta, but her parents moved to London two years after having her, so she spoke in a polite, raspy English accent.

Kareena asked if Kajal was free and suggested they walk to the Hungarian Pastry Shop together to chat over coffee. Kareena was done with classes for the day and had nothing for the rest of the evening.

When they arrived at the cafe, they sat down and ordered a slice of the dobos torte cake they saw in the front window display by the entrance, and shared it each with their own fork. Kajal ordered herself a lavender oat milk latte. Kareena, a decaf Americano. When the drinks arrived, Kareena showed Kajal the Google calendar on her phone, which exhibited her weekly schedule. Every hour was color-coded to represent where she needed to be, all laid out visually on her phone: TA office hours every other weekday or student association meetings she needed to attend. For the current day, Kareena had organized sections for her study group at the library and the rest of the time she planned to spend however she wanted.

See, this is you here, said Kareena, pointing to a space on her calendar that was rendered the color green. Green means I can be here. I can be wherever I want to with the color green. It's my favorite color.

A waiter approached their table and poured them each more water without asking permission. Conversation between the two had ebbed for a moment. Kareena sat across from Kajal, concentrating heavily on her phone. She was in several group chats but wasn't responding to any of them. Instead, she watched an argument unfold between two strangers in a chat group of twenty students, letting her phone buzz constantly in her hand.

Kajal sat calmly across from Kareena, sipping her lavender latte. She wasn't in the mood to talk and wished she could excuse herself from the table and leave comfortably, but she didn't want to come off as rude to her new friend. But she felt depressed. Dale's face popped into her mind then, and she remembered they had plans to go to the movies later.

She wished now more than ever she had a more organized calendar.

Kareena looked up from her phone and mentioned that a friend of hers had moved into a new apartment and was throwing a housewarming party. She asked Kajal if she wanted to come along.

Where is it? Kajal asked her.

With her fork, Kareena ate the last piece of the dobos torte cake before answering. She put her fork in her mouth, that held the final piece of the cake slice, and let the clang of her fork ring out as she slid its metal spikes against the front of her teeth.

125th Street and Broadway, said Kareena, chewing. It would be nice if you came; you could meet the rest of the group from the upstate retreat.

I'll text you the address, Kareena continued. Did you have other plans tonight?

Kajal had plans with Dale to see a revised 35 mm print of *The 400 Blows* at the Metrograph Theater downtown. Dale insistently asked Kajal if she wanted to go weeks in advance, and when she agreed, he immediately bought them tickets. She hadn't seen the film before, but it was one of Dale's favorite movies. He wanted to show her the film on the big screen, he said: The way it was meant to be seen!

No, I can come, said Kajal. I was going to head back to the library to study more, but I can come by afterwards.

Cool, said Kareena.

Kajal drank the last of her latte. Looking past Kareena, she noticed how dark the city had become. Outside the cafe, Kareena and Kajal hugged goodbye and went their separate ways, confirming they'd see each other later.

On her way to the library, she told Dale, over the phone, she'd no longer be able to attend the movie with him. He called her not long after she departed from Kareena, asking if she wanted to grab a bite to eat, and before she said anything, she had become anxious, knowing her news would upset him.

In the library, Kajal sat in the same seat as she did before. Outside, where once the whole student body played, she saw no one now except one or two students walking the pathways through the lawn in the dark. The library was quieter than it had been before. The absence of the bodies walking the hallways beyond the library's doors, made the silence in the library seem somehow more palpable.

A receptionist was at the front desk now, a young female student on her work-study hours who failed to notice Kajal as she walked by. The young receptionist was writing in her notebook and listening to music loudly through her headphones.

About an hour later, Kajal could no longer read the words of a review sheet in front of her. The words on the page started to blur, and her eyes sent tears down her face, ruining the mascara she put on in the morning, and now black streaks of pigment marked her cheeks.

She was tired and wanted to go home to sleep and see no one but her bed. She had no interest in going to this party alone, but home was the last place she wanted to be. She looked at her phone and thought of Dale sitting alone in a theater and felt guilty. She always felt guilty.

Kajal pushed herself away from her desk. A wave of grief passed through her and she cried for real. These crying episodes started to become more commonplace after her father passed. She'd be fine one minute, and then an image of her father's face would appear in her mind, and a blanket of grief would come over her.

Going home wasn't any easier than going to a party or a dark movie theater to sit alone in. It was all the same to Kajal. She wanted to be nowhere and everywhere at once.

Kajal put the stray books in her locker and walked out into the city streets. Not knowing what to bring to the party, she crossed the street to a French pastry shop that was closing and bought a dozen Canelés, a dessert she had tried in Bordeaux and loved when she and Dale had traveled to France. She loved the pastry and thought Kareena would appreciate the gesture.

Kajal entered the apartment building half an hour later. It was an old pre-war building typical on this side of the island. Kajal appreciated these older buildings, which held more character and beauty than the fragile glass sculptures she saw people living in more and more now, that were popping up in the Williamsburg and the Midtown areas.

When Kajal entered the apartment, it felt more like she was entering a party her family would host rather than one hosted by her friends. Food was on a foldable table, and paper plates were in the corner, aligned with plastic silverware. The ceiling lights were turned on, light music played, and people sat on the floor in circles, talking and cackling in the glow of mixed cocktails.

When she entered the living room, all heads turned towards her. She continued, ignoring the silent stares, and walked past a slew of abandoned shoes in the corner. Kareena greeted her and introduced her to the crowd from the door. Everyone's faces turned towards Kajal's and smiled as they welcomed her, with small hand gestures and non-synchronized hellos.

Someone she didn't know but vaguely recognized came over with an extra beer in his hand.

Shoes off, please, he said laughing. This is an Asian household. The guy with the two beers was white, and Kajal could not tell if his joke was in good taste, but she was too shy to challenge him on it.

He handed her the beer, and they chatted for a while. She thought he was cute and flirted with him but felt guilty as she was doing it. Did Dale not do the same thing? His name was Marc, and he was a Columbia grad, but not one Kajal knew very well. They never talked longer than two minutes before, but had a few mutual friends in different circles.

They talked about school. He was interested in international education, something she told him she was interested in as well. He was too drunk to talk about it in detail, though in the back of Kajal's brain, she thought he might be trying to say what he thought she wanted to hear. He said getting a degree in education seemed more stable than getting his master's degree in journalism, which was what he originally wanted to study.

Great, another writer, she thought.

They found themselves alone in a corner of the apartment talking. For some reason, no one had interrupted them. The party continued on. Feeling less reserved, Kajal surprised herself and mentioned that her father had passed away last year.

Marc said, mine died too. Sounding almost happy they had found something in common.

Oh, I'm sorry to hear that.

It happened when I was younger, though. He died in a car accident. I don't remember too much of it, to be honest. I hardly think about it at all now.

That must have been really tough for you, though. I'm sorry.

They continued talking for what felt like hours. It was effortless to speak to him. She didn't struggle with the uncomfortable silence that happens in between conversations she had with new people. Also, when one topic ended another one soon came up. She wanted to know what it felt like to be past the constant awareness of her father's absence. She had no one she trusted to talk about her grief with. It felt good to talk to someone who she felt would understand her pain, the pain she thought her boyfriend or friends couldn't relate to. And pain her family refused to acknowledge.

Someone dimmed the lights and raised the music. Kareena poured tequila into as many shot glasses as she had. When she ran out of shot glasses, she eyeballed it and poured a little more into red plastic cups. Everyone took a shot. A dance circle formed. Kajal stood up next to Marc. He looked at her, and she allowed him to put his right hand on her lower back and pull her in closer. His right leg went in between hers. Kajal felt awkward at first. Her initial reaction was to run away. Her body turned stiff as Marc rubbed the front of his pants along the top part of Kajal's right thigh. She didn't know how to move her body with his. But she felt the warmth of the tequila rise from inside her, like a heat wave, and when she lifted her head to see the room, it spun around her in a blur. She noticed all eyes were on her and Marc. Everyone cheered them on, and then Kajal let herself go. She liked the attention from the crowd of the party. She hadn't been touched this way in what felt like months, and she let herself fall into his arms, moving with the music and the rhythm of his body against hers.

He was a good dancer and tall, she noticed. She didn't know how to dance. Though, with him, she didn't need to. There was a song change, a popular Spanish pop song that Kajal liked and wanted to dance to.

Dale never liked to dance to this type of music with her. He was too self-conscious, too self-loathing.

She turned around on Marc, aligned her spine with his chest, and grabbed the back of his neck. The rhythm of the song influenced the movement of her hips. He placed his hands on the front of her thighs and they slowed to the song's pace together. She was sweating. It was loud. More tequila was poured into everyone's cup.

Drunk now, Kajal excused herself from the impromptu dance floor in the living room and entered the kitchen. She walked by a dessert plate and picked up a flaky coconut Thai dessert she tasted and thought was delicious.

Marc came into the kitchen after her. Kajal poured

herself a glass of water. He was too drunk to talk but could not stop smiling. She noticed how well-trimmed his beard was, the overhead ceiling lights in the kitchen giving his facial hair a spotlight. He gently moved a few strands of hair out of Kajal's eyes and traced the top of her skull with his fingertips, both of them giggling. What? Kajal asked him.

You're a good dancer.

No, I'm not.

Sorry, I'm so drunk.

Yeah.

He kissed her, and Kajal didn't move. She was frozen in that space in the kitchen. He put his tongue in her mouth and pulled her closer. He was hard, and Kajal could feel his penis rub against the side of her thigh.

Someone had dropped a wine glass behind them and shattered pieces of glass fell all over the kitchen floor. Kajal panicked and pushed Marc away from her, hard, like she was the one who had to explain herself. Kajal looked behind her to see the face of whoever had broken the glass, but no one was there. It was just the two of them and the shattered glass on the floor.

They caught their breath. He had his hands on his chest where Kajal had pushed him, and he looked at her with disgust and mumbled what she thought was the word *bitch* under his breath and walked out of the kitchen and disappeared into the party.

A complaint is what ended the night. Someone from the floor above theirs had come down, and Kareena, who opened the door, was met with a screaming mouth.

She cut the music and announced to everybody: Help clean up or get out. It was 4:00 AM.

Kajal's dance partner left without saying goodbye. She volunteered to clean the dishes to get her mind off things.

The remaining few were hungry and did not want to go home. Kajal followed the new group down the street to the corner for a pizza slice. Sitting in the pizzeria, Kajal quietly went over the events of the night in her head, lost in thought. She could not engage in conversation fully, embarrassed by what had happened in her friend's kitchen. Afraid someone in the group might have seen her and Marc together, but no one had said anything. They knew she was in a relationship. Kajal had become worried everyone in the group knew.

She realized everyone she sat with was a stranger, and Kajal came to, like out of a bad dream, and woke up sitting at a table amongst a group of foreign faces, not knowing how it was she had gotten there.

Tired and without money, she hailed a cab to take her home, using her credit card to pay for it. She wondered how Dale's night went, hoping he enjoyed seeing the film, even if he saw it without her. Her eyes were tired, but her heart was racing. She entered the apartment, which was caked in darkness, and walked past her mother's bedroom, the bedroom her father took his last breath in, to her bedroom down the hall, where Dale was sleeping. The clock on her phone read 5:00 AM. Dale would soon be waking up to leave for work, and still, she could not sleep.

She watched Dale lying in the dark, turned away, her childhood cat resting against his forehead. A token from her life in the past merging with her present.

To help her sleep, with Dale's silhouette turned, Kajal slipped her fingers into her pajama pants. She closed her eyes and thought of the heat that emitted from Marc's body as they danced, her arms wrapped around his neck, pulling him in closer.

Kajal grabbed the door knob for support as she muffled out a silent orgasm, drying her wet fingers against Dale's oversized sweatshirt he let hang from the hamper.

Quietly, she slipped into the sheets and laid beside him, facing the other way with her back turned towards him.

She was dehydrated and could use a glass of water but was too lazy to get up and do the short walk to the kitchen. She stared at her dresser for a while until her eyelids started to give in. Her mind raced with thoughts until, eventually, just as Dale's alarm went off to wake him for work, she drifted off to sleep.

III

The 400 Blows

Dale woke up with the cat sitting on his stomach, kneading the blanket that covered his body, meowing for food. It was a little after 5:00 AM, and Dale's alarm would soon go off. Dale touched the cat on its forehead and rubbed with his thumb the tiny white patch of fur that stained the section between the cat's two eyes. The cat's eyes squinted half closed, and he began to purr up on Dale's chest. Lying down, Dale looked outside the window to his right and saw the sun had not yet risen and the sky was a pitch black dark.

He removed the cat from his stomach so that he could get up. Dale sat up in bed, shifted his feet to the floor, and held onto the mattress tightly with both hands, wanting to do nothing but lie back down.

Dale noticed Kajal only then. She was fast asleep behind him, covering her body with their blanket. He was startled, not having seen her just a moment ago. Her shape slowly took form in the bedroom's darkness.

Since their move from Brooklyn, on nights when Kajal was out with her friends, Dale would wake up intermittently, throughout the night, to see if she were beside him. He'd sit up as if waking from a bad dream and move his hand around the bed, finding only the flat cold surface of the mattress.

He'd search for his cell phone on the floor, to check for text messages she might have sent him. Often, Kajal would not update Dale on her whereabouts. She was not required to text him, but since she started grad school, he would hardly see her. When she did remember, she'd send him a goodnight text or a *I'll be home late* text, and he'd force himself not to call her with questions, or get angry and text her back, or look on any of her social media platforms for information she was not willing to give herself.

He'd force himself to go to sleep, alone in their new home, anxious, no longer tired, and confused about who he was in this person's life. He didn't know who he was to Kajal anymore.

But in the morning, just before the sun would rise and Dale's alarm went off to wake him for work, Kajal would always appear beside him in their bed sleeping, and his shoulders would soften, relieved again to see her.

Dale got off the bed, put the kettle on the stove for coffee, and packed himself a lunch. He went back inside the bedroom to get ready. He tried to make as little noise as possible. He was unaware of the time when Kajal had arrived home, but he assumed it was late. He knew she had school later in the day and didn't want to wake her.

In the dark, he struggled to put one leg into his jeans as he hopped on one foot, trying to prevent himself from falling over. On the floor, things lay scattered around him: clothes he discarded and refused to organize and fold and place neatly inside his dresser drawer. A hamper sat by the door stuffed to the rim with rogue pieces of fabric creeping out of it.

Dale had to be careful not to trip or fall over anything. Down the hallway, in the kitchen, the kettle began to whistle, and observing from the bed, the cat watched Dale's silhouette struggling to put his other foot through the cool slip of his jeans.

Dale walked out of the bedroom into the hallway, past the room where Hussein took his last breath in. He could see through Ruksaana's bedroom window the sun rising behind the Ward's Island Bridge. The alarm on his phone went off in the back pocket of his jeans, projecting its synthetic sound in each room inside the apartment.

Kajal opened her eyes briefly, then slowly shut them closed again. Too tired to move.

Dale dropped the clothes he was holding and reached behind him to swipe his thumb along his phone's screen in order to quiet it. From Dale's point of view, no one in the house had moved.

Dale grabbed his keys and put the lunch he had made in his bag, slipped through the heavy metal door of the apartment, and headed downtown on the train to work.

Dale walked into the lobby at a quarter to seven.

The company Dale works for, Sam, Richard, and Paul (S.R.P), was named after the three douchebags who started the company in Sam's garage two decades earlier in Los Angeles.

The company started as an experiment. Three wayward boys, not wanting to commit to living lives similar to that of their parents, who shot and edited music videos for their friends post-college while living in a two-bedroom apartment in Silver Lake. Sam got a job as an assistant editor on a feature-length film that went on to win an Academy Award, and Sam leveraged the film's success to sign clients to a company run by three pre-adult males, neither of whom had yet to pay their own phone bills.

They promised each other that art would be made. An oath to work on projects they found provocative and that would change the world and the culture.

But after achieving their first client, an affluent and trending skater shoe company, they shifted their business model to editing commercials for boutique companies to make a quick buck, and they got rich.

The elevator doors opened, and Dale walked past the empty receptionist's desk. He continued down the hallway to the back of the office, put his bag down in one of the chairs that sat along the cherry red acrylic kitchen tables, brewed more coffee, took a seat, and started to type.

Through the kitchen window was a view of 23rd Street and Broadway, facing downtown, towards the Flatiron Building. He felt even with the time he took in the mornings, there was never enough time in the day to write well, with all of his other responsibilities. Dale tried for years to wake up earlier than he did but always struggled with the snooze button on his phone. Sometimes, he'd wake up hours after his alarm went off and the sun was higher in the sky than it should be, and he'd start his day with a feeling of dread that overwhelmed him.

This morning, Dale wrote for over an hour. He didn't have a plan for this new script. He just started typing dialogue last week, going in no particular direction but liking the tone and feel of the voices of the new characters he was writing in. Dale had finished a draft of another screenplay the week before but was sick of looking at it, and put it away, not to be looked at again, for a while.

Later that morning, he could hear distant sounds of people coming through the elevator from the other side of the office. He felt paranoid doing non-work related things while at the office. Not believing his employer not to use his writing against him from progressing at his job.

Just as he stood up, one of the editors came in through the loading dock elevator behind him. The editor ignored Dale as he walked past him, listening to music loudly through his headphones, holding his speed bike on his shoulders, and singing out loud to a song by Roberta Flack. Dale jumped as the editor passed him, having not seen him until then and watched until the editor turned right at the corner and disappeared down the hallway.

He put his laptop away in his bag, sighed heavily, and went into the bathroom, closing the door behind him, relieved again, for the moment, to be alone.

On his way out of the office, Dale texted Kajal. He wanted to know when she'd be done with class in case she wanted to meet and grab something to eat. Dale had two tickets to see *The 400 Blows* at the Metrograph Theater, which was screening a restored print of the film as part of a retrospective of the director's work. The film was one of Dale's favorite movies, among a few others made by the filmmaker, and he was excited to see the restoration in a theater and show it to Kajal, who had never seen the film before.

Dale wished he could spend the entire week watching the films in the retrospective. There were film's screening that were rarely played inside a theater and some of the movies could not be rented at home.

He made a list on his phone's notepad app of all the films he planned to watch at the theater with their scheduled showtimes and the days of the week they were screening, listed besides the films title. He looked forward to crossing off each one he watched from his list, each film that he crossed out a reward to Dale, giving him a false sense of accomplishment, adding to the ever-evolving Rolodex of movies he collected in his brain.

When he arrived at work this morning, he remembered seeing the sun just starting to rise, and now walking through the lobby, he caught a glimpse of the day's last strands of light. Dale walked through the building's revolving doors and stepped out onto the street. A group of tourists was to his left, taking a photo with the Flatiron building behind them. Standing next to them, Dale took his first breath of fresh air since the morning. The sky above was fading but you could still see the light protrude through the buildings on the avenue; the sun slowly descending behind the Hudson in the distance.

He had a few hours to kill before the screening and was tired from the day and wished he could go somewhere private, that was his own, to rest. He didn't want to return home to the apartment where Kajal's mother and brother were. He didn't want to be left alone with them, waiting for Kajal, as he did daily since they had moved into Ruksaana's apartment.

He didn't have anything against Kajal's family. But it never felt suitable walking into their apartment after work, to put his feet up and relax, making their home his without Kajal's presence. He felt like an imposter being there without her, and because of the language barrier, Dale didn't know how to keep a consistent flow of dialogue with Kajal's mother. He tried learning a bit of Urdu to speak with Kajal's mother more fluently. But he could never remember the words he learned or master the silent *h* sounds in the language. The conversations between him and Ruksaana were always short but polite, ending with them laughing to signal to each other the conversation was over.

Dale crossed the street, leaving the block he worked on, and was stopped by a crowd of oblivious tourists who blocked the crosswalk of the adjacent sidewalk. He stepped into the curb lane to get around the crowd who took turns looking down at their cell phones, their faces perplexed, deciding on which direction to take.

He stepped onto the curb with confidence, to show them. The stalled crowd now behind him as he texted Kajal and headed south towards a coffee shop he frequented on Bleecker.

Dale liked this particular coffee shop because it reminded him of cafes he'd seen in movies, and read about in books on Paris in the late twenties. On a good day, he'd come to this cafe to write and have a hot cup of coffee or a glass of wine, depending on his mood.

He pulled a chair to a table adjacent to another that seated several college students discussing the current political climate. Their laptops and notes spread out before them on the table they sat around. Dale put his jacket on the back of his table's chair, took his bag with his laptop in it to the bar, and ordered himself a glass of red wine.

Next to him was a couple talking about a film they had just seen at the Angelika, a movie theater he used to work at in college just a few blocks south of the cafe. He didn't pick up on the film's title but could tell by their conversation the film was a French film and politically charged.

The barista brought Dale his wine, placing it on the counter before him without saying a word. Dale nodded *thanks* to the barista's back, grabbed his bag from off the floor, and walked over to his table, holding his glass of wine in his right hand and sat down in the chair that had his jacket resting on the back of it.

Some of the students who were sitting at the adjacent table had left, and those who remained were smiling, engaged in what seemed to be a less constrained conversation. Dale opened his laptop and read over what he had written in the morning, taking a sip of his wine and started to make corrections.

He wrote for about an hour, and checked his phone, not realizing the time. Kajal had yet to respond to his text message. This infuriated him. Not texting him back was part of a trend of Kajal leaving Dale feeling unseen by her in the recent months. He felt as if Kajal didn't care about his bids for connection. He spent all his time thinking about her. Inviting her into his life, and she was able to pick and choose when she'd want to participate. But if she asked him to be anywhere, or do anything, Dale would show up despite his own plans or agenda and never leave Kajal waiting. Never having her second guess if she'd be attending an event alone that she thought they'd be attending together.

The cafe was far from the theater, and if he wanted to get a bite to eat before the film, he had to head out soon.

The phone rang a few times before Kajal picked up. He could tell she was outside based on the noise in the background. It was loud in the cafe, the group of students next to him obviously drunk; speaking loudly and banging on the table in their banter with harsh laughter. Dale had to duck his head underneath the table with one palm over his ear in order to hear Kajal speak.

There was something in the way she spoke that told him something was on her mind. She was distracted by her thoughts. He would've asked her *What's wrong?* but from past conversations he knew this question to be a trigger for her and he wanted to have a good night.

I don't think I can go to the movie tonight Dale, said Kajal.

He knew now where this conversation was headed but continued to talk, and he grew disappointed. This was how things were between them now.

What do you mean? He asked, playing along.

Something came up…I feel like I should study more.

Okay.

A friend invited me to a housewarming party…

Dale stood up from his chair, growing infuriated. He had to stand to avoid saying something he might regret. He kept his head down to block out the noise and walked a few feet back over to the bar where he ordered his wine.

You couldn't have told me this earlier? I could have given the ticket to someone else. Now I've wasted money.

See if you could get a refund or if one of your friends could go, said Kajal.

Did you hear what I said? Kajal. The movie is in an hour. It's not enough time. The theater doesn't give out refunds.

I'm sorry.

Dale could hear an ambulance in the background from wherever Kajal was walking. The noise of the ambulance made it more difficult to speak, but it didn't stop him. He kept sharing his feelings with Kajal, even though he knew it wouldn't change anything. She wasn't coming. He could hear her silence in his ramblings but kept talking anyway until the sound of the ambulance dissipated, and he ran out of breath, and there was nothing more to say.

I'll see you tomorrow then? When I wake up, he said annoyed.

Don't be mad at me.

I'm not mad. I'm disappointed.

We can watch the movie together another time, okay?

It's fine. How late will you be?

I don't know, Dale.

Okay.

Don't be mad.

You said that already.

Goodnight.

Goodbye.

The two hung up. Dale grabbed his bag from underneath the table and left the café, angry. There was a loneliness inside him that wasn't there before he spoke to Kajal on the phone. When he left work, he was content inside his body and was looking forward to his evening. He was happy that he was to see Kajal later. But their conversation made him feel different. He was alone as before the phone call, but the conversation rendered a shift inside him that deflated his good mood.

He took money out of an ATM and got a falafel sandwich from a hole-in-the-wall he frequented on MacDougal Street, then took the train downtown to Ludlow and arrived at the theater 30 minutes early.

Dale walked into the theater and sat on the distressed vintage furniture in the lobby. The furniture at the Metrograph was uncomfortable to sit on and sitting on the uncomfortable furniture had somehow worsened Dale's mood. He would have much preferred to have no choice to sit at all and stand in the lobby than to sit on a couch with no cushion, and that looked like used furniture bought from the 1800s that someone had died on.

He didn't even bother to remove his coat or the backpack from his shoulders. He just plopped down on the sofa, depressed, and stayed there frozen still, staring at the empty space inside his mind, utterly unbothered by those in the theater with him who could see him.

He thought he should pee before going into the theater, so he did and washed his hands. He paid for a Bruce Cost Ginger Beer and a medium-sized popcorn flavored with parmesan and truffle oil. Altogether, twenty bucks spent on concessions to supplement his mood and more money spent on things he did not want or need.

He held the popcorn under his arm and the ginger beer in his right hand. He ate the popcorn with his available fingers and floated through the lobby of the theater like a ghost who was haunting the place.

The door guy announced the film's title to the theater's lobby and opened the door to the theater. Dale showed his ticket from a screenshot he took on his phone and went into the theater to find his seat, with no one from the lobby following him inside.

Silent advertisements for films and upcoming screenings showed on the screen. When he walked into the theater, it seemed like he was the only individual attending tonight's screening until a woman came in and sat down in the chair beside him. The woman was around Dale's age. She wore a short dress, painted white and spottily decorated with yellow flowers that floated down from its seams. Her hair was a brunette color and cut short at the neck. She was tall and thin, wore a light black turtleneck over the dress, and a hunter-green leather handbag hung over her shoulder.

Is this seat taken? The woman asked him.

Dale looked at her and could not hide the question mark written on his forehead. When he arrived at the theater, he was reminded the tickets he bought had assigned seating and forgot he had chosen the seats manually online when he bought the tickets several weeks ago. There was no need to rush here like he did. It would make sense if the woman who walked in had chosen this seat ahead of time, was stuck sitting next to a stranger, in an empty auditorium and didn't want to commit to choosing another seat until before the movie started. But she had asked Dale, *Is this seat taken?* So either the door guy failed to tell her where her seat was located, like he did for Dale or she didn't care and took free range of the theater and decided to sit next to the only other living person inside the theater with her.

This, also, would have been Kajal's seat if she were here.

No, he answered honestly. It's not taken. He curled his lips and changed his body's direction to face the opposite way from the woman with the flowered dress.

She sat down, and Dale focused on his breathing.

I'm guessing you're a fan of Truffaut? The woman asked him.

She must not be from here, Dale thought. Of course, he would get stuck with a chatty tourist on a day like today. Dale was not in the mood to socialize with a stranger. Though he knew ignoring her wasn't an option. So, he shyly turned his head towards her, knowing what he was getting himself into, and answered the woman calmly: Yes.

Same! I've always preferred him to Godard, the woman continued, but don't get me wrong, I love Godard but I prefer Truffaut's work because his films are closer to the types of films I would make if I were a filmmaker, I guess? I don't know. She laughed. I mean, I love a good suicide film but I can relate more to Truffuat's work. Godard is so brainy and intellectual. He's obviously trying to challenge his audience, you know? It's like he's mad at you for watching. Love his earlier stuff, though. His first ten films are amazing.

You're not a filmmaker? Dale asked. Or you are? Pretending he didn't hear her right.

No, I'm not. But I go to the movies a lot. I work primarily from home.

Doing what? Dale asked.

I work freelance as a software engineer. I always wanted to make movies, though. My parents are huge film buffs. We'd watched classics and old horror films together when I was a kid. Growing up, I mostly watched films in black and white until I graduated from middle school and started to watch more of what my friends were watching. In college, I took a few film courses but decided on something more stable for a career.

Yeah. Good choice.

You went to film school, I guess?

Yeah. I did. Good guess.

That's pretty cool, she said. Made any films?

A few shorts. Nothing fancy, said Dale. I know people who work in the tech world. Where did you go to school?

Harvard.

Harvard, really. Wow.

Yeah, the school was okay, but I'm happy to be out of Boston.

Do you work for Google by any chance?

I did! I wanted to work in a more ethical space that aligns with my creativity, you know? I left to do freelance work so I could travel more. I don't know what I want to do next. I used to work in the office just outside of San Francisco, which was cool. I loved California, but I felt like moving around more. I didn't like being stuck in one place. What made you guess Google, by the way?

I guessed Google because it seemed like the obvious place to work for someone who majored in your field at Harvard.

That's what they thought, too! It was a good job, but I don't know... I wanted more life experience. And if I already made it through the door, I felt, if I leave, I could always go back. Computer software engineers make a lot of money.

So I've heard. Have you been in New York for a long time?

Not long, no. Just a couple of months. I've been roaming around the city. Watching movies. Not really doing anything specific. I have no plans. I walk everywhere. I'm alone most of the time. Which I prefer. My family was originally from here.

What's your name?

Clara, the woman said.

Dale introduced himself as the lights dimmed and the trailers began to play.

I'm working on creating an app for film enthusiasts, Clara said, whispering now. My goal is to help people interested in seeing more independent cinema in the theater before it's too late, and the only place left to watch films like these is on your iPhone or your smart TV. It'll show you what's playing and where and update you on special screenings, like Q&As or new restorations happening inside the city the location point on your phone picks up on. I want to work with film festivals, too. It's easy to find places to watch good cinema in New York, but in other cities, finding a film culture could be more challenging. Even in this city, people don't always know where to look, and I think something like my app could help!

Sounds interesting. I'm sure it would be helpful for the theaters too, said Dale, acknowledging the empty seats around them.

Exactly! I have a meeting with the Criterion Collection next Wednesday, which is very exciting. I'm just excited to go into their office, to be honest with you. I've been in conversation with them for months now. Finally got through the door. I like their streaming platform a lot, and if I could connect with them, it could be a massive push for me to get funding.

It sounds like you're making some headway. I'm definitely interested, said Dale truthfully.

Thank you! Yeah, it's exciting. I think the app could be beneficial to cinefiles. And who knows, maybe we'd have a few more seats in the theater tonight if something like my app already existed. I think of it as my contribution to the film industry since I'm not an artist. I can use my skills to get more people to come to the theater.

Yeah. Sounds exciting. I'm intrigued.

Here's my card.

She pointed her phone towards Dale as if asking him to take it.

You have to scan the QR code, said Clara.

Dale looked at her phone's screen and understood. He took his cell phone out of his pocket and scanned a QR code that appeared on Clara's phone's home screen.

I'll be quiet now, said Clara smiling.

Dale looked at Clara's card, which now appeared digitally on his phone and he saved it to his digital wallet, clicked the phone screen off, and put it back in his pants pocket.

Clara settled into her seat, placed her green handbag on the floor, and turned away from Dale to watch what was left of a trailer playing.

Black and white images of the Eiffel Tower appeared on the screen before them. The opening sequence of Truffaut's *The 400 Blows* had started to play. A few late stragglers stumbled through the aisles to their seats. Dale and Clara looked at each other and shared a smile paying homage to the late comers and turned their heads back towards the screen and watched the rest of the film's opening sequence.

Dale settled into his seat more, and the further he got into the movie, the more relaxed he became. The movie had taken him out of himself. Despite the shift in the evening's plans with Kajal, he was happy he had come tonight. He was grateful for the short conversation with Clara. It helped him get out of his head. She had surprised him.

When the movie ended, Clara and Dale walked out of the theater together. When the ending credits started

Dale was shy to continue their conversation, fearing Clara would not want to speak with him because of the attitude, he feared, was too apparent in the conversation they had when she first sat down. But when they exited the theater, it seemed Clara did not have such feelings toward Dale, and he was relieved.

They walked out of the Metrograph together, engaged in conversation that felt effortless to him. It was nice for Dale to feel that someone was listening when it was his turn to speak, instead of making him rush to the end of his sentence before the person he was talking to either lost interest or moved on to something irrelevant to what he was in the middle of saying.

He lied about his direction and walked twenty minutes out of his way to her subway station so they could keep talking. Dale followed Clara down the West 4th Street station, swiped his MetroCard, and said goodbye to her as she went towards an uptown A train, and before they left they shared a hug before parting ways.

When she was out of sight, Dale exited the subway and walked the same streets he had with Clara, minutes before, from the Eastside, to a catch a train to take him back home to Harlem, where he would sneak into Ruksaana's apartment to sleep.

IV

The Celebrity

Dale didn't wake up from his alarm on time, and Kajal turned over from her side of the bed, grabbed his phone, and silenced it for him. She nudged him on his shoulder to wake up, and he softly lifted his head from the pillow and kissed her lips in the dark. The kiss woke Kajal up, and she touched him. Dale closed his eyes and paid attention to how her lips felt. He was tired and almost let the name Clara leave his lips. She continued. There was something about Kajal he did not recognize. It had been a long time since the two had been intimate that the experience of being together felt new. He pulled her hair, and she continued, and he flipped her onto her back, went in her for a little bit, and almost came. He stopped himself, pulled out of her, and touched her with his hand before using his tongue.

From his tongue, she shook and covered her mouth to avoid making any sounds that would wake her mother, who she knew was in the bedroom sleeping next door. They both didn't want to wake her. Kajal came and said to do it again, and he did. This time it took her a little longer to come, but she thought about the party and how she felt dancing with Marc; his cock touching the back of her leg, and he kissing her, their tongues touching, all of the grad students watching them and she came for the third time that morning; her orgasm more powerful than the first.

The sensation afterward overwhelmed her, and she took a deep breath, waiting for the ache in her stomach to pass.

After, Dale sat up in bed and let his feet touch the floor. Kajal laid down in the spot Dale was in and closed her eyes to sleep. Outside, the city had not yet begun its day. The streets were still dark, but the sun was budding in the background of Dale's view.

How was your night? Dale asked her.

Good, she said with an exhaustive sigh.

He wanted to talk more. To investigate her night a little. He wasn't satisfied that she had orgasmed by his touch. In fact, he did not feel responsible for the pleasure she felt during sex but more like a tool used to make her come. It wasn't just in bed he no longer recognized her but outside, too, and Dale had become paranoid. He was more interested in knowing where she'd been without him and with whom but was afraid to ask any questions that would lead to a fight. So, he fought the urge to ask and took this rare moment of physical intimacy as a gift.

Dale stood up from his side of the bed, bent down, and kissed her simply on the forehead. She closed her eyes and fell asleep almost instantly. Then he walked out of their bedroom to use the restroom. He woke up too late this morning to write. Dale packed a quick lunch in the kitchen, then his bag, and ran out the front door without drinking a sip of coffee.

Dale got off the train at 23rd Street and crossed the avenue to his building. He started work early. He knew there would be a full house today at the office, and he wanted to set up the rooms before anyone else would arrive. He put a water carafe in each room and cleaned the mess from the previous night. Whoever was the closing PA didn't do their job because garbage had been left out, and the entire office was a mess.

One of the rooms had leftover pizza slices and half-eaten BBQ chicken wings sitting, rotting in an old white china bowl; bones and crust lying half-eaten in an abandoned, oily, opened pizza box left on the table that welcomed Dale as he walked in. Little black gnats swarmed the mess, dispersing in various directions, flying insects looking for an escape, some gunning towards Dale like locusts as if he were Moses in *The Ten Commandments*.

His good mood from seeing the film the night before and his conversation with Clara had dissipated. On observing the mess in the editor's room, Dale grew angry at himself for not having done better with his life. At age 29, this was how he participated as a productive member of society. He thought at this age, he'd be way more established then he was. But because he possessed the innocent aspiration to want to tell stories, picking up other people's garbage was how he was rewarded.

Dale entered the kitchen, grabbed a large black garbage bag, put on red rubber gloves, and returned to the room. He opened the windows to let out the pungent smell that now spread throughout the office. One by one, he picked up the half-eaten BBQ chicken wings with his now gloved hands and the entire pizza box, which he found still had half a pie in it. He opened every window to let the air blow in and out of the rooms. He lit candles and scrubbed every table and chair he thought a client might sit in, and by the time the first editor arrived, the office smelled like lavender and watermelon.

Dale could feel a building tension from within the office. A meeting was being held for a commercial S.R.P. was editing, that was to be directed by a notable celebrity. Word was the celebrity was coming into the office. Still, staff must not talk about her with the other clients or, at any point, make eye contact with her, or take breaths when around her, and maintain a professionalism none of them had if she were to come into the office.

More people Dale hadn't recognized continued stepping out of the elevator. The receptionist was late and had not called in to say where she was or when she'd be coming into the office, giving Dale no choice but to step in and take over the front desk for her. Dale sat down behind the desk reluctantly, knowing other things around the office needed to get done. Dale was the only PA on sight and now the receptionist, and had to balance taking phone calls and babysitting every adult who either worked at S.R.P. or was visiting, all from behind a desk inside the lobby while trying to maintain a calm and polite composure.

On an average day, the best Dale could do was replace his anxious personality with a false, over-positive, and hyper-stimulated one. If anyone were to turn their heads three-quarters of an inch towards their right or left shoulders, Dale would be in the background of their view, waiting to respond to a request they may have. This is how he made up for his limitations, by being everywhere at once. But he could not do that sitting from behind a desk.

Newcomers continued walking past Dale as they stepped off the elevator. If the clients were cognizant enough, Dale would be the first person they saw when the elevator opened its doors, and they took their first steps out into the lobby. But despite Dale's big hand gestures and open smile, nothing could get through the brains of some of the clients as they stepped into the lobby, juggling in their minds matters far superior to what Dale could assist them with. They managed to mute his presence and turn to do god-knows-what down a hallway in an office they had never before been to.

For the few clients who did stop for him, Dale took their breakfast orders down to reward them. Though, still, the orders were dictated to Dale in a rush. The clients never giving Dale the proper time needed to confidently write down every detail of their order. Not sure if he was getting the person's name right, along with any allergy issue mentioned or specifics to their keto diet.

This is what I went to film school for? Dale thought.

Dale's chest started to tighten with each new client that came in through the elevator; the number of clients accumulating in the kitchen growing in his mind to irrational proportions, with no one to lead them. His head began to ache. The phone started to ring. He could do nothing to release the tension other than write a brief transcript of each conversation he had with a client to his mother to see if he could have said or done anything differently in the moment.

Later, he was on the phone with the deli guy when the receptionist arrived. The receptionist looked disheveled and hung over. She had not bothered removing her sunglasses when stepping off the elevator, ensuring her appearance looked worse than how she felt so that no one would question her tardiness. It was just obvious why she was late when you looked at her.

Dale looked up from his list of breakfast orders and saw his boss, Ava, walk past the front desk then, paying him and the hungover receptionist no mind.

Ava held her long cylindrical water bottle with half a lemon cut. Particles from the lemon's cadaver drifted toward the top as she floated through the office.

On seeing Ava, Dale replayed the list of things he had accomplished that morning, hoping he had done everything he had to before the clients arrived and that Ava would notice he had done it alone.

He wouldn't think about breathing normal again, until Ava had passed him. He was frozen with intrusive thoughts that orbited in his mind like stars encircling the head of a cartoon character who was hit with a large polo mallet. If he didn't move, he thought, she wouldn't see him.

Ava disappeared down the hallway, and Dale sucked the air back in through his mouth again and from the phone's receiver heard a voice he had forgotten saying, *Hello*, followed by a *Will that be all, sir?*

He didn't know then how to answer the man's simple question with the thoughts running through his brain.

Then, out of nowhere, BANG! A swift, dry breeze of room temperature air hit him straight in the face as a golden leather purse fell down hard onto the desk before him.

You can go now, said the receptionist, who then took her scarf for a walk a few times around her neck, attempting, it seemed, to take it off. She threw it on the back of Dale's chair and walked away.

The man on the phone repeated, Will that be all, Sir?

Yes. Yes. Sorry, Dale said into the phone.

Okay, give us twenty minutes. And the phone signal dropped.

Dale placed the phone onto the receiver and watched the receptionist walk toward the women's restroom in slow motion. From his chair, he could hear the crowd's loud, boisterous echoes bouncing off the walls inside the kitchen, each voice waiting for him to satisfy a need.

Dale's eyelids started to close. He wanted to put his head down on the brown leather desk mat, to rest his head, but fought the urge to.

A producer stepped out of her office, exuding the energy of nails being scratched onto a chalkboard. She walked the short distance from her desk towards Dale.

Conference room, she whispered, and pointed in the direction of the crowd in the kitchen, then redirected her hand towards the conference room where Dale would take them.

She was a thin middle-aged woman with dark, straight, black hair and had eyes half closed, squinting at you disappointed.

Dale gave her a head nod, showing he understood the language it was she was speaking to him in. Then she turned and walked away, disappearing behind the door she came out of that enclosed her desk.

Dale stood up from behind the receptionist's desk and passed the receptionist in the hallway, who gave Dale a silent head nod of approval. When he arrived in the kitchen, he saw the accumulation of people that had passed him.

No one noticed Dale at first. They were all busy with their own conversations. It was loud in the kitchen. Each voice contributed to a booming noise that ricocheted off the walls, making it sound like a high school cafeteria during lunchtime.

Excuse me! Dale screamed over them, attempting to project his voice over the accumulating noise. Dale's legs started to shake from the nerves of the inevitable attention coming, and he regretted not having put anything inside his stomach other than two cups of strong black coffee.

Excuse me! Dale tried again, this time getting a few dumb stares and looks directed his way.

Your meeting will be starting shortly, said Dale, smiling to the crowd who stared back at him with blank faces.

If you'd like to make your way towards the conference room, it's just around the corner. If you need further assistance with anything, I am here. Thank you.

Only inside Dale's mind did he hear the sound of a standing ovation, like he was Pavoratti performing Don Giovanni for the last time. The room stayed quiet a few moments longer before the noise of chattering voices incrementally started up once again.

A few rogue clients left the crowd to walk to the conference room alone. As they passed him, Dale gave more specific instructions on how to get to where they were going without him, adding desynchronized hand gestures and a nervous, delicate laugh.

After a few minutes, Dale led those who remained in the kitchen to the conference room, like an adult leading his Scouts troop to a reserved campsite. There were about twenty people behind him. All followed Dale's lead through a hallway they had already walked earlier that morning. When they arrived at the conference room door, two new people were speaking to the receptionist at the front desk.

The receptionist was sitting down, leaning over her desk, her two fists resting softly underneath her chin, flirting with the Distinguished Gentleman of the duo. And standing next to the Distinguished Gentleman, Dale noticed, was the commercial's notable celebrity.

The celebrity dressed incognito, wearing a gray hoodie and a logoless blue and white baseball cap, and on her eyes, she wore tinted Aviator sunglasses. Dale had become starstruck on seeing the celebrity. From her presence he gasped out loud, placed his right hand over his open mouth and stopped short; the line of clients behind him now stalled.

For a quick moment, everyone's eyes were on Dale. Waiting for him to slip. To speak the unarticulated and say what everyone was thinking: *Oh my god, it's YOU!* But he's been here before and stopped himself, placing his right arm, again, by his side, and pretended his reaction was that of a cough or a sneeze he had interrupted.

The line of clients behind him took the initiative and walked the rest of the way, without him; the route to the office's conference room's door now apparent.

The celebrity stood next to the Distinguished Gentleman, whom Dale could only guess, based on their physical chemistry, was the celebrity's male partner. The celebrity wasn't talking; she was more watching the man she came in with, babbling relentlessly towards the overzealous receptionist.

Dale stepped in front of the conference room door and led the last few clients inside. As the clients passed him, Dale maintained a smile and a constant nodding of his head, listening to the conversation that took place by the receptionist's front desk.

Dale heard the receptionist make a joke, and the Distinguished Gentleman laughed. And the Distinguished Gentleman put out his fist for a pound, to which the receptionist responded with great nervous giggling.

Dale could tell the conversation was coming to a natural close. The Distinguished Gentlemen said *Good day* to the receptionist and turned away from her desk and walked towards the conference room door where Dale was still standing.

The celebrity followed behind the Gentleman. Dale stood patiently waiting, holding the conference room door open for them, with his right hand, giving himself a reason for still being there.

His stomach gurgled as the famous couple approached him. Dale held with a nervous excitement a brown jewel he crowned inside his clenched asshole. His knees weak, standing in front of the conference room door.

Before the famous couple entered the conference room, Dale knew this to be his one shot with the celebrity. He looked only in the celebrity's direction, pushing his gaze past the Distinguished Gentleman, who attempted to make eye contact with Dale and flashed a grin that an issue of *People's* magazine anointed as The Most Charming Smile of 2019.

Along with his smile, the Distinguished Gentleman held out his fist for a pound from Dale, an attempted distraction away from the office's honorable guest. Dale saw this and ignored the Gentleman's gesture, keeping his gaze on the celebrity's tinted Aviator sunglasses as she trailed behind the ageless man before her. Dale's reflection in her silver lens.

As he approached Dale, the Distinguished Gentleman felt a cramp in his upper bicep, having never before experienced rejection for this long in his life; having no choice but to lower his arm back to his side; his bid for connection unconsummated. He inched closer and closer to the door, eventually passing Dale, with a   face showcasing a frown that was recognized by everyone.

Dale said a quick *Hello* to the celebrity, as she passed him. His voice was barely audible but she noticed him and lifted her head up and smiled back, dropping the brow bar of her sunglasses to her nose and, like a slingshot, reverberated the word he said to her back.

When she passed him, the celebrity entered the conference room. Dale didn't remember him closing the door behind her or every client who he was invisible to, standing in her honor as she sat down in her seat like a judge entering her courtroom. He didn't remember walking back to the kitchen, exuding a joy only a child could hold, with a grin that showed nothing bad could ever happen to him. How he felt was impenetrable, light on his feet, as his heart ceased pounding like a drum like it had been all morning, and now rested in his chest with ease.

Dale was unloading the dishwasher, when Ava surprised him by sticking her head out from around the corner wall and asking him to join her in her office.

He had only visited Ava's office a few times before. His second interview was the most time he spent there. He'd pop his head in whenever Ava needed to order something or if she had mail she wanted him to carry out, but otherwise, that was it. He had no business in her office.

About a year ago, Dale had been sitting at the front desk, and he saw Ava crying in her office while on the phone. Dale jotted a question onto a post-it note, and he opened her door and held the note for her to read; the note asking if she was okay. She looked up at him, staying on the phone, and quickly, with her eyes, read the note in his hands, not changing her facial expression, and looked up at Dale, giving him a vague head nod to convey he should leave her office immediately.

There was a caste system at S.R.P, and Ava was at most a puppet for whoever it was that pulled the strings behind the curtain in California. But showing empathy was a power move, and Dale knew it. He didn't go in there without thinking about how it could benefit him.

Ava never said anything about the call. He never learned why she had been crying. It turned out his act of bravery was just a fleeting moment, a dot in the time bubble, and when it was over, it had been killed and buried and stayed between only them.

When he entered Ava's office this time, she was typing something into her computer, and she told him politely to sit down. He sat in the guest chair, waiting for her to speak first. He tried to stay calm, smiling and showing those who walked past her office that what was happening was just a casual encounter between a boss and her employee. There was no reason to think otherwise.

Ava finished typing and walked over to the seat next to Dale, sat down, and before speaking let out a giant sigh.

Well, said Ava, busy day. How are you?

Good. Good, said Dale, nervously.

Pretty exciting, our guest today, no? I rarely care for celebrities. I never get starstruck anymore. But her? I just love her movies.

So do I.

We rarely get female stars here. Have you noticed that? It's primarily famous men who come into our office. That entire room is filled with men who are rich because of her talent.

I bet that's true. Yes.

You probably don't know what it's like to be the only person like you in a room, do you? But she knows. And I know. And because of that, I have a tremendous amount of respect for her. She's welcome here anytime.

Yes. Yes. I agree, said Dale, trying to smile.

Are you okay? Do you need some water?

No, no. I'm fine.

I wanted to chat with you, Dale, before I left for California next week. Sorry for calling you in on such short notice. I know it's been a busy day, but I don't know when I'd have time otherwise.

Uhm, uhm, mumbled Dale, shaking his head in agreement. No problem, he said.

Are you sure you're alright?

Yes. Yes. I'm fine.

He changed his position in his chair, realizing he'd been sitting like a child giving a confession to a priest with his hands folded, lying on his knees, one leg crossed over the other. He separated his arms slightly and spread his legs out wider, hoping he could give off a more relaxed impression.

I wanted to talk with you about your future here, Dale, said Ava.

Here it comes, Dale thought.

There was a plastic clock on the wall by the door, which Dale then became aware of. In the center was Minnie Mouse holding a smile like his, with her arms twisted unnaturally, even for a cartoon, all just to tell you the time.

Where do you see yourself a year from now? Asked Ava, sitting with one leg folded over the other, meaning business now apparently. Her polite manner gone. This was serious.

Well, I'd like to continue working at S.R.P...

Doing what, you think?

I'm not sure I understand the question, unfortunately.

Ava let out another deep sigh, a pocket of air that had been stored inside her since Dale entered her office. For a moment, Dale thought she was about to laugh, then noticed she didn't.

Dale, people should have the opportunity to find out what they want to do with their life. I still haven't figured that out for myself yet. Don't you think you should have that opportunity, as well?

Uh, yes...

You do?

Yes?

Well, we just don't know if there is a place for you here that is a proper fit. Long-term, I mean.

You don't like the work I've been doing?

It's not a question of your work ethic, Dale.

I know what I want to do with my life. I don't think I have that problem.

Okay, can you achieve that here?

Dale paused for a moment before answering, Yes, he said.

Ava extended her smile even wider now. Dale could see the wrinkles in her face form in rows around her eyes and mouth.

Okay. Even so, the problem still remains as to what I should do with you, Dale. People have started to talk...

Talk? About what?

About you, Dale.

About me?

Yes.

Why?

They feel uncomfortable, Dale. Even worse, our clients have started to express the same opinions...

Uncomfortable how?

Do you want to be a PA for much longer, Dale?

I was hoping that I could be promoted to an Assistant position at some point. That's how I've come to understand, from other Assistants here, how one grows at S.R.P. I thought I was doing okay as a PA. What have people said about me exactly?

Have you noticed that other production assistants who were hired after you were promoted to...how can I best put this... *different* positions here at S.R.P.? While you're still only fulfilling the duties you were initially hired to do?

Yes.

Has that been a concern of yours, Dale?

No.

Interesting.

Is the problem that I continue to do the work you ask of me?

Obviously not.

Hmm.

Do you know how to use any of the editing systems we have here, Dale? Premiere? Final Cut? Do you know how to use Avid, Dale?

I do not. But I could learn.

You've never really brought it to my attention before this moment that it would be something you're interested in learning. Why do you think that is?

I might have expressed it.

Nope. I don't recall.

Well, I have experience with a few different editing systems. But I haven't had to use them since college. I'm not an expert on film editing. I have more experience as a writer. But I'm definitely familiar with the software. I thought, at least, if I did a good job with the position you hired me to do, we'd be having a different conversation.

Me too, Dale. Me too.

No one has given me any constructive criticism on how I should do my job differently. Even now, I still don't know what it is you want me to do other than what I'm already doing. What have people started to say about me?

There was a knock on Ava's door. Dale's head pivoted to the left to see who it was. A different producer walked in, and came over to Ava, and whispered something into her ear, and left the room.

I'm sorry, Dale, but we will have to continue this conversation another time, okay? After I come back from California, probably.

I don't understand. Are you saying I still have my job?

Did I say otherwise?

I really can't tell.

Look, we'll continue this conversation when I get back. I shouldn't have called you in today. We've just been too busy. I'm sorry. Everything's fine, okay? There's no need to worry. I just think I have to find a better way to communicate what I need from you to help you grow here. So that maybe we can both understand each other's needs more. Okay? I'll make sure to do that when I get back. As long as that's something you actually want?

Yes. Yes, it is. Dale lied.

Okay, great. We'll speak again soon. Just be patient with me, Dale. Now, if you could close the door on your way out, I'd appreciate it. Thank you.

Ava stood up from her chair, and headed back towards her desk, sat down, and started typing again. It was like he was never there.

He sat on the seat for a moment longer than he should have until he was pushed by some unknown force to stand up and walk to the door to exit. He felt his legs shaking from nerves, afraid they would not support his weight to the door. He managed to pass by Ava's desk without saying an additional word; her body language no longer registering his presence.

He wanted to cry out loud, in front of her, like a child, scream and shout in her face, punch and kick the walls to show her his rage, impress her with his anger, and give his tears as a parting gift. He should have stormed out of the office then. And quit his job. But he didn't know how.

Instead, he put his tiny paycheck before his pride, and walked out of her office to clean something and act like what she had said had little to no effect.

V

Happy Birthday Kareena

To make up for not going to the movies with Dale, Kajal invited him to go dancing, with a group of friends, for Kareena's birthday. Kajal didn't tell Dale what happened at the party. She didn't know how to tell Dale that she had been kissed by another man, and liked it. She was afraid to admit this to herself, even. Afraid, also, to hurt Dale. Afraid to lose him. Afraid to get screamed at; all of the above could apply, so she chose to stay in her silence.

The club Kareena chose, whatever it was - club, bar, nightclub, restaurant - was a speakeasy, dressed incognito as a taco shop.

The couple followed a group to an address, and from the sidewalk, the venue seemed to be a regular hole-in-a-wall taco joint, familiar to this side of the neighborhood. But out of place, and sitting next to a functioning kitchen was a man who wore all black, who sat on a stool next to an enlarged soda machine, unphased by the group's sudden appearance, asking with an almost dead-pan look, for the group's IDs. Dale was holding Kajal's wallet in his backpack. Kajal did not have a purse to match her outfit and asked if he could hold of her's what was necessary for the evening. Kajal searched for her ID and when she turned back around the enlarged soda machine was opened, to reveal the entrance to the nightclub the group had all come here to visit.

Inside the nightclub, Dale stood beside Kajal on the dance floor with his backpack hanging from his shoulders, his laptop inside weighing him down. Kajal danced among her friends, off to the side of Dale. Dale was on his way home when Kajal texted him, informing him of her evening plans; inviting him if he wanted to tag along. He didn't want to go dancing, not after the day he had at work. But if he didn't go, it would be another night spent alone in Ruksaana's apartment. He took his bag with him because he did not have the energy to drop it off in Harlem and head back down to the Lower East Side. He had already left work and did not want to go back into his office to show his face again, just to drop off his backpack. Afraid, showing his face would give his bosses a reason to ask him to stay later.

So, there Dale swayed, pathetically, holding onto the straps of his bag with both hands, like a highschool student, pivoting his legs to a song he did not know, trying to find its rhythm. Trying to hide his natural born, stoic, unenthused face to everyone around him who screamed the lyrics in his ears with great fervor.

He could feel the day's unspent dread resting inside him, looking at the only person he felt could help him release it. Kajal's eyes were closed, her head bent forward as if she was focusing on the floor. She danced with herself among the group. Dale was self-aware of his bid for connection, resting inside his chest and just a few feet from him, his reward, but he knew there would be a great cost if he were to spend it right then and there.

The group formed in a circle on the dance floor. No one taking the center lead. It was crowded inside the club. Intoxicated individuals shoved members of the birthday group aside in search of someone in a similar state of mind to be with. Walking to the bar or the bathroom wasn't an option; it was more like you moved through the crowd like a cell in a clogged artery, and only if you were lucky did you find yourself where you intended to be.

For most people, coming to this dance hall was not a chore, like it was for Dale. But for a way to avoid being alone. Everyone wanting to find some connection with a stranger to go home with and feel wanted for just one night. To orgasm but not by their own hand, but by the hand or mouth of another and fall asleep lying on their chest buzzed, knowing it wouldn't last forever.

It was all worth the discomfort of the space and the expensive drinks, their parent's credit cards paid for, and the loud music that played until 4 AM. It was always 4 AM when the clubs turned their house lights on and sent those still on their search to find connection elsewhere.

Dale landed at the bar. It was his turn to buy everyone drinks. A few people were in front of him, sitting on stools, drinking martinis with olives in their glasses, their faces unphased by the loud music and frustrated crowd behind them. To Dale, it seemed the people in front of him were in their natural habitat and he watched them like animals, as if he were a visitor inside a zoo.

They were better dressed than he was and he had come to feel insecure in his decision to come dressed comfortably in his white t-shirt, that he had also worn the day before, with jeans and the black Nike running shoes he liked to wear for work.

One of the bartenders made eye contact with Dale, and he ordered three cocktails, which came out to be $37 with tip. No one followed him to the bar, so he bought what he could carry back with him. He sighed and handed his card over to the bartender, who asked if he wanted to keep open a tab. He did not.

From where he was standing, the mass crowd behind him exuded the authority of a ten-foot brick wall. And Dale was already conjuring a plan on how to bring the drinks back to Kajal without making a fool of himself. It was too tight in the club to walk comfortably back without spilling anything.

The two people in front of Dale left their seats at the bar, and he moved in closer. He leaned his body against the bar's wooden counter, finally able to take a calm breath, now having some space between himself and the crowd on the dance floor behind him. He placed his forearms on the counter, realizing too late the surface beneath his arms was sticky from the continuous splash of sugary cocktails that were passed back and forth all night.

A voice from behind Dale vaguely made itself known through the volume of the music of the club. Hey! Boy, with the bag! Said the voice.

Dale didn't know the voice was directed at him, so he kept his gaze ahead, minding his own business, wanting a napkin to dampen his sticky arms with.

Excuse me! the voice said again. Dale still had not registered the voice wanted him until two rogue fingers tapped him hard on his padded shoulders, making him turn around.

Yes? Dale asked, annoyed, turning his body away from the bar.

Dale saw now where the voice had come from. Behind Dale stood a thin man around Dale's height, dressed in a red jumpsuit, wearing a camouflage bandanna around his neck, like a country singer, with burgundy-colored high-heeled shoes on his feet, staring Dale in the eyes.

I said, do you mind putting your bag down! It's too crowded in here for that! You bumped me.

Sorry about that! Pretty crowded in here!

It's pushing me away from the bar! It's hard enough to get the guy's attention as is!

Sorry, there's no place for me to put it! What would you like me to do?

Dale could hardly hear him. The music was too loud. The man in the red jumpsuit continued to speak, looking Dale straight in the eyes as he spoke. His eyes were dilated, his lips moving fast, but nothing audible came out. The man's lips stopped moving, his face changed, and he smiled at Dale as if he had completed a full sentence.

Dale leaned in closer to the man. I can't hear you! Said Dale, moving his ear down closer to the man's mouth.

I said, could you get my drinks for me? Since you're already at the bar and have the guy's attention! And you can put your bag down with my friends! Your bag! He repeated, pointing.

With your friends? Asked Dale, confused and unsure if he had heard the man correctly. Dale raised his left eyebrow unconsciously, thinking of what to say back.

Would you want to come over? Asked the man. We're just over there in the lounge section! We got a table! If you buy us a few drinks, we'll Venmo you? Do you have Venmo? If not, we can find another way to pay!

The man smiled at Dale and gave the aura to that of a kindergartener trying to receive a reward from their teacher.

No, that's okay! I'm okay! Said Dale, trying to smile, understanding the man now.

Are you alone? Asked the man.

Why would I come here alone? Dale thought.

No! I'm here with my girlfriend and a few of her friends! Dale explained, pointing to the wall of people behind them.

You have a girlfriend? I see!

Yeah!

So, you can't buy a couple of drinks for a few friendly fellas who might want to have a conversation with ya? Is that it? Because you have a girlfriend?

What?

Because you have a girlfriend!

Yes, I do!

I see!

Yes!

Did I offend you, sir? Mr. Straight Whiteman in a crowded bar with a backpack on?

What?

You don't like me? Is that it? I saw your judgmental eyes the moment I saw you! You have hate written all over your face! You don't want to buy me a drink, right? It's you who's missing out, Mr. Whitey, sir! Who came out to this particular club on this particular night from Long Island, probably, just to waste other people's time? Is that it? You wouldn't want to talk to me? You wouldn't want to talk to my friends? I'm a good dancer! I'm a good friend to have! It's your loss, Mr. Whitey, Sir!

It's my what?

Your loss, bitch!

Dale opened his lips to try and respond, but his words were intercepted by the man's right hand that came down hard and fast on Dale's right cheek. A tempo change occurred over in the DJ's corner, and the man in the red jumpsuit laughed and disappeared into the crowd behind him like a cartoon character in a dream sequence.

Dale stood there frozen still, holding the right part of his face, shocked, hunched over; lost in shame and exhaustion. He wondered if he had bad luck or if some sort of cosmic energy subjected him to these types of interactions with strangers.

No one happened to see his altercation with the person, and if they did no one said anything to him. Too embarrassed to look and see his face in the mirror, he stayed put and waited for his drink order to arrive. The side of his face started to sting red. He touched his cheek and used his phone to observe the mark that now appeared on the right side of his face, while others gyrated obliviously behind him. The bartender placed the three cocktails he ordered down on the counter, along with his debit card and receipt. Dale turned and noticed he had moved a few feet from his spot along the bar. The bartender called out to him to make sure he knew the drinks were his. Dale didn't know how the distance between him and the bar had formed, which disoriented him. He held his marked cheek, keeping eye contact with the floor, and excused himself back to the bar, where he signed his name, picked up one of the cocktails he ordered, and took a sip.

The crowd behind Dale moved in a wave-like motion symbiotic to the DJ's track. The man in the red jumpsuit appeared again and, by the crowd's force, pushed Dale against the bar's counter, causing him to drop his drink.

As his drink fell from his hand, Dale watched it fall in slow motion through the air past his knees. He watched the rim of the glass touch the floor, making at first just a crack and then exploding around him into a thousand pieces. Glass and tequila covered his and the surrounding people's legs and feet. He followed, for as long as he could, each individual piece of glass, that went in its own unique direction, without feeling; accepting that wherever each piece landed was out of his control. If he could rewind time and pause the scene right before the glass fell, he would stop when each piece came back together, to make the glass whole, again, in his hand.

Dale stayed, leaning against the counter with his head just under the bar. More aware than ever of the bar, the crowd, and the room.

He tried to breathe. He tried to stop the room from spinning and return his vision to normal. He lifted his head up and held in his anger. An image of Kajal's face came to mind. He blamed this incident on her. He wanted to get back to her. He grabbed the two drinks off the counter and excused himself through the crowd, not caring if he shoved a little too hard to get through. When he returned to their spot, they were gone.

He looked over the heads of the bodies that surrounded him and saw no recognizable face. He saw his new friend dancing at the bar, alone, waving him back over like a genie in a Disney cartoon.

Dale stood on the dance floor, holding Kajal and Kareena's drinks, avoiding making eye contact with his new friend. He put all his focus inside his shoe, moving his toes around to ring out the tequila that had absorbed inside his sock, as the bass from the speakers pulsated through his veins like an additional pulse.

Outside, on the curb, Kajal held Kareena's hair as she vomited into the street. Cars sped by them, just missing Kareena's head. Fellow night strollers walked past them, making rude comments or gestures or walking past and not seeing them at all. The rest of their friend group had left. Some stayed dancing, unaware of Kareena's condition, while others decided to call it a night at the site of Kareena's vomit.

The two entered a diner down the block and sat at a booth. Kajal ordered french fries and two ginger ales for her and Kareena, who looked pale and slumped across her seat.

Was it something you ate? Kajal asked.

I don't know, she said.

Kajal wanted to text Dale their whereabouts, but her phone died, and she had not memorized his number. Kareena sat across from Kajal sipping the soda, feeling bad for herself.

When Dale left for the bar, Kareena had become light-headed and short of breath and told Kajal she felt sick. The scene had become overwhelming. From her vantage point, there was no place for them to go comfortably. Around them was nothing but bodies and no clear pathway to exit.

Kajal turned from Kareena and looked towards the bar. She could see Dale and even tried to wave him back over. She called out his name, but her voice was no match against the DJ's speakers or the crowd surrounding her. She turned back, and a security guard was walking through the crowd, holding a fainted woman in his arms.

The guard towered over Kajal. For a moment, she panicked and thought the woman in the guard's arms was Kareena, but was relieved to find Kareena behind her, cushioning herself against Kajal's back holding on to her shoulder's.

The diner was filled with young people on a food break before making their way out to the clubs. Kareena excused herself to the bathroom, and Kajal sat quietly eating the french fries she ordered, dipping each fry into a blob of gleaming red ketchup. Kareena made it to the bathroom, went into one of the stalls, and stuck a finger down her throat to conjure whatever it was inside of her that made her feel ill. She waited for the stall to stop spinning, before getting back up to wash her hands and mouth and then went back out to the table where Kajal sat and slumped back down into the booth.

You alright?

Yeah.

After Kareena said she could handle it, they left the diner to return to the club. Kajal tried to get back inside, but the bouncer wouldn't let her enter without paying the after-midnight $40 fee. For some reason, they missed having their hands stamped, and after a specific time, the club charged to get inside. She tried to explain her situation to the bouncer, but he didn't have the memory or energy to care. She told him her future husband was inside waiting for her, and there was no other way for her to reach him.

Kareena stood by a slew of large garbage bags, smoking a cigarette, waiting to see what commenced between Kajal and the bouncer. Kareena cocked her head upwards and blew smoke out into the open night. She was tired but started to feel a little better than before and even a little hungry. The club was on a busy street. Across from them was a parking lot, and next to it a college dorm. Kareena blew another cloud of smoke into the air and watched as people passed her, feeling slightly disassociated from the scene and the people on the street.

Kareena knew she didn't want to be out much longer and that her birthday night was ruined. She wanted to go home to bed but was annoyed at the prospect of leaving early on her birthday to spend the night alone.

Kajal borrowed $40 from Kareena and re-entered the club, pissed off. She passed the entrance and squeezed herself through the club's crowd to the bathroom, where she peed and washed her hands. She walked back out onto the dance floor and saw no sign of Dale still.

She continued towards the bar and passed a section with red leather couches and tables holding tall bottles of Ciroc and baskets of fried chicken. Kajal walked past the tables and found Dale sitting alone at another booth with two untouched cocktails before him. She walked over, noticed the red mark on his cheek, and gently stroked it with the back of her hand. She could tell he had been crying when he looked up. He still looked like the boy she met so long ago. Looking into his youthful eyes, she remembered her own innocence, a feeling she knew would never return. She picked up his bag, moved it to the empty bench across from him, sat down and listened to whatever he had to tell her. Before they stood up to leave, Dale projected as loud as he could into her ear, over the music: *I want to quit my job!*

VI

The Weather was Changing (Again)

The weather in New York was changing. The air had turned from a cool, dry breeze to a crisp, biting cold. The first snow of the year had fallen. A soft white bed lightly covered the streets of Manhattan, gracing every corner from the government housing building Kajal's family lived in, across the hilly path across Central Park, to the Soviet-style building of her school where she walked to attend classes.

A few hours after Dale left for work, Kajal woke up and left her home and walked north along 5th Avenue. Sometime after Kareena's birthday, Kajal accepted a part-time position working at a café on campus. She started her mornings by making coffee, taking out the frozen pastries and quiches from the freezer and putting them on a display shelf by the window near the front door. She wore a uniform that consisted of a black hat that displayed the cafe's logo, a white t-shirt, and a thin black apron with navy blue jeans that she purchased with her mother on a trip to Costco. On her way to the cafe to start her shift, she ran into an army of families, all leaving their homes to take part in the snow that had just begun to cover the sidewalk. The children of these families were dressed for the cold, excited to see what the snow looked like on the dead trees and pathways that interweaved themselves throughout the park. It was not the crowd she usually saw on her way to work. It was often much quieter at this hour.

She went out the night before with Kareena and a few other friends. Maybe it was her headache or the lack of sleep that caused the slight discomfort in her. Still, she felt uneasy at the sight of these families walking in the same direction, perfectly spaced apart on the sidewalk as if they were each assigned a specific metric of distance from one another, all clones of the same molecule.

She nuzzled her head inside her coat for warmth and walked through the families, holding like a shield in front of her, her mug of hot black coffee; the coffee Dale had brewed from their French press before he left for work.

They all crossed the street, unafraid of the incoming traffic. The cars slowed for these families. Each family white and affluent, appearing in the falling snow as pale silhouettes. Watching them cross, Kajal was reminded of a zombie parody film Dale showed her a few years back when they first started dating. She couldn't remember the title but remembered liking the film. The zombies here were all doctors, lawyers, and diplomats, all wearing the same Patagonia winter outfits. A more modern type of horror.

Kajal, who already suffered from poor eyesight, did not find relief in the beauty the snowfall brought to the neighborhood this morning. She missed the charm of the city's winter aesthetic due to the fatigue made from last night's outing and the subtle pounding of her head from her hangover. She wanted to be confined inside the walls of the cafe and feel protected behind the freezer's cool titanium door, ritualistically selecting the days-old frozen pastries, as she did at the beginning of each shift.

The families continued to come. Each pod contained the same monogamous group of alabaster offspring with two parents, one male, one female, and two children of the opposite sex and three years apart.

Kajal took a sip of her coffee to help distract her from the pain in her head. She kept her head down and walked north. She was thankful the coffee was hot. She twisted the cap off her mug and let the steam break out and move fast past her face, forming droplets of moisture on her eyelashes.

Behind her, a family of four caught up and began to pass her on the sidewalk. Her chest tightened at the sight of them, and her breath fell short, having not seen them coming, and she feared an oncoming panic attack.

When she had her first panic attack, she thought she was going to die. It happened when she was arguing with Dale in her mother's living room. Both Ayad and Ruskanna hid in their bedrooms with the doors closed as if they were children hiding from their parents, who were in the middle of a fight. Kajal could feel a tightness knotting in her chest. Her throat closed, and her vision dimmed. Dale was screaming over her. And when she tried to suck in air to breathe, a thin wheezing sound came out of her throat. She could not control her breathing, and the room turned white.

The family behind Kajal passed her as her vision began to wane. She looked behind her to see if any more were coming, afraid she would pass out in front of the families. The parents of the children smiled apologetically as they passed Kajal, hoping she'd excuse their over-buoyant children who had run up ahead, screaming piercing sounds into the air, excited to enter the park to play in the snow.

The perfect family, she thought.

Kajal slowed her pace to let the family gain some distance from her, not able to accept with grace the noise they made. She watched them disappear through the park's entrance and then up a hill and stayed put until they disappeared from her vantage point as the snow continued to fall, already covering their tracks.

When she finally arrived at the cafe, her headache had worsened and she drank a large glass of water. She played music from her phone as she set up, drank more coffee, and ate a frozen pastry she warmed while humming to the music that reverberated out of her cellphone.

This was how she spent her mornings in the cafe. A respite from the crowds of students and tourists alike. Kajal learned to appreciate the quiet, reflective time working in the cafe gave her. Unlike Dale, getting a head start to her day was of little importance to her, having been used to her whole life waking up and entering the chaos of the day as soon as she heard the first sounds of her family moving about their morning, and feeling pressured to join them.

When she finished her shift, she walked to the SIPA building for her first class. She stamped her feet down hard onto the weatherbeaten mat beneath her. She still had a slight headache from her hangover and thought about buying some pain medication to help relieve it. The snow from her boots fell off her like white powder, confining her inside a circle of the white gleaming substance. The lobby was empty, aside from a small group of disheveled male students who sat separately from each other in beige, rigid arm chairs sanctioned off inside the designated workspace for students. Each student had their heads tucked into a textbook. A laptop somewhere close by to each one. The sound of an email rang in the dull open air of the lobby. Kajal walked anonymously to her locker and took out the books needed for her evening's lecture.

She entered the lecture hall early and realized she was unaware of the time. The professor had yet to arrive, and only a few students were present for the class.

It had been weeks since Kajal attended the housewarming party at Kareena's friend's apartment. She still hadn't told Dale yet about the kiss she received that night, and had started to question, as the days passed, if the kiss had actually happened. She was so deliriously drunk when it happened, that she had become comfortable with reducing the moment as a figment of her intoxicated brain. But on seeing Marc in the lecture hall, sitting two rows ahead of her regular seat, all the memories from that night had returned with extreme clarity, like that of fragmented clouds in the process of welding themselves into a forecasted sky.

She realized she was still wearing the cafe's hat from her shift, and she ripped it off her head so violently that the velvet strap broke, and her hair became more knotted and entangled.

Marc had his head down, sleeping on the desk, unaware of Kajal's presence as she walked by him to get to her seat.

She contemplated leaving and missing the day's lecture. She had not seen him in this class before and was confused by his presence.

In the bright fluorescent lighting of the lecture hall, she realized she had no feelings towards the boy who slept with his head down on the desk before him. He was so pathetic. Whatever feelings manifested between them happened due to the rare cosmic timing of tequila, dancing, and grief, all of which had dissipated since he Irish goodbye'd her at the party.

Kajal looked outside the hall windows, waiting for the professor to arrive, hoping he never would. Kajal wished she could be anywhere other than where she was. Outside, the sky hung over the campus like a white flat board, which made Kajal think of a film set, which made her think of Dale, and she wondered if anything was real or if anything that happened to anyone mattered.

After the lecture, Kajal made her way down the steps to exit. Marc had seen her stand up from her chair, and he stood waiting, staring as if he was confident nobody else in the room could see him. He slept through most of the lecture, and nobody bothered to wake him, so he had a pink line running across his face that was an imprint of his left arm.

Hey, she said to him.

Hey, he said back, never diverting his eye contact.

She realized she couldn't say his name out loud. Marc. The name sounded strange, rolling off her tongue or, if said, quietly in the inner sanctum of her brain. She noticed he had gotten a haircut since they had last seen each other. The back and sides of his head were shaved, with a slight fade showing more skin the closer you got to his neck.

Marc asked how she was doing.

Good. Not bad. Why?

Nothing.

You're in this class now?

I'm missing a credit for the semester. The school fucked me.

How?

By making me miss a credit.

She didn't know why she was speaking to him. She could feel herself playing dumb when talking to him. She kept talking about nothing, all just to be polite and hide her true feelings as he stood over her, watching her, unable to speak.

A different professor walked into the room then. A new class would soon be starting. Kajal looked behind her, towards the door to exit, and she quickly thought of an excuse to leave. She said goodbye to Marc and walked past the professor she didn't know to exit, doing everything she could to stop herself from running.

Kajal met Dale at a Vietnamese restaurant on MacDougal Street to share a bánh-mì and a bowl of lemongrass chicken Pho. Kajal reached out to Dale to meet. Because of her moment with Marc, she craved human connection. She wanted to know if she could connect with another human being and be loved and cared for.

It had been their first meal together, alone, since Kajal started grad school. On the train down to MacDougal Street, she thought about the kiss with Marc and how it felt to be desired by another human being, rather than being resented by one. It had been too long since she felt at peace with Dale. It wasn't so much Marc as a person Kajal wanted; she barely knew him. But he was someone new, and she found this exciting about him. He understood her grief. He was not entirely known, but someone who might know how to hold space for her.

Kajal walked into the restaurant and found Dale waiting by a female hostess who brought them to a table that just opened up. Dale had been writing at a café near the restaurant and came by early to put his name in with the maitre'd. And when Kajal entered his name was called. They sat in their seats in what would have been, at another time in their life, a comfortable silence. But as they sat down and looked through their menus, both could feel a void neither knew how to address.

We should schedule more time like this each week, said Kajal, looking up for a moment from her menu. It's nice to be off campus.

I would love that, said Dale.

Do you want to see how I organize my calendar?

Dale didn't answer but watched Kajal take out her phone with a child's enthusiasm as she flashed him the coded color calendar on her cell phone.

What color would you like to be?

What do you mean?

On my calendar. What's your favorite color?

Her question made Dale look away from his menu. The restaurant was packed with people. Dale and Kajal sat next to the Pho bar, which had a brick wall behind it with shelves with campy dishes displayed and three different colored Buddha statues Kajal questioned the appropriateness of, judging by the all white staff in the kitchen.

It was freezing inside the restaurant. The heat was on, but the line for those waiting to be seated extended out the door, keeping a consistent path for the freezing air to make its way inside the restaurant, helping maintain a persistent chill.

Do you need to put me on your calendar to remember to spend time with me? Dale asked her.

No...

Why do you think it's not automatic? To see me, I mean.

Automatic? What does that even mean?

To find time to be with me. Why isn't it just something that you do?

Because I'm busy.

You're so busy you need to color-code me into your calendar?

Yes. I can't do everything like I used to. I'm in grad school. You know this.

It's not only because you're in grad school. I understand you're busy with school. But it's something else. I feel like you're avoiding me. And you don't want to admit it.

I'm not avoiding you, Dale.

Why did you reach out to me today? Did something happen?

No.

It's not very like you. I was surprised to see your text.

That hurts my feelings.

Why? It's true. You don't text me. I text you. I reach out to you to do stuff. I invite you to do things and involve you in my life. You do not.

This is all because I didn't go to the movies with you?

You know it's not just that. It has nothing to do with that. You're never home.

Then what bed do I sleep in at night?

You come home when I'm asleep, and you're there when I wake up. How is that us seeing each other? I work. I leave in the morning. I barely know what's going on in your life. You're never there when I come home. Nor do you invite me out. It's like I live with your mother. It's awkward for me.

I invited you to Kareena's birthday party.

That was one time, Kajal. I don't know why you're acting so ignorant about this. You know we never see each other. I don't know why you're minimizing this.

I'm not minimizing it. I'm just busy, that's all.

You're using school as an excuse.

I'm not.

There are parties you don't want me going to. You spend late nights studying in the library when you could be home at least some of the nights. Where were you last night?

I was with Kareena.

Always with Kareena.

Studying at home is distracting for me. I'm more productive in the library.

Okay, but you weren't studying in a library last night. You were drinking in a bar.

Why don't you live with your mom and dad in the suburbs if you're so unhappy living with my mother, who doesn't ask a dime of you to stay there.

I don't want to live away from you. I love you. Do you want me to do that? Move out?

No. But if you're going to complain about living somewhere rent-free, move out.

I used to feel like you always wanted me around. That you liked spending time with me. That I was the only person you wanted around you. Everyone else was background noise then. At least that's how you made me feel. And now I feel like I couldn't matter less to you. It's like this school changed you. Like you think you're better than me or something.

You don't not matter, Dale. I don't know why you keep saying that.

Well, something's different. Things are not the same. I'm trying to be as honest about my feelings with you as I can, and then when we speak, you act as if everything is normal. It makes me feel crazy.

Nothing is normal for me. I'm busy with school. I don't know how many more ways I can say it. My father just died, I moved out of my apartment too, and I miss it, and you keep making this shit all about yourself and your inconvenience.

That's not what I'm doing. That's not fair. You can't put those two things together. They're separate. We can talk about our relationship separately from your father's death.

You're selfish. You're being a selfish asshole right now.

Okay. You're getting upset. Now we can't talk. Do you want the Pho or a Banh Mi?

Don't be condescending.

I'm not. You don't want to speak seriously. You want to pretend like everything is okay, and it isn't.

That's not what I'm doing. Stop saying that. Stop acting like you know everything.

Kajal said nothing afterwards, and looked at Dale with such rage that he knew if he said the wrong thing, she'd stand up from the table and walk out of the restaurant.

A waitress finally approached the table, and Dale ordered the lemongrass chicken Pho and a pork Bahn Mi sandwich.

I don't eat pork, said Kajal.

It's not a Bahn Mi if it doesn't have the pork paté in it. I wanted a Bahn Mi. Everything else is just a sandwich.

But I don't eat pork.

Then we'll order the chicken sandwich and the lemongrass Pho.

Okay.

The waitress took their menus, walked away from their table and an awkward silence ensued.

Is it wrong of me to be nostalgic about our life before Columbia? We were a lot stronger a year ago. Or something's different. I may not know how to articulate it well.

Oh, so you're afraid to say something?

No, I'm just saying I may not be using the right words.

Maybe it's you who is afraid to say something. Ever think of that?

I just have a feeling, that's all. A feeling I don't have the words for.

We had our problems before I went to grad school, Dale. Things weren't perfect at any point in our relationship.

I know. But when are things ever perfect, though? Who doesn't have problems in their relationship?

Yeah, I agree. But we've been together for 11 years. That's a long time to be with someone.

You always sound defeated when you say that. 11 years coming out of your mouth sounds like you survived a prison sentence.

It's been a long time! That's all I'm saying.

What's your point, though? I value how long we've been together. I think it's a success we've been together that long.

I do, too. But haven't you ever wondered what else is out there? You never thought about what it's like to be in another relationship?

Have you?

Not seriously. But I've thought about it.

See, that sounded like you just retracted from what you really wanted to say. Because you're afraid of how it sounds, when it comes out of your mouth.

I'm not retracting anything.

No? That you want to break up?

That's not what I said.

You said you thought about it.

No, I didn't. I said I've wondered what having been in other relationships is like. I've only really been in one. And it's this one. I've never dated. We've been together since we were 17. I'm just saying that's a long time.

Okay. We've been together for a long time and...

Nothing! I don't know what you want me to say. I literally started this conversation by suggesting we spend more time together. And you've turned it into an argument.

Fine. Have it your way. We won't talk about it. And you can use the color blue for me.

What?

For your calendar. You can use the color blue.

When they finished eating, Dale got the check and paid for their food. The two went outside the restaurant and walked the streets of the West Village, freezing. Dale noticed the line to get inside the restaurant had shortened. They looked up and saw stars in the sky. It was a rare clear night in the city.

On the train uptown, Kajal was on her phone. Dale was tired from the day and sat quietly beside her. He looked out the window and watched as the express train sped past the other stations, the setting changing rapidly through columns like a film strip through a projector.

When they entered the apartment, it was quiet. The cat was waiting for them by the door. Kajal picked up the cat and kissed him on his forehead. Dale turned on the television.

Dale asked Kajal if she'd like to watch something before bed?

No, I'm tired, she responded. I think I'm just going to sleep.

Okay.

And with that, Kajal took her cat to their bedroom and laid down with things on her mind she was afraid to admit, afraid to say out loud, that kept her from falling asleep.

VII

Gentrification

Dale woke from a bad dream he was having.

Kajal was lying still with her eyes closed beside him, and he sat up on his side of the bed, sweating, looking down at his legs thinking of his own death. He was still in his pajamas and groggy from his slumber. The moon's light was potent, shedding the last of its energy down onto the city before the sun would rise and erase it.

He turned to see if his shuffling woke up Kajal. It didn't. She lay there still, sleeping beside him.

Death was not an uncommon theme to Dale's anxious mind. It has happened before, Dale woke himself up saying the words *I am going to die* in his sleep. The words left his lips as his head lifted from the pillow, waking him, as he watched the last of the muttered words leave his lips.

Afterwards, he'd find himself sitting upright in his bed, staring down at his own two feet, sweating. Not remembering what he dreamt about that brought him to this new angled position, sitting upright in his bed.

His tone when speaking the words that woke him felt similar to that of an epiphany. As if whispered by an apparition into his ears, unwanted, while hovering over his bed and leaving before he could ask a follow-up question.

He never remembered the dream that came beforehand. The transition from dream to waking life happened too quickly for him to remember anything, as he came to just when the words *going to die* left his lips. He could only remember the words he said and how they felt coming out of his mouth and the ambiguity of the source to his dread so early in the morning.

To calm down, he'd stare at his feet and try to slow his breathing. Hoping to get a minute or two more of sleep before his alarm went off to wake him.

Dale moved off the bed and looked out the window. There was a biker riding north along Third Avenue. There wasn't traffic at this hour, just a few cars driving alongside the lonely biker. He was so tired and wanted to sleep but knew he could take advantage of having woken up this early to write.

Dale grabbed his toothbrush from out of his top drawer, took out both parts of his retainer, and put them away inside its case. He crossed the room to exit. Through the small opening of their bedroom, his eyes still adjusting to the dark, he could sense someone standing in the hallway watching him.

He did not expect to see Ruksaana's silhouette in the doorway so early in the morning. He wished she had made some type of noise or gesture to show she was standing outside his bedroom door just as he was about to get dressed.

He was usually the only one up at this hour and did not need to think much about respecting the boundaries of others. Now, he and Ruksaana were up, watching each other in the dark.

He slowly started to transition away from his spot in his bedroom, careful not to embarrass her. He gathered his things for the bathroom and opened the door slowly to leave. Ruksaana stood there, still, watching him.

Good morning, Dale, said Ruksaana, chuckling, feeling caught. Dale stepped outside of the bedroom. Ruksaana shifted her body to face her own bedroom down the hall, not knowing how to move comfortably in the situation she put herself in.

The cat came out from behind her and stood between them in the hallway, acting as a mediator.

Good morning, he said to her in a tone that required her to answer back with some sort of explanation.

Is Kajal inside? She asked him.

Yes, Dale whispered back. He opened the door a few inches further, enough for her to see inside.

Okay, she said, not looking further in, trusting him.

Do you want me to wake her up?

No, no. That's okay.

Are you sure?

No, that's okay. I think bad dream, yes.

She smiled at Dale shyly. He didn't know if she was talking about his dream or hers. Ruksaana's smile reminded him of Kajal's. Like her daughter, she had eyes that could light up a room, even in the dark.

He glanced at her kindly, no longer mad, but hinted with a physical gesture that he needed to use the restroom.

Ruksaana turned and headed down the hallway towards her bedroom. Dale passed the cat in the hallway and entered the bathroom, wishing he had been more helpful to her. He knew she was worried about Kajal, but he felt there was nothing he could do to make her feel more at ease about whatever had caused her stress.

Dale picked up the seat from the toilet bowl, turned the shower nozzle towards the hot water, and started to relieve himself.

When Kajal's father died, Ruksaana never showed a tear to anyone, even when alone with her daughters. It was her silent intention to move on and hide her pain till it passed. But what she kept hidden was seen in other ways by her loved ones. She had grown more concerned for her health. Making an attempt to eat better and go outside more for exercise. She feared more for her son, who still hadn't found himself a job or gone back to school. What would he do after she was gone? Who would take care of him?

When Kajal would reminisce about their father to her siblings, Ruksaana would sit quietly, listening, consoling her children when she had to. But she always segued into isolation or sat in the corner of the living room alone to sew or watch TV as they talked.

Above him, Dale could hear muffled sounds of a couple arguing through the vent above the showerhead. The couple's screaming conjured a scene inside Dale's mind of two knives being dragged along the other's blade. He could not understand their words but heard the pitch and force at which the two were speaking. Dale could hear objects being thrown around the apartment through the walls. The sound of glass shattering penetrated as he threw water onto his face to try and wake himself up.

He wondered if he was still dreaming. Was he the only one in the building who heard this?

There was a dog inside the apartment, too. An older dog. By the depth and volume of its slow intermittent bark, he could tell the dog was out of breath and agitated by its owner's arguing. Without any conscious effort, Dale could visualize the dog's face barking at its masters, screaming at them to *Stop... Stop!*

Dale spit toothpaste from out of his mouth into the sink. He turned the faucet on to rinse again.

He turned on the showerhead and stepped under the hot water. He let the hot water run down his back. Even through the sound of the harsh running water he could hear the couple still. He closed his eyes, listening, doing whatever he could to block them out.

At work, he was reorganizing the supply closet. Noting what they needed, he made a list for the receptionist every two weeks to order more supplies to restock the shelves. Sticky notes. 2 terabyte hard drives. Pens. Pencils. Pink latex-free erasers. It was still early in the work day. Dale had a cup of coffee with him and a John Coltrane track playing from his cell phone. He was comfortable. He was alone. A rare moment of peace at work.

An editor had come into the office early, accidentally leaving a hard drive with footage he needed for the day at his home in Brooklyn. The receptionist asked Dale if he could go and get it. The editor was apparently too busy to go himself.

Not really having a choice, the receptionist called Dale an Uber. The car picked him up in front of the building and took him over the bridge into Brooklyn to a newly renovated apartment complex in Williamsburg that had a doorman in the vestibule and a Whole Foods across the street.

Dale entered the building's lobby and noticed first how tall the ceiling was. Dale took note of an abstract sculpture placed by the building's entrance and questioned its purpose for being there. His eyes took him past the sculpture to a slew of long decadent shelves with a small keyhole and a placard displaying a name on one line and an apartment number on the next. Next to the shelves was a small seating area that contained two long red leather couches and a coffee table with expensive magazines stacked equally together into two piles. Two tall green ferns stood on either side of the table with a rug underneath that looked like it was the hair taken from a Komondor dog.

The apartment building reminded Dale of hotels his family would visit on vacation. Where you could expect the smell of chlorine in the air when you walked in through the lobby. Dale did not smell chlorine here, just the scent of lavender essential oils trying to cover up the smell of citrus cleaning solution that could clear one's nostrils.

He walked towards the doorman's desk, who was engaged in a conversation with two people Dale assumed were residents of the building. The doorman stood beside his large marble desk talking to the couple.

The doorman saw Dale enter the lobby through his peripherals but paid him no mind. He did not think twice about if the boy who stood in the lobby questioning the purpose of the abstract sculpture was of any concern. He knew right away he had never seen the boy, but took his time leaving the conversation with the building's residents.

Dale inched his way closer to the front desk. He noticed a small dog standing beside the couple on the floor, patiently waiting with its tongue out; echoes from his memory of his time in the shower that morning. Dale stood a few feet from the main desk, reading his notes over as they spoke. Trying to memorize what he had written so he would know what to say when he got his chance to speak.

The couple in front of Dale exited their conversation with the doorman and Dale got the man's attention by saying Hello, politely.

The doorman moved his eyes upwards, finally acknowledging Dale. His face was not kind. Dale said what he was there to do, mentioning the editor's name and apartment number.

The doorman asked if Dale had a key, in an accent he just then noticed.

Yes, said Dale.

It was apparent this was not a common request asked of the doorman. He questioned whether it was a good idea to let a stranger into the home of one of his tenants without some sort of prior verbal confirmation. If Dale had just walked past the marble desk with confidence, the two might have had just a small exchange of words. But because he could pick up on Dale's nervous energy, he felt obligated to investigate further.

An older couple entered the lobby, and Dale watched the doorman's face change from a frown to a bright smile.

The older couple waved hello as they passed the doorman and continued behind the wall that blocked Dale's view of the elevators. As Dale watched the older couple pass him, he thought what he and Kajal would look like at their age. He wondered if they would grow old together, and if they did, would they live in a building that had a lobby that smelled nice or had fern plants next to rugs that looked like dead dogs as you walked past and had pointless sculptures in the lobby that did nothing but stand out as eye sores, in an attempt, by the building's architect, to create a novel and sophisticated space, to band-aid the wounds in a town whose reputation now stands on those who did the kicking out.

The doorman asked Dale to wait beside his desk for a moment. Dale did as the doorman asked him to and stepped aside, waiting by a blank white wall decorated with a floor-length mirror. Dale watched the doorman briefly walk away from his desk and quickly return. In his absence, Dale turned to see his reflection in the mirror, looking at himself staring back at him, and he contemplated the purpose of his existence.

The doorman picked up the phone and dialed in a number. Dale could not tell who the doorman was speaking to based off of the few words he heard him say. After about a minute, the phone call ended, and the doorman waved Dale over, using only his index finger to address him and saying to Dale in his ambiguous accent, *You can go*.

The elevator in Kajal's mother's building smells of dried-up piss from drunken, wayward men who, in the night, wandered into the building, mistaking the elevator for a convenient bathroom stall, and pulling out their cocks to urinate onto the silver panel walls.

The carpeted elevator Dale was in now, riding up to the third-floor apartment in a luxury complex building in Williamsburg, smelled like flowers and played music by the Beach Boys.

During his time with the doorman, Dale had grown curious about what the editor's apartment might look like. His family did okay, but he assumed no one in his immediate family could afford to live alone in a luxury building like this.

Dale was let out onto the third floor. The windowless hallway was quiet and carpeted, dimly lit by overhead ceiling lights. Dark pink wallpaper covered the walls. A dry vacuous air lingered. Walking through it, one could expect an employee with a trolley cart of fresh towels and cleaning supplies to come from around the corner to enter one of the many doors to volunteer their cleaning services.

He noted a small placard on the wall that listed the floor's apartment numbers and continued in the direction he thought was correct.

In front of the editor's door was a welcome mat that read *Fuck You* in large golden-brown letters. Standing on the welcome mat, Dale envisioned loud punk rock music coming from the other side of the door, shaking the door off its hinges. The apartment's door was black, glistening like it was newly polished. Tiny white light bulbs from the ceiling reflected off the door like white flowers that swayed depending on which direction you moved your body in.

Before Dale entered the apartment, his cell phone vibrated from inside his coat pocket. He pulled it out quickly, anxious to see the message and glanced at it quickly just to see his mother's name on his phone's home screen. He clicked the button on the side without reading the message, turning the phone's screen black, and then used the key he was given by the editor to enter the apartment.

The apartment was not as clean as the lobby. Laundry was thrown about on the living room floor. A Prince Street Pizza box with the remaining slices of a pie sat on the kitchen counter, with concave pepperoni disks gathering grease from its time throughout the night. He looked outside a sliding door window, which stretched from floor to ceiling, and saw a small porch that faced the street. On the porch, there was a small round table for one, and in its center sat a used ashtray with a few abandoned stubs of cigarettes left shriveled and ashy.

It was clear the editor lived here alone. It would surprise Dale if two people lived inside the apartment and left it looking like it was. He walked through the kitchen, making sure to avoid stepping on anything he might come across that was fragile. He looked at his notes for directions, turned right at the corner he was supposed to, and walked in through a door down a hallway that was left ajar.

The room he entered was clean. Light came in through another sliding door window. There was a small bed made, and outside the sliding door was another outdoor space, though much larger than the one in front that held the round portable table.

Against the wall, Dale saw a desk that had a computer monitor setup. A screensaver of a cartoon human skull bounced off each corner of the screen; it's bloodless face laughing at Dale. Dale walked over to the computer monitor, swiped right on the mouse, and entered a password he was given by the editor. He disconnected the hard drive and double-checked everything was in its proper place. He double checked the footage the editor needed was all there. It was. He logged off the computer, shut it down properly, and headed back out into the living room.

When he entered the living room, Dale saw a light flurry of snow had started to fall out through the porch's sliding door windows. He took out his cell phone to call an Uber back to Midtown. The wait time was fifteen minutes. This was much longer than he was used to waiting for a car. He thought about canceling but didn't. Dale sighed, sat on the couch in the living room of the editor's apartment, and contemplated his next move.

He didn't want to go outside to wait for his car in the cold. He watched the snow fall for a few seconds more and decided to kill time by perusing around the apartment.

He poked his head inside a second bedroom door. Nothing was interesting beyond the door, just a disheveled bedroom he assumed was the editor's. It was the second most lived in space aside from the living room inside the apartment. Dale wanted to walk in further but fought the urge. It had dawned on him then he might not be alone. What if someone had been sleeping inside the bedroom he had just walked into? How would he explain that to the editor? He hadn't thought about what he would do or say if he did find someone sleeping on the other side of the bedroom door.

Of course, no one told him another person would be inside the apartment when he got there. He knew right away there was no one inside the bedroom, but still, the thought that there could have been made Dale paranoid. What was it his business if someone had been inside the apartment anyway? He didn't live there. They didn't have to explain themselves to him.

He closed the door back to the width it was before he opened it. He felt he had passed a threshold he shouldn't have, but who would know? Still, he was nervous. He loudly cleared his throat in an attempt to call out to whoever might be inside the apartment with him, if anyone was there. He stood still in the hallway, waiting for a response.

With the lingering silence, he decided it was safe to look around some more. But as he was head deep inside the editor's refrigerator, face-to-face with a carton of heavy cream, did the feeling of being watched again resurface. He did not know where this feeling derived from or why, but it kept showing up.

He closed the refrigerator door quickly and walked to the middle of the hallway, passing the old pizza box, and stood still, listening for any new signs of movement. There were no new sounds. No new movements. He called out: *Hello?* Using words to communicate this time. Assured in his solitude, he grew paranoid still.

Dale checked his coat pocket, making sure he had everything on him that he needed; the hard drive, the reason for him being there, the apartment keys. Dale zipped his coat up and left, barely remembering to look behind him as he closed the door to wait in the street for the car in the cold.

The elevator doors to his office opened. He walked past the receptionist's desk, and the producer's room. Dale walked down a hallway where on the wall hung a photograph of a man holding the corpse of his dog to a hole he had plans to bury it in. Dale passed the large photograph and continued towards the kitchen. Coming out of one of the rooms was the editor, whose apartment he just returned from. The editor laughed when he saw Dale, something Dale did not understand then but went along with, laughing back awkwardly. When Dale saw him, he took the hard drive out of his coat pocket and handed it over. The editor took the hard drive from him and muttered a thank you knowing it would be the last time the two would ever speak.

About twenty minutes later, Dale walked out of the office, onto the busy avenue, carrying more stuff than he had come in with. In his backpack, he stuffed a second coat, a pair of sneakers, his laptop, two hard drives, and food that Kajal's mother made for him to take that he had never gotten the chance to eat. It was all just stuff he left at the office over time and forgotten about.

He stepped out onto the street. Traffic was moving as usual down Park Avenue South. It was the shock at what had happened that caused the embarrassment that now reverberated through his entire body. Dale had no thoughts. His mind was quiet. There was a reluctance to tell the people he had to about what just happened at work. How could he put into words the shame he felt? If he could see inside his chest, he would find a miniature version of himself collapsed over in the fetal position.

His legs took him to a nearby park just above Twenty-third Street, and he sat on one of the benches and stared at nothing. He took out his cell phone to call his mother and finally read the message she sent him. The message made no sense. Just words put together at random from what could have been a butt dial or a message meant for someone else. It took two attempts to reach Carol, his mother. He couldn't speak about it at first, but she knew something was wrong with his tone.

She asked him if everything was alright.

He told her slowly. Letting the words figure themselves out.

They were watching you the entire time? Carol asked him.

There were cameras.

Why?

I don't know. For security reasons, I guess. What does it matter?

He had cameras inside the apartment? That's very unusual.

Yeah.

And everyone inside the office was watching you?

Yeah. On the editor's phone. They were watching inside the producer's room.

Everyone?

Yes, Ma.

But he asked you to go inside the apartment, right? You didn't break in or anything?

No. They asked me to go and pick up the hard drive. I told you.

Why did he have to show everybody? I mean, what was the reason for that?

I don't know.

But why did you...

I don't know.

The refrigerator?

I don't know, Ma.

Well, I don't know what to say. Really. The whole thing confuses me. I'm left without words, to be honest.

I thought I was alone. I've never done anything like that before. I just wanted to see inside the apartment. The Uber...

And you told her that?

Yes! She said it didn't matter. She said she couldn't trust me again, that after what I had done, and what people knew, they could never work with me. She said she's never had to do anything like this before in her career. I fucking hated that she said that.

That she never had to do what? Fire someone?

I don't know. She made it seem like her firing me was somehow harder for her than it was for me.

Did they show you the footage?

No... I'm sorry.

Don't apologize to me. Did you say something to him? To the editor?

I tried. They wouldn't let me see him.

Jesus.

They just rushed me out of the office like I was some criminal. Like I hadn't picked up after them for the last two years of my life. The babysitting. The long weekends.

Yeah. I don't know what to tell you, Dale. This sucks. This really sucks.

It's so embarrassing.

Now I have to tell your father. Isn't he going to be pissed?

You don't have to tell anyone anything, thank you. I'll tell them.

Have you told Kajal yet?

No.

I wonder what she's going to think?

I just want to fucking die.

Stop talking like that.

I do. I want to fucking die in this stupid fucking park. With these oblivious, smiling fucking assholes around me with their stupid fucking smiling dogs.

Why don't you come home tonight, Dale?

I'm going to Harlem.

No, you should come here. We can talk more.

We're talking now.

You know what I mean, Dale. In person. With your father.

What would that do?

Just come home, and we can figure it out. You can relax here. You can start over again tomorrow.

He eventually hung up on her. The conversation was going nowhere and became unproductive for the two of them. Ending it was the only thing he thought he could do. He wanted to call Kajal next but decided against it. He didn't want to explain again what had happened. Not right away. He just wanted to be somewhere quiet. It was too crowded in the park.

Whatever he didn't want, he threw out. The hard drives, the old notebooks, the food. Everything he hadn't seen or thought about in months was thrown away in a garbage can near the West Side entrance of the park, south of the office. He left the park with only his winter coat and the backpack he had on his shoulders that held his laptop. His dad called his cell phone twice. But he didn't pick up. He just let the phone ring in his coat.

A light snow had started to fall again. The events of the day ran through his mind as he walked uptown, thinking about each moment since he left the storage closet. It felt like it was all planned, set up for him to fail.

He made a right at a corner street and continued uptown. The snow was gone, but the sky remained a continuous white cloud. He wanted to be next to water. He walked until he arrived at Riverside Park. He had made it all the way uptown without realizing it. He imagined Kajal was somewhere on campus not too far away. He continued through the park and made his way across an overpass to the West Side Highway, which he had been to only once before.

It had been a while since he had walked through this park. He sat on a snow-covered bench, looked across the river, and gazed ahead at the cliff face of New Jersey.

There were a few joggers, but it wasn't crowded. A light bed of snow remained on the uphill lawn opposite the water, which would lead you to the street. To his right, he could see the George Washington Bridge, and for a moment, he was transported out of New York and placed inside a memory of when he had visited San Francisco.

Dale developed a chill but didn't want to go home. He left the park to warm up. He made his way further uptown into unfamiliar territory. He could feel a slight pain in his calf muscles from the walking he'd done. He could have gone home then but continued until his anger was gone and replaced by a slight exhaustion.

From where he was standing, he could see Yankee Stadium in the distance. There was a strong breeze, and he walked over a bridge that led him into the Bronx. He turned and looked behind him and felt sick looking over the Harlem River at the island he had just come from. He didn't know what neighborhood he was in. It was then he remembered the dream that woke him up in the morning and he thought of Kajal's sweet face and felt better. She was all he wanted and so he went to her. He texted her the words *I love you* and walked back over the bridge into Harlem to go home.

VIII

Diner: Part 1

K ajal wouldn't read Dale's text message until hours later. That morning, she finished her shift at the cafe and was on her way to class when she came across a vigil happening on campus for a student who had recently passed. She didn't plan on attending a vigil that morning for a girl she did not know. But felt compelled to stay when she saw the mass crowd on the steps of the main library, holding posters with pictures of a young woman's face she had recognized.

A small choir sang a few songs a cappella. The crowd listened patiently, with their heads down in discomfort, all fighting the chill from the cold. The wind had started to pick up, and the voices of the choir had to compete with the bustling sound of the breeze. There was a moment of silence before the vigil ended. Kajal was in the background, shivering, holding a small rose someone gave her.

Kajal recognized the girl's face from an article she read from a free newspaper stand in the subway. The headline read: COLUMBIA STUDENT FOUND DEAD. She didn't personally know the deceased, but anyone in the city the week of her death would know her name. Alison Towers was a freshman at Barnard College. She was born and raised in Kansas City, Missouri, and moved to New York at the beginning of the school year. There was a quote in the paper by the student's mother, saying Alison's four-year plan was to graduate and pursue research abroad in the development of climate change.

Alison was found on a Tuesday morning by the entrance of a nearby park close to campus. An off-duty security guard found her on his way home after working an overnight shift. The guard saw Alison's body lying on the sidewalk through his car's foggy windshield. He almost kept driving, mistaking the student for a sleeping bum on the sidewalk. But the guard said what made him stop was Alison's blond hair and pink-colored sweater.

When the vigil ended, the crowd dispersed from the library's steps. Kajal joined a small group that had plans to make a memorial where Alison's body had been discovered. Most people left due to the cold, but Kajal stayed put and searched the crowd for a familiar face to drag along with her. A small part of her felt she was intruding on a private service, though everyone was welcomed. This was for the students.

Kajal saw no one she recognized and stayed at the back of the new group, holding onto the rose she was given, and followed the group down a familiar path off campus.

When they arrived, Kajal realized she had been to the spot where Alison's body had been found. It was only a short walk from the steps of the library where the vigil had taken place. They walked past the Rodin sculpture and her father's magnolia tree and down a private street to the scene of the crime, where Kajal could see the front door of the building where she attended most of her classes.

From the street was a small outcrop with a garden that acted as an entrance to the park, which held a single staircase that led you south onto the park's main grounds.

A new voice brought Kajal's attention back to the service. There was a leader of the group now. Cassandra, a tall white woman who wore a pink thermal jacket. She addressed the crowd near the iron fence. At her feet lay bouquets of carnations and a variety of different colored roses. A Barnard teddy bear sat next to a vintage girl-pop-band t-shirt, and a string of unplugged LED lights with tiny polaroids clipped on dangled across the chipped black iron fence.

Kajal guessed Cassandra and Alison were friends, though there was no indication the two had ever met during the service. But she was the only one who had shared words.

Cassandra thanked the small group for coming and made them stand together in a half circle around a bench. One by one, as Cassandra spoke, people from the small group placed additional mementos down along the fence that Cassandra stood in front of. When it was her turn, Kajal placed her rose by another's, returned to her spot in the half circle, and stayed there with her head down until it was over. No final words were said, but after a moment of silence, each member of the group left in their own time in their own chosen direction.

Kajal wasn't in a rush to leave, so she stayed put and sat alone on the bench, observing the collection of roses and candles that were left behind. Cassandra bent down slightly, touching a photo of Alison with her fingertips. She lifted her hand to her mouth, gently grazing her fingers along the edge of her lips to reenact a kiss.

Anyone who passed Kajal could have mistaken her for someone close to Alison. She sat on the bench, at first with no thoughts, then tried to envision Alison's attacker and what might have led to the event of her death. No one had the story of Alison's final moments, yet. It was not even mentioned in the paper where she first read the story. But it was not lost on Kajal; someone's life had been taken in front of the bench she so calmly sat on.

She took an incense stick she had bought, at a bodega store to bring home to her mother, out of her bag. She had a box of matches on her and bent down slightly, placed the incense stick next to a bouquet, lit it, and for a few moments, from the bench, watched it burn.

She had no class after the one she missed, and though it was cold out, she was not in a rush to leave the bench, with the sun's light gently penetrating through the cracks of the shrubbery behind the park's cracked fence.

Kajal stayed put, lost in thought. Frustrated over the in-justice of Alison's life and how it was taken away from her, so young, and she could sit there miserable about her own life, in front of photos of Alison smiling, as she laid face up in a morgue somewhere.

The cold forced Kajal to eventually stand up and she headed back towards campus. She walked past her father's magnolia tree again and said a short prayer. Afterwards, she walked the grounds of the campus alone. The cold kept everyone away and she appreciated the solitude.

Kajal came across a group entering a tiny chapel on the east side of campus and she followed them inside.

In front of the tabernacle, a quartet played a piece from Vivaldi's *The Four Seasons in E major*. Kajal welcomed the opportunity to sit and listen in the warmth of the chapel in one of the back pews. She had yet to listen much to Vivaldi or had much interest in classical music, but watching the musicians play their instruments in a half-empty room of people had moved her.

It didn't faze the musicians; the room was half empty. It seemed to Kajal they would play just as well if nobody were there to listen to them. Kajal sat in her pew in the back, taking note of each player with their instrument, silencing the other members of the quartet out as she went down the row of them, observing each one. She watched each player's face and took notice of the look of concentration each one had and their own enjoyment in listening to the sound waves that would not exist without the collaboration of their string, wood, and hands.

She stayed there until the quartet played their last piece. The musicians turned into regular people once the spell of their music faded, and the small crowd applauded them, and the musicians stood and bowed, accepting their praise.

The crowd began to disperse shortly after the quartet finished their last piece. Kajal watched the musicians pack their instruments, quietly engaging in benign small talk in front of the altar. Kajal could not hear the details of their conversation. She wanted to say something to them as they passed her, hoping to compliment them, for she was grateful for stumbling upon their music. But she was shy, and as they exited the chapel, they walked by her without her saying a word.

When she was alone in the chapel, and able to pay attention to her body, she felt the space the music had created inside her, that stayed long after the music had faded, due to the chapel's palpable silence. She missed the days when she felt free like a kid. Though nothing was easy about those early days, she did not know then what grief was. She didn't know what pain was either. True pain. She just knew her life the way it had been, and in her youth, there was no reason to question it.

A few of Kajal's friends met at the Harlem Tavern for happy hour. She didn't want to go home, so she went to the bar, telling herself it would be for just one drink. The bar was loud when Kajal entered. Her friends sat drunk at a table at the back in a secluded corner on the left side of the tavern. The table was filled with half-empty beer pints. A slew of silver tin trays lay across the table with the remains of bones of eaten chicken wings and grease stains of now phantom beef sliders.

Kajal approached her friends and thought about getting her own tab out of fear of having to split the check.

One of them asked, Where's the waiter? We need to make room for Kajal to sit.

This was David, who snapped his fingers towards the direction of the bar with what could be seen as both a stern and drunk expression.

We've made a mess of ourselves, said David. No one's come to pick up after us!

Sorry, Kajal, said Adam softly. We've been here for a while...as you can tell.

Someone call over a waiter, please. I'm getting annoyed. Someone needs to clean this up, said David, chewing on a french fry.

David's getting annoyed, guys. Someone needs to do something.

How long have you guys been here? Kajal asked, shedding an uncomfortable laugh. She pulled an empty seat from an adjacent table and sat with the group.

It's been a long time, I think.

I have a class later, said another.

Someone call over a waiter, please.

Garçon! Garçon!

David's drunk, guys.

I'm fine. I'm not drunk. I'm just trying to help Kajal find a seat!

She's sitting, David.

I mean before. I was trying to help her find a seat before she sat down. When she first walked in.

What's the line you say for the word *garçon*?

What line?

From the movie? You know that film with the actor who's a Scientologist.

I don't know what you're talking about.

Fuck, I can't believe I forgot...

Garçon! I want a garçon, god damn it!

No, that's not it.

Anyway... Kajal, honey, dear, moon pie, sweetcakes. How are you doing? Adam asked, trying to change the subject.

You guys are wasted, said Kajal, laughing.

NO. Whatever gave you that idea? Asked David. We've only been drinking alcohol!

What were you guys talking about?

Adam has a new fuck boy, said David, taking another sip of his beer.

I wasn't going to say it like that, David. Jesus Christ. Do you need some water, honey? Adam said, rolling his eyes and looking over at Kareena for help.

What? What did I say?

You're dating someone new? Kajal asked with a smile.

Yes. He's very sweet. We met on Grindr, and it's super chill. Last night, he came over, and we cooked, watched a movie, and snuggled.

That's all you did, huh? David asked, staring at Adam with a drunken expression.

Well, no. But I'll leave the rest to your imagination, said Adam, laughing uncomfortably.

I want details, Adam!

I'm going to get a drink. Do you want one, Kajal? Asked Kareena.

Sure! Thanks. I can Venmo you.

No, I got it! Kareena said, giving Kajal a quick wink and walking towards the bar.

Adam asked, Did you guys hear about that girl from Barnard?

Yes. Oh my god. So sad.

Yeah.

It's so fucking tragic.

I actually went to the vigil they had for her on campus, said Kajal.

Oh, you went to that?

Did the school do something for her?

Friends of hers set it up, said Kajal.

I didn't hear about it. Wish I did.

I was looking for you guys!

The Dean emailed all Columbia students yesterday, saying it would happen today on campus.

And you went?

Yeah.

Apparently, they found the guy who did it, said Adam.

Really?

Yeah. He was just a kid, apparently. He lived in one of the project buildings just north of the school, and the cops followed a blood trail to his front door.

You're kidding. I haven't heard this yet.

His mother answered the door when the cops showed up. She had no idea. The cops found blood on the kid's jacket he had hung on the coat rack by the front door to their apartment. He was in his room playing video games when they arrested him.

Wow, really?

The poor mother.

Kareena asked, What are you guys talking about? And put down the beers she bought at the bar.

Thanks, said Kajal, smiling.

The girl from Barnard, said Adam.

Oh yeah, I heard the school did something for her today.

Yeah, I went to it. Kajal repeated. So sad. There's a memorial now in the spot where they found her. I'd go with anyone who wants to visit. It was really lovely…

I would go. I'm sorry I didn't, but I don't do well at those types of things, you know? I have no relationship with death. I'm terrified of it if I'm being honest. I still have my grandparents, said Kareena.

Wow, that's amazing. You're very fortunate.

Yeah. It's something I've always felt guilty about. I've never even seen a dead body before. The thought of it creeps me out. I don't think there is a way to prepare yourself to lose a loved one or to understand that each person at this table will one day die. I know we know. But we don't really know, you know what I mean? I mean, I'm lucky to still have everyone in my family who is dear to me alive. But, still, I avoid the subject with friends. I'm terrible at funerals. I've never known what to say to someone who is grieving. What could I possibly say that would make someone mourning feel better?

Yeah, I don't know either, said Adam. I lost my grandfather when I was six, but it's been that long since I've lost somebody. My parents tell me stories, reminding me of how close I was with him. There are photos of us together, but still... I barely remember him, Adam continued. Apparently, his death was hard for me to cope with, but to tell you the truth, I don't remember ever mourning him. He was just gone from my life one day. Like, I remember when he was there, and we did things as a family, and then one day, he was gone. There's no feeling of loss. Just this void, you know? When I told my mother this, she felt terrible. It made her so sad to hear. She insisted I was so upset when he died, which I believe. But isn't that terrible? That despite how much he loved me, it did nothing to help me remember him better? It's just kind of super fucking tragic when I think of it...

Well, he doesn't know because he's dead, Adam, said David.

David!

What? It's true. You don't have to feel bad about not remembering your grandparents. That's your mother's problem. It happened over twenty years ago, man. What are you expected to do? Mourn forever? That's how the world works. We live. We die. And then we're forgotten about, and another group of unlucky souls who come out of their father's dicks get to live in the world we built, or should I say are destroying, for them. That's what happens. I'm sorry to say it. But it's true. We're in grad school, guys. We should know these things. We go to Columbia, for God's sake. Now, I'm going to get another drink. Does anyone else want one? On my father's credit card?

The night did not end at the Harlem Tavern. They spent another hour drinking at the bar. Kajal drank one beer and then another and then another after that, and when the group left, they walked south down Frederick Douglas boulevard.

Kajal felt a buzz that hugged her from the inside. She loved the group of faces she was with, happy to be among them. With each step she took with her friends, she became more grateful for their existence. With each drink, the heavy emotions felt more and more like a distant memory. Kajal wasn't aware of time's pull. She didn't know where Dale was. She did not feel the absence of her father.

Kareena knew of a small club close by where they could dance. In the day, the club was a hole-in-the-wall street Indian food joint where Columbia students would get a quick bite in between classes. A secret door would open at night beyond the restaurant's entrance. Students would walk past the empty kitchen, go through the door, and find themselves inside a space that looked like an abandoned Irish pub.

When the group arrived, they paused at this second entrance before entering. The club looked more divey than they expected. Music played at a high volume that distorted the sound that came out of its speakers, and its spinning disco ball did what it could to erase the bleakness from the space, but could not save it from it. Adam bought the first round of beers. The club was relatively small. The group could maneuver easily through the small crowd of individuals to get to the bar.

They tried to ignore the dingy vibe of the nightclub, happy to be drunk in a place like this. They found humor in dancing underneath the spinning disco ball, maintaining eye contact with those in their group, and keeping a barrier with their bodies to avoid outsiders who tried to get in.

Later, Kajal followed Kareena into the bathroom. When she came out of the stall, Kareena handed her a small pill and told her to swallow. Without thinking, she did so, trusting her friend. Afterward, the two stepped outside the bathroom, waiting for whatever they took to kick in. They discovered Adam had left to meet someone else, and it was just David who stayed behind to dance with a girl neither Kareena nor Kajal recognized. The two joined David and his new friend on the dance floor and danced around them, laughing like two witches around a burning cauldron, knowing the night could conjure up anything.

Marc materialized out of a cloud made by the bar's fog machine. He held a bottle of Bud Light in his hand. He went behind Kajal and tapped her on the shoulder; when she turned and saw him, she let out an involuntary gasp. The strangeness of the club had started to dissipate during their conversation. What was once foreign about the place had become more charming after the night went on.

Under the disco ball's light, Kareena forced Kajal closer to Marc, taking them away from the bar they had disappeared to and back out onto the dance floor. Kajal turned her backside along the front of Marc's waist. She kissed his lips, her head tucked up and sideways behind her right shoulder. He leaned over her and kissed her back, taking turns using their tongues to touch the upper parts of their mouth. Kajal had forgotten the pill she swallowed in the bathroom, but on the dance floor, a warmth crept up inside her, forcing her to remember. Everything she rubbed against felt like a hug to that distinct part of her body. She danced against Marc, using him like a bear does a tree when trying to scratch an itch.

David and his new friend left the club. Kareena invited Kajal and Marc over to her apartment. They all left the club together, talking. It was cold outside. It was cold inside the apartment. Kareena handed out little blankets, which Kajal happily took over to Kareena's oversized golden armchair. They each had a beer and talked for a while, speech slurred, and fatigue appeared behind their eyes. Then they shared a kiss and kissed until they undressed. Kareena invited them into her bedroom. Kajal followed them inside, nervously letting the other two take the lead. Marc held Kareena's breasts in his hands and kissed her mouth as Kajal watched from the bedside. Kareena watched Kajal watching as Marc licked the skin just under her right ear. Kareena turned her attention towards Kajal.

Marc watched them kiss, and after Kajal agreed, Kareena opened Kajal's legs and slowly started to lick her clitoris. Kajal was hesitant but didn't stop Kareena from doing it. She just watched her friend move her tongue around her labia's lips. Marc put his face between Kareena's ass cheeks, using his finger's to rub her pussy and he licked her there for a while, standing by the bedside table. Kareena lifted her head up from between Kajal's legs in order to let out a small shriek from the back of her throat.

Kareena put Marc in her mouth. They played with each other for a while in that frozen position of intimacy and then Kareena took Kajal's head and replaced her mouth with Kajal's. Then Kajal and Marc took turns pleasuring Kareena who came twice by the both of them. And when it was over, Marc left with his shoes and backpack on just as casually as he had come.

When Kajal woke up the following morning, she was lying in Kareena's bed, half-naked, not remembering putting on the top she now wore. Kareena's back was facing towards her, and she was lying in a tight space between a cold white wall and Kareena's body, thinking of ways to get out of the bed without waking her.

Kajal found her phone underneath her pillow. She had a pounding headache and felt like she would throw up. She massaged the sides of her temples with her thumbs and could see the rhythm of the pulsating colors inside the closed lids of her eyes. She wanted to drink water but feared anything she put inside her stomach would come up. Kajal looked at her phone. The time showed it was 2 PM. She had a slew of missed calls and text messages from Dale.

Kajal got out of bed. She slowly pushed herself downwards towards the end of the mattress and stood up, careful not to wake Kareena. She went into the bathroom, closing the door behind her. When she felt safe, she let out the remains from last night into the toilet bowl. After, her head was still pounding, and she started the shower without asking Kareena for permission. She wouldn't allow herself to think about what happened the night before. She couldn't properly process the events that occurred in the moment.

Already bottomless, Kajal removed her top, stepped underneath the showerhead, and allowed the warm water to hit her face. She stayed under the water for a while. She hoped the steam from the showerhead would help relieve her of the horror she felt inside. She washed her face with soap. She could feel the dirt from the night before on her skin and hoped that once clean, she would feel new again.

Kajal left Kareena's apartment and met Dale at a diner. The diner was somewhere in Harlem, close to her mother's place. She felt slightly better after the shower and had enough energy to walk through the park to the east side. She felt a little nauseous still, and didn't have much of an appetite. The fresh air helped. She ordered a coffee and some French toast, hoping the bread and caffeine would help her.

When Dale entered the diner, Kajal noticed the glum expression on his face. A brass bell that hung from the diner's door dinged as he walked in. He sat in the booth across from her and ordered a coffee. She tried to appear happy for him, smiling when he entered. Dale would have no idea what kind of night she had by the face she used to look at him.

Kajal asked if he wanted to order any food. He said he didn't, and they shared her French toast.

They didn't say much to each other. Dale was afraid to say what was on his mind, hoping she would explain first why she had not come home the previous night. He didn't want to tell her about him being fired, afraid she would get angry. If she did, it would only double down on his shame and embarrassment. She was still processing her night through her hangover. She knew she had been unfaithful but could not think of the words he needed to hear while sitting across from him. She would need time for that.

They continued to sit eating their breakfast. Something silent was building between them. They didn't know then what. Kajal cut a piece of her French toast with a fork and cradled it with her hand into Dale's mouth. He swallowed the sweet bread, feeling restless, not wanting to sit down any longer, and thinking of when it would be a good time to speak.

IX

A Day in the Life (Last Year)

———⟡~⟡———

On the day Kajal's father passed, Dale planned to meet his two friends to see a film. He and Kajal were living together, and that morning, as most mornings, he made her coffee while she made the bed. They showered together and moved around each other getting dressed for the day, a ballet they performed for each other to no audience.

That afternoon, at the office, Dale found himself missing Kajal, thinking of her sweet face, and canceled the plans he had made with his friends. He would wonder what made him long to be with Kajal that afternoon. What would have become of their relationship if he had not been with her, that evening when her father passed? When he woke up, he had no reason then to think the day would be unlike any other. And yet, he decided to cancel with his friends and meet Kajal, who he lived with, for dinner instead.

Kajal was excited about her recent acceptance to NYU and was set on going to grad school part-time while keeping her full-time job and apartment. She applied to NYU early, though it wasn't her first choice. She organized her letters of recommendation from her now ex-colleagues, reviewed her statements of purpose, and sent the application to the admissions panel for NYU and moved on. She thought, if she ignored what she wanted long enough, it would lose its excitement and maybe she wouldn't want it or care about it anymore after some time had passed.

Kajal's father had his surgery in the morning. It was minor, but she called him on her lunch break to make sure he didn't need her to come with her car to pick him up.

No, you don't have to worry about me, Beta. He said to Kajal over the phone.

Are you sure, Papa? I'm coming to the city tonight anyway. I can pick you up.

No, I'll be home before you get out of work. Ayad is coming. The hospital is only two blocks away. I'll be fine, my love.

Okay, Papa. Love you, see you at home. Khudahafiz.

I love you too, Beta, okay.

Dale left work and decided to take advantage of the crisp winter evening and walk downtown instead of taking the train. The two decided to see a film together. *The Mystery of Picasso* by Clouzot was restored by Janus Films and played for a limited engagement all week at the Film Forum.

Dale texted Kajal throughout the day ideas for what they could do with their evening, including seeing the film. Seeing a movie at the local cinema was not something Kajal would do in her spare time. But Dale mentioned the film to her anyway because it was only out for a week, and she accepted, swayed by the promise of splitting bao buns at their favorite Japanese restaurant and not spending the beautiful evening in their apartment alone.

Near the end of her day, Kajal was running out the door when her boss, Nicole, asked her to run a last-minute errand. It was to drop off a package at the post office on her way home.

Not a big deal, her boss reassured her.

The post office was in the opposite direction from where Kajal lived; still, she had to drive through rush-hour traffic to get home, park her car, and change for her date in the city with Dale.

It was a favor that derived from Kajal asking that morning if she could adjust her working hours in the fall due to her attending grad school. This was how Kajal started her day, thinking of ways to approach the subject of her going back to school to her boss, knowing ahead of time it would be a difficult conversation.

When she told Nicole, the look on her face showed that she was disappointed. Nicole hadn't seen this coming. She didn't say anything off-hand to Kajal; she just gave her a weak congratulations, took a breath that helped suppress her annoyance with Kajal, and said they'd talk more about it in detail another time.

Then she disappeared for half the day.

This was what Nicole did when she was upset about something. No one ever knew where it was she disappeared to. She would reappear later in the day, casually walking back to her desk, smelling of cigarettes, acting as if nothing unusual had happened. There were times when she would disappear for hours. And in her absence, her employees would have to manage the Science Center without her. Her staff had to make excuses, on her behalf, to the teachers who were chaperoning class trips and had payment questions, or vendors who were there to fix the aquifers in the catfish tank; questions only Nicole would know how to legally and professionally answer. Employees complained of Nicole's behavior to her higher-ups for years, but nothing ever came out of it. Faces of the staff would change with each season. Those who stayed learned to cope by gossiping to their coworkers, building a trauma bond among them in the quiet corners of their office. But with Nicole at the lead, a community of enthusiastic career-long science educators was gaslit, via microaggressions, blatant prejudice, and narcissistic abuse, to the ashes of a failed and apathetic team.

To the staff, it seemed Nicole could treat her employees however she wanted to. Comments made on Nicole's behavior to her higher-ups made little impact. Those who worked underneath her felt they had no choice but to quietly continue their work with their heads down in silence, knowing they had no advocates in the department's bureaucratic web of carelessness, job turn-overs, and apathetic civil servants.

I'll let you know when it's time for you to leave, said Nicole, to Kajal on a different day when she hinted at her plans for a greater future. Nicole was furious with another subordinate who decide to quit that morning. Kajal knew about Michele's plan for months but was unaware of what day it would happen.

I'm just not going to show up one day, Michele told her during their lunch break a few months prior, let the bitch sweat.

The two sat outside eating store-bought salads at a long wooden picnic table in the Center's garden. Michele did end up coming to work but decided, on her own time, when it would happen. Once she gathered the children for the day's field trip in the adjacent classroom, Michele went to her desk, grabbed her purse, jacket, an extra Patagonia fleece emblazoned with the DOE logo from the storage closet, and sage she clipped from the Learning Garden that morning, and walked out the Center's steel doors without saying goodbye to anyone.

Kajal connected the dots when she heard Nicole screaming Michele's name through the hallways. If Michele hadn't already quit, she would have most certainly been fired then on the spot.

None of Michele's coworkers held the decision to leave against her. They envied her courage to walk out like she did, instantly earning this new abundance of freedom. Michele knew she could start a new chapter of her life once she mustered the courage to walk out, even if it meant depending financially on her affluent grandfather for a few months. And though that brought on its own set of obstacles, from the perspective of everyone who stayed behind, there was something exciting about this new chapter of Michele's life. For everyone else, her options seemed limitless.

There was traffic on her way to the post office. Kajal knew she was going to be late for Dale. She had to change out of her work clothes. She wanted to look cute for their date. She didn't like her hair and her work clothes smelled of animal feces; she wanted to change. When Nicole reappeared after Kajal broke the news about grad school, she put her to work in the Learning Garden. There was a small farm behind the science center where turkeys roamed, ducks quacked, and fresh produce grew. Three chickens had died in the night, and a pungent smell seeped through the Center's halls, stinking up the place. She had to find the source of the smell first, then put on two red rubber gloves and an N-95 mask, and for the first time in her life, grabbed two chicken carcasses by their shanks and threw them in the compost bin with the confidence of a white, middle-aged farmer.

Dale had bought tickets for the 8 PM screening and had time to kill. He walked around the west village for an hour, then went to the restaurant to wait in line, hoping they could both sit without waiting. He hadn't heard from Kajal in a while but assumed because of the time, she was now on a train in a tunnel, where, due to lack of signal, she could not reach him. To Dale's surprise, there was no line when he got to the restaurant. They had chosen a popular ramen spot near the theater. Dale put his name down with the hostess, who directed him to an old wooden chair, where he was to wait until his entire party arrived. He noticed there were only a few tables taken then. He was hungry, annoyed, and tired from being on his feet all day.

He was only twenty-eight years old then but already held the presence of an aging old man.

He took a book from his bag and started reading as a queue formed slowly behind him. He had just beaten the evening crowd. Dale tried to focus on the words from his novel but was distracted each time a different patron who came after him walked past him to a table to ponder the pages of their menus, deciding on what to eat.

An hour had passed and he looked up from his book and confirmed with the time on a mid-century wall clock behind the bar that Kajal was most certainly late. His eyes became dry from reading as slight tears streamed down his face. He texted Kajal again. She had not answered any of his previous text messages.

Dale closed his eyes to rest them and placed his book down gently onto his lap when, almost immediately, a presence appeared before him; darkening the light behind his closed eyes.

Kajal? He thought. Dale opened one eye lid at a time, slowly revealing the upper torso and head of the hostess who had sat him there. Dale noticed how attractive she was, and he would have smiled flirtatiously back if it had not been for the bothered grin on her face. She asked Dale if he wouldn't mind sitting at the bar. It was getting crowded in the restaurant, and Dale had become just what he had tried his whole life in becoming; a total nuisance. She told him he could sit on any of the available stools (there were only two), and before Dale could muster a response back, the hostess shifted her attention to a woman waiting in line behind him, taking her name down and adding it to a list.

It would be another twenty minutes before Kajal came up from behind Dale and tapped him on his shoulder. He had ordered himself a Kirin beer while sitting at the bar, and he sat, slowly sipping it, feeling like the biggest thing in the room. There was something about the open setting of a bar that made Dale uncomfortable. He didn't like to feel seen, though nobody was looking at him, which he also had a problem with. He wished he could be more like his literary heroes and sit comfortably with a stoic confidence, drinking a beer in a dimly lit space, content and happy. But getting drunk alone and making friends with the barkeep was not in his bag of tricks.

Kajal had fixed her hair and makeup and changed into clean clothes. She wanted to look pretty for her date with Dale, and that she did. When she had exited the subway and found herself on a familiar West Village street, an excitement she had not expected revealed itself.

Dale thought she looked beautiful and wanted to tell her so, but his feelings towards complimenting her were trapped in his resentment of her tardiness and lack of communication. A numbness rang through his body from waiting, sitting at the bar alone, and when she approached him, he could do nothing but look her in the eyes with a glum and disapproving stare.

She felt awkward leaning in to kiss him. She touched his shoulder warmly and kept a disingenuous smile as he stayed cold seated on the bar stool.

Sorry I'm late, she said, already knowing what he was upset about.

What took you?

Long story. I got caught up at work.

I don't think we're going to make this movie. It's in an hour, and we still have to eat.

Do you just want to go?

No, I'm starving. Aren't you?

Yes, and I much prefer to eat than see the film, but I know you already bought the tickets...

It wouldn't be the first time.

I can pay you back. It's not a big deal.

That's not what I'm asking, Kajal. Let's get the hostess' attention.

Dale stood up and walked past Kajal to interrupt the hostess as she spoke to a different customer. Kajal waited alone by the now empty bar stool, disappointed. The distance she felt from Dale when she first approached him at the bar surprised her and made her regret coming. All the effort she put into coming into the city, dealing with her boss, and dressing up for Dale made her feel unseen by him.

Dale walked back over to the bar where Kajal waited. The hostess said it shouldn't be much longer. She stood beside him silently, not waiting for an apology but upset that her evening was ruined.

They didn't wait much longer for a table. They pulled out their chairs, hesitant to say what was on their minds, and sat silently, looking over their menus.

You know if you're going to be late, you could at least tell me. I don't understand why we have all of these technical devices, and I can't get just one message from you saying you're going to be late.

My phone was dying Dale, and I was rushing to get here. I'm sorry. It was a difficult day at work for me and I lost track of time.

I shouldn't have bought the tickets. It's not like it was going to sell out. I don't want to fight with you, okay?

I'll Venmo you for the movie, said Kajal, taking out her cell phone.

I thought your phone was dying.

I have just enough battery to make you feel like a dick.

Don't Venmo me, please. I don't want you to pay for the movie.

Done, declared Kajal, slapping her phone down face-first onto the table. Great night we're having, she continued. Glad I was having a shitty day at work, and now I'm here in Manhattan arguing with you.

What happened at work?

Nothing. I don't want to talk about it now.

They both ordered a bowl of ramen, a beer, and a few pork bao buns to start. When the bao buns arrived, Kajal was reluctant to have one because of the pork. But the smell was so intense it made her stomach ache. She was hungry. She picked one up and took a bite, shamefully enjoying it.

A waitress brought over the two bowls of ramen. Dale ordered two shots of sake with another beer for himself. The ramen looked gorgeous in its swirl of red and white colors. The aroma of garlic and pork broth wafted past their nostrils, like a ghost haunting their table, flying towards the hungry customers waiting in line, eager to have their turn with the soup. The couple thought of nothing but the food in front of them; the movie was forgotten, and the argument finished. It was just the two of them and their food, connected and present in the moment, silent and speechless, hungry and in awe at the presentation before them.

He wanted to take a photograph of her. She was embarrassed and didn't want to pose for a photo, but Dale insisted and snapped a few of her laughing in her drunken state with his phone. It was dark on the street they found themselves on. He told her to stand on the steps underneath a light. She climbed three steps up, and he took a few more of her with the school's purple and white flag flapping in the wind in the dark. Hurry up, she said with her teeth clenched as people walked behind her in and out of the school's front entrance.

While Dale took the photo of Kajal, back in Harlem, Ayad was attempting CPR on their dying father. Ruksaana watched the scene unfold from the kitchen. Afraid, she put a scarf over her head and lit an incense, reciting a prayer she knew by heart and had repeated in hushed tones, underneath her breath, her entire life.

Kajal fell asleep on Dale's shoulder as they sped through the boroughs on a train back to Brooklyn. Dale tried to read from his book but was distracted by the weight of Kajal's head on his shoulder. The arches of the Brooklyn Bridge stood tall in the distance; its silhouette outlined by the bridge's lights, like a children's puzzle, waiting for someone to connect the dots.

Dale's phone vibrated inside his pocket, but he didn't notice. They tried to reach Kajal first, but her phone had finally died. When someone did get in touch with them, they were off the train a block away from their apartment. It was Kajal's oldest sister Blanche's sobs Dale heard first on the phone when he picked up. Without thinking, he handed his phone off to Kajal, somehow knowing already what the call was about.

They grabbed what they could from the apartment. They knew they would not be returning. Kajal was shaking in the alcove, where Dale's desk sat, as he packed a bag for them and looked around for their car keys. Anger was the first emotion Kajal felt before fear. She was angry, but not with Dale but with herself for not being home, and eating pork, and drinking with Dale when her family needed her.

Dale did what he could to calm her. He tried to be her strength. They rushed out of the apartment, found their car in the dark, and drove out of Brooklyn together to East Harlem. This would be Kajal's introduction to death. Driving up the FDR, a calmness had come over her. Dale was in the driver's seat, repeating the words, *We Don't Know*, *We Don't Know*, hoping she'd use the words as a mantra with him.

But Kajal did know; she just didn't want to accept it. They drove underneath the Brooklyn Bridge and headed north. It seemed like they were just there.

The device used to try and resuscitate her father was left penetrating out of his mouth as he lay lifeless, surrounded by his grieving children.

Hussein was on a bed in the emergency room's main floor, next to several unused machines. They walked by him but had not known it when they entered. Dale and Kajal were led by a doctor, who told them the news in a room on the other side of the hospital, from where Hussein's body lay. They parted the blue curtain that hid him from the public and stood beside his corpse quietly. Kajal's siblings soon followed, with Blanche's then fiancé trailing behind. They were given the courtesy of seeing the body 15 minutes before the shift rotation started. The doctor who took them closed the curtain for privacy, the receptionist's desk stood not one hundred feet away. A plastic sheet covered his body up to his neck; only his face was exposed. Kajal noticed the gray hairs that grew out of his ears. He would shave his ear hairs, embarrassed by how long they got.

His children held each other's hand, surrounding the part of the bed where Hussein's head stuck out of the white sheet that covered him.

Dale stood on the other side of the bed with Blanche's fiancé, both of them, observing the corpse's children, questioning whether it was appropriate to still be there. Blanche placed her hand on her father's shoulder. Kajal kissed the top of her father's head, crying. Ayad stood beside Kajal, staring at his late father with no readable expression on his face.

They still had to tell their mother and each child worried who would break the news. Blanche and Kajal depended on the other to take the lead. They asked the nurse if they could have more time. The staff wanted to take the body down to the morgue in twenty minutes, at 10:30. Which was not enough time to break the news to their elderly mother and have her walk the three blocks over to the hospital to view her dead husband's body. The staff allowed them until midnight. They had no choice but to leave the hospital; neither of them looked forward to returning. The children walked in synchronized steps to their mother's apartment, each one growing a little older with each hesitant step they took next.

Kajal heard herself say *mother's apartment* for the first time in conversation with her sister on the walk up to Ruksaana's apartment. It felt unfair to say and register as truth, already, as if her father were a thing of the past.

They took the elevator up to the twelfth floor. Kajal's stomach twisted in knots. She had to go to the bathroom. Someone pissed in the elevator's corner, and it reeked, but no one addressed it.

Questions ran through Kajal's brain as they slowly progressed through the building's floors. Would her mother have to move out of the apartment? Could they afford to stay? Where would they be relocated to if they had to move? The building her mother lived in was government-funded property. If you didn't need the space, they moved you. There was no special treatment.

When the elevator arrived on the twelfth floor, the sound of a small bell dinged in the hallway. Kajal's heart started to beat fast. Inside the apartment, the cat ran from the arm of the couch to the front door in preparation to greet them. Telling their mother would be admitting a truth they did not want to accept. They entered the apartment slowly. Ruksaana stood up from the couch she had been praying on; she knew her answer when she saw her children's faces. Being the older sister, Blanche instinctively stood in front of Kajal and broke out in tears, saying the words for the first time out loud:

He didn't make it. He didn't make it. Papa didn't make it.

X

Diner: Part 2

Dale couldn't stand the silence any longer. He'd been looking absentmindedly at a photo on the wall to his left of a middle-aged white man holding a four-foot marlin, smiling. He was trying not to say what was on his mind. Kajal sat across from him, looking at her cell phone, taking a break from eating her breakfast. There was a cold sensation in the pit of Dale's stomach that he found hard to ignore. He looked over at her. She laughed at a text message someone had sent her, and he resented the slight smile on her face.

Are we going to talk about last night or not? Dale asked, annoyed that he was the one to bring it up first.

Talk about what?

They were still at the diner. Kajal took a small bite of what was left of her breakfast.

What do you mean, *Talk about what*?

Dale took a breath. Fighting the urge to throw his coffee mug across the diner and watch it splatter into a million pieces.

Why didn't you come home last night? You didn't answer any of my phone calls or text messages. Like, where did you even stay?

I stayed at my friend's apartment.

Whose apartment? Kareena's?

Yes, said Kajal.

And you couldn't pick up your phone once to tell me that? I don't understand.

Their waitress came over to pour them more coffee but quickly walked away, noticing the look on each of their faces.

I lost my job yesterday.

You what?

I lost… my job…yesterday, he said condescendingly. I no longer…. have an income… I'm not sure how many ways I can put it.

How?

Long story.

Well…what are you going to do?

Get another job, I guess.

Kajal cracked up laughing.

I'm sorry. I'm sorry. I know it's not funny.

Why are you laughing?

We're such a mess. I'm sorry. It's not you. She laughed harder.

You're cruel. You're so cruel. You have no idea, said Dale, disgusted.

How was I supposed to know you lost your job? Kajal asked, after a beat of silence. It's not my fault.

If you cared to answer your phone, you would have known.

Well, I'm sorry. That sucks.

Tell me, do you think it's selfish that I needed you last night? Honestly. Like, after the year we had, is it possible that I, also, could get emotional support in this relationship? Or are you the only one who's allowed to get it?

I find it funny you think you give me emotional support.

Are you kidding? Are you saying that I don't?

How do you give me emotional support, Dale? You belittle me for not coming home at night like I'm your child. You resent me for going back to school and having us move out of our apartment.

It's not that you didn't come home. It's that you never come home, Kajal. You don't communicate. And I don't resent you for going back to school.

Yes, you do. And you're jealous I go to an Ivy League.

Jealous? You're friends with a bunch of drunk idiots, and you're miserable. You're so lost within yourself I don't even recognize you.

They're not idiots. You don't know them.

Kajal, we moved into your mother's apartment so that we could be together. That's what we both wanted when you started school.

I can't always be home, Dale. I don't know why you keep bringing that up. I'm busy. I told you. I'm busy.

So, what are we gonna do? I don't see you anymore. I'm not an idiot. You're not doing homework till so late that you can't pick up your phone once to text me where you are. Or that you're so far away you can't take an Uber back home. I'm sorry. But that's not the situation you're in. You're avoiding me, and I know it.

What do you want me to say, Dale? You're not the only one going through shit. I'm sorry you lost your job, but you hated working at that place. I lost my dad, okay? There is no way your problems can compare to mine. You can get another job.

I'm not comparing me losing my job to you losing your dad, but I have needs too, and they're not less important than what you're going through. They're just different. It's what I need. I was there for you when your dad passed. I drove you to the fucking emergency room. And I'm here to listen and talk about your dad whenever you want; you just don't want to open up to me. But I'd sit and talk about him all day if you wanted. I care about whatever it is you're going through, but I'm not a mind reader.

I'm allowed to mourn however I want to, Dale. You still have both of your parents. How could you possibly know what I'm going through?

I won't know until you share it with me. I didn't say I could solve your problems, but I'm more than willing to listen.

I don't want to talk to anyone about my problems, Dale. I'm too sad to talk. Okay? I'm sad all the time. Is that what you want to hear? You don't know what I'm going through. You can't help me, so stop trying. This year was supposed to be great for me, and it isn't. It sucks that my dad's not here. He was supposed to be proud of me. On top of all of that, I'm supposed to be jumping around like a great girlfriend while you watch me under a microscope like I'm some fucking amoeba.

Kajal couldn't keep her tears back. Just the mentioning of her father made her cry. It had been a while since she had spoken about him to anyone. The people in the diner stopped pretending not to notice their conversation. Some even looked over their shoulders, finding it hard not to make eye contact.

Dale realized their waitress never returned to check on them; he had finished his coffee and wanted more. He started to feel embarrassed, sitting there with Kajal, drawing unwanted attention. He felt as if they were everyone's entertainment for the evening.

Dale said nothing while Kajal cried. He didn't know what else to do but grab her hand. She pulled her hand back and picked up a napkin to blow her nose with. They sat in silence while she tried to gather her breath again.

Maybe I just need time, said Kajal after a while.

What do you mean?

I don't know.

From me? Do you need time from me?

Yes. Maybe. I don't know.

You asked me to move in with you to your mother's apartment. I did. We had our own life and our own apartment, and now you want me out?

It's not like that, Dale.

You never expressed anything like this to me before. Ever.

I know, but things are different now. I don't know what to do. I need to be home, and I don't want you to be there, said Kajal, surprising herself.

You don't... want me...to be there, he repeated.

They said nothing after that. Dale asked for the check and paid the bill. She kept her head down, staring at her plate, feeling ashamed. They sat for a few moments longer in silence. Dale looked out the window, holding his empty coffee mug, not knowing how to move or stand up.

The couple parted ways at the diner. Kajal walked the few blocks home alone, heartbroken, not having believed what she had said to Dale. She didn't plan to break up with him. Kajal had never ended a relationship before. She had no plans to tell him about her night at Kareena's apartment. Maybe if they stayed together, she would feel obligated to tell him she had been unfaithful. But now that they had parted ways, she felt it was a thing of the past, and she had no intention of explaining herself.

She entered the building she lived in, exhausted, wanting nothing more than to lie down and sleep. There was an older man in the elevator. On hearing the creaking sound of the building's main entrance, he threw his arm out the elevator door, giving Kajal time to enter. She slid into the elevator, thanked the man, and pressed the correct button to her floor, all in one motion.

The elevator doors closed, and the elevator proceeded upwards. Kajal stood beside him, quietly looking down at her feet, aware of the thoughtless mind she now possessed. A feeling of disassociation rang through her body as if she were inside herself, trapped, detached from her surroundings. She had only a passing thought that she might not be well, blaming her last moment with Dale responsible. Why hadn't he fought for her?

She could feel him moving beside her. The old man was pacing in his corner, mumbling words incoherently under his breath. This only brought Kajal to a more heightened state, her heart beating a little faster each growing second she was in the elevator. She tried to direct her gaze towards the man to better see him. She wished another person had been in the elevator with them, making her more angry at herself for not having Dale walk her home.

The elevator passed the fifth and sixth floors. A hum from somewhere inside the elevator shaft revealed itself. The old man swatted with his right hand at the open space above them as if there were a fly Kajal could not see taunting him.

She tried to keep her gaze pointed in the opposite direction. Afraid the old man's quick and violent swings might accidentally be turned and focused on her. She contemplated a plan of attack in case she needed to defend herself. She found her keys in her coat pocket, grabbed the largest one, and slid the tip of its blade in between her clenched fist, knowing, only in her head, this plan of attack would work.

She took a risk and looked at the man standing beside her. He was just taller than she was. His clothes were disheveled and unclean. He wore ripped jeans and an old dirty sweater that was long, warm, and inviting but stained from something that left a pattern similar to two clouds floating along his chest. On his head, he wore a beret that was a hand-me-down and meant for someone else, someone younger. It barely fit him and looked tight on his head.

The elevator passed the seventh and eighth floors. The man swatted again at the air above him, visibly growing more frustrated. He stomped his feet hard onto the floor. The sound of his foot against the plastic tiles made Kajal jump in place. She put her arms up in defense of the man, blocking her chest and abdomen from him; she had one leg up and squinted her eyes shut so that it looked like she planned to fight him blindly if he were to attack.

The intensity of his swatting slowed down long enough to make Kajal ease into the idea of lowering her guard.

The ninth and tenth floors passed, and they made eye contact. Kajal was taken aback then. When the old man turned and looked at her, she noticed how beautiful his eyes were. They were a gorgeous green with a golden jagged line circling around the old man's iris. She could see herself reflected, taking the place of a boy being called back home to his mother's house for supper, a scenario that ran through her brain at the moment, and she had no idea why. She could see the house in the distance, behind her in the man's eyes. She turned to look back, but behind her was only the car's silver panels, which she had expected. When she turned back around, the old man had his eyes looking away; he was the one who was afraid now.

A calmness set over Kajal. It had been over a year since eyes like his looked into hers. Goosebumps crawled up and down her skin. The man's presence now relaxed her, taking her to a place she had never been but was nostalgic for. She didn't overthink her feelings. The images of her daydream faded the closer they got to their destination.

She dreaded the growing numbers now. Kajal relaxed her grip on her keys, her hand still inside her coat pocket. She had so many questions she wanted to ask him. The man stared impatiently at the red static numbers changing shape, now calm as if the episode that just transpired had not happened.

Before the old man left the elevator, she wondered, as he passed her, if she could get away with wrapping her arms around him, squeezing his torso tightly, and nuzzling her face inside the small pocket underneath his right shoulder. This was how she wanted to be held and how no one else could hold her.

The elevator doors opened to the eleventh floor, and the old man walked out, paying her no mind. Without thinking, she followed him, slowly stepping out of the elevator and watching him walk down the hallway.

She grabbed her keys, this time to use as a prop. The elevator doors closed and went up to the twelfth floor without her. She moved slowly down the hallway, not taking her eyes off the old man as he wobbled his way down the hall. The hallway was identical to the one her mother lived in, aside from the same graffiti marks made on different sections of the wall. She even walked in the same direction she would if going to her mother's apartment.

The man stopped at the last door on the right, apartment 11K. He fiddled inside his coat pockets for his keys. Kajal stopped and stood still at a distance and watched the man. On the opposite side of the hallway, a family exited their apartment; a woman with her two daughters dressed warmly for the day, arguing loudly over something the older child had said to the younger. Their high-pitched vocals bounced off the poor acoustics, making a piercing sound that echoed into Kajal's ears.

What day was it? Kajal asked herself. Seeing the two girls with backpacks, she wondered if they were being taken to school. The two girls and their mother walked towards the elevator, approaching Kajal. The old man found his keys, opened the door to his apartment, and stepped inside. Before he closed the door, he glanced at her. He stood momentarily, holding the door open as if waiting for something to happen. The two stayed in their positions, watching the other. Kajal made the first move and smiled. She lifted her hand slightly to wave it. The elevator doors opened behind her, and the two girls and their mother entered. On the elevator's harsh bell sound, the old man shut the door hard and locked it from the inside.

She could smell her mother's cooking from down the hallway. Before Kajal entered the apartment, she guessed the special occasion, knowing her mother cooked her famous biryani only when they had guests over. Kajal entered the apartment and could tell that there were more people than usual, because of the extra pair of shoes at the front door. Kajal walked a few steps into the apartment, passing the kitchen. She poked her head into the living room, expecting Dale to be there waiting to lecture her. A pending rage then sat underneath her chest. But when she could see inside, it wasn't Dale who was there but her sister, Blanche, sitting in a chair next to their mother, who sat on the couch, drinking chai from a mug that displayed a recipe of tomato soup.

Blanche and Ruksaana turned their heads simultaneously towards the living room's entrance and greeted Kajal; a relief had come over her. Both Blanche and her mother shared the same enthusiastic smile.

After their father's death, Blanche's values in life changed. It was only a few days after her father's passing that Blanche and her then fiancé, Henry, made their engagement official. One random morning, they headed downtown to City Hall and married. It was a shot-gun wedding; no one from their families knew or was invited. They had a friend of Henry's be the witness, and when the ceremony was over, they had dinner at an Applebee's. Afterward, Blanche called her mother and informed her she now had a son-in-law.

Blanche finished laughing at something her mother had said to her in Urdu. This was the first sighting of her sister in months. After Blanche married, she and her new husband dropped their lives and moved out West. They headed to nowhere specific. They just got in their car, threw out everything they didn't need, broke their lease, and left New York. They hadn't planned much on the possible consequences of leaving their life behind, communication being neither of their strong suit. They both knew though they wanted out. Blanche only considered a discussion relevant after Henry pulled over on the highway and experienced a panic attack somewhere outside of the Philadelphia area. But whether it was out of shame for marrying a non-Muslim man, or quietly leaving New York without telling her family, out of fear of having to confront them about it, Blanche did not know. The two quit their jobs, got married, and left their life, asking no one for their permission.

Hi Kajal, said Blanche happy to see her younger sister.

The two sisters lost whatever little dialogue they had after Blanche left. Not long after, Kajal found a group chat had been created in her WhatsApp with every member of their family, minus their father, in it. The only message ever sent was the word *Ohio,* which Blanche wrote when passing through the state, along with a photo of a corn field next to an adjacent gas station they were using.

Whenever Blanche spoke to Kajal, even before their father's passing, she would come off as resentful or rude to her sister and reveal her disappointment whenever she spoke to her. As the older sibling, she resented Kajal for how little, in comparison, she was responsible for helping with their parents. She often gave Kajal shit for having a social life and a boyfriend and not dedicating more of her time at home. When Blanche left, Kajal resented her sister for leaving so soon and getting married without inviting her. But when Kajal saw her sister sitting in their living room, in a chair next to their mother, smiling, her immediate reaction was not anger but excitement from not seeing her older sister after so long.

Heeey, Blaaaanche, exclaimed Kajal, elongating her words consciously, almost hinting at their past tension.

Blanche's eyes were wide open and inviting, a genetic trait she shared with both Kajal and her mother. Kajal could see a change in her sister's appearance. She was thinner now, and her skin was more tan. An obvious metamorphosis had occurred on the road, wherever Blanche had gone to out West with Henry. She looked older to Kajal but more confident and inviting than she had been before she left.

Is Ayad here? Kajal asked. Did he see you?

He's sleeping, said Blanche, keeping her smile. I see some things haven't changed.

Kajal come sit. I made Hyderabadi biryani, Ruksaana beckoned.

And it's sooo good. Right Mama? Blanche affirmed, putting her arm around her mother and smiling with even more affection; she was happy to be beside her.

Very good this time, said Ruksaana, I'll make you a plate.

She started to stand. A visible discomfort showed on Ruksaana's face. Kajal told her mother to sit, but Ruksaana ignored her and limped her way into the kitchen.

So, what are you doing here? Kajal asked.

I wanted to see you guys. I missed you.

Yeah, I missed you.

Talking hurt Kajal's head more. The smell of the biryani had started to make her feel sick.

I've been wanting to talk with you, Kajal, said Blanche.

About what?

We don't have to talk now. I'd rather do it without Mama listening.

Okay. I think I'm gonna need to lie down for a bit first. I was up all night at a friend's house, studying.

Mama said you didn't come home?

Yeah, you'll be here?

I rented a room in a hotel not too far away, said Blanche, shaking her head yes. Go rest, she continued. We don't have to talk now. I'll tell Mama to put your food away. I'll be here for a bit.

You rented a room in a hotel? Why?

I know you and Dale have the other room, and I didn't want to kick either of you out.

You could have slept in the room with Mama.

I'm married now, remember? Blanche said, laughing, showing Kajal her wedding ring. Go rest. We'll talk another time.

Kajal nodded, thankful to her sister for letting her off the hook. Kajal left the living room and walked down the hallway towards her bedroom. The bed was unmade and beaten up from a restless night. Dale's pajamas' lay disheveled in the center of the rippled sheets. She sat on the bedside, touched one of his pajama legs, and clutched it tightly in her fist, wanting to cry.

Kajal laid down on her back, wishing to sleep, but could not due to the constant noise inside her mind. She wished the bed would fold inward and take her away, down into its deep darkness, and consume her.

She looked up momentarily and noticed something yellow in the corner of her eye. She sat up in bed and looked at it more closely, squinting her eyes to adjust them from the blurriness she was experiencing. A yellow post-it note had been placed in the center of the mirror of her dresser. She got up off the bed and walked closer to the note to read it. Maybe Dale never planned to come back to her mother's place. Maybe Kajal being honest with herself and telling Dale how she felt had done the work for him.

She took the yellow note off the mirror, held it in her hands, and read it out loud in the room to no one.

The note read: *I'll always love you.*

Blanche was the name she chose for herself. Her parents gave her the name Samina, which she used until she graduated into high school. Samina was born and raised in Pakistan until the age of three when her family moved to Brooklyn just before Kajal was born. They moved from their home in Pakistan - where Samina had her own bedroom - to a bedroom they all shared in a home owned by an uncle she had never met before, who already had roots in New York.

Samina was put into her first institution within a year of moving to the States, a Catholic children's daycare center right around the corner from where they lived. Ruksaana had started helping their aunt clean houses in

Coney Island, and Hussein started work as a cab driver. The daycare center being the closest and cheapest option they could find near their home. Samina did not handle the transition from Karachi to Brooklyn well, hating New York, and the strangers she spent all day with and the strange language she could barely understand.

On their recent trip, Blanche and her husband befriended a therapist named Valerie, for a short time somewhere in Taos for a much-needed break off the road. They rented the therapist's guest house as an Airbnb and bonded after she helped Blanche and her husband with a flat tire.

Valerie lived retired for the past twenty years in New Mexico where she was born and raised. Her home was made out of adobe brick and had a Portuguese-style red clay roof, two thin spiral columns outside, in the front, with cacti plants sitting by the front entrance, and two gas lanterns hanging on both sides of the arched door. A tiny hummingbird feeder hung beside the old mailbox, and two old white wooden rocking chairs sat on the porch whose purpose was to sit on and look out into the great nothing.

They weren't ever invited inside Valerie's home, her guest house supplied everything they needed: a small kitchen, a working bathroom, and a cozy bed.

Blanche and Valerie had developed a friendship separate from Henry, sipping wine on her porch in the evenings. Blanche only returned to Henry in the guest house when the starlit night sky revealed itself to them. On the porch was where they had these conversations, mostly analyzing the early period of Samina's life, helping her better understand her parent's decision to leave their home when she was young and releasing the narrative, she told herself, of that time turning her into a frustrated and reserved adult.

She had not questioned this part of herself until her father's passing, thinking there was nothing she could do to change the stoicism she felt that rested both inside her body and on her face. She described these reserved feelings to Valerie as *numb* and that they had followed her throughout middle school and into the early stages of adult life. She always observed other people and wondered what it felt like to be inside their bodies, assuming they were normal and something inside her was not right.

When other people showed joy, Samina was always curious about why they were so moved by mundane occurrences as a blossoming flower or a descending sunset. Knowing she was no poet, she still desired to enjoy more of what she thought other people liked. One of the reasons she went on this trip with her husband was to nourish that curiosity she knew she held within her.

It had been a while since Valerie had a patient. One of the goals of retiring was to incorporate more of a community of friends into her life. At one time, her social life involved only the conversations she had with her patients. However, the years and experience of being a therapist consistently seeped into the conversations she had with people she met. People often described Valerie as easy to talk to and easy to be around.

Blanche was always skeptical of seeing a therapist. She inherited her mother's innate aversion to opening up and involving people in her personal life.

When she graduated from middle school, her family saved enough money to move into their own apartment. Around that time, a teacher recommended to her parents that Samina talk to someone. She started to isolate herself from the other students in her class, and her grades started to slip, making her teacher concerned about her mental health and questioning what life was like for her at home. Ruksaana did not see the point in her daughter talking to someone who wasn't a family member or who did not speak their own language. She was insulted by the teacher's recommendation and feared her daughter was being outed for the wrong reasons and from the other students in her class.

What could a therapist do that she, as Samina's mother, could not?

Even at the young age of three years old, Samina was aware of the uncomfortable lifestyle her family was leading. They slept in the same bedroom together in the first year of moving. Her father used a yoga mat to sleep on at night, while Ruksaana and her daughter were given the gift of two blankets to use as their mattress.

There was no actual furniture in the beginning, except for the crib her parents slept next to on the opposite side of the room Samina designated as her own. When Kajal was born, she was loud and sucked all of her parent's attention away from Samina. Even as a child, Samina was confused as to why her family wanted to leave their home in Pakistan and move to such a strange and foreign city like New York and give themselves the burden of caring for an infant all at the same time. Samina would conjure plans in her *Hello Kitty* diary on how to get rid of her little sister. She once took her outside, without her parents' knowledge, and left Kajal to sit alone on the curbside next to a pile of garbage like she was furniture, left for someone else to take. She even thought of dialing 9-1-1 which she heard you do when you need help.

Even as she matured in age, Samina could still quickly sink back into that frustrated perspective she had as a kid. She did not understand what her father meant when he said moving to New York would lead to a better life. Nothing showed promise about their new life in New York. There was no safety net for her to hold on to, no comfort zone for her to feel protected by.

The first year of living in the States felt akin to a prison sentence she held without trial. When she graduated from middle school, Samina found herself relating to the punk/goth/emo kids the most. She was attracted to their dark and rebellious energy and for the most part, they accepted her into their community. They were the first real friends Samina made in America. She started to look forward to waking up and going to school in the mornings. For the first time, she had a reason not to go home straight after class. She started listening to rock bands like Good Charlotte, Linkin Park, and Audioslave, music her mother would call noise and turn off anytime Samina put in one of the CDs her friends had lent her into their uncle's treasured high-definition stereo system he had at home.

She finally learned what being a part of someone else's crew felt like. They were the same kids she was intimated by when she had first arrived, who hung out across the street from the school in front of the wired fence of a parking lot; all of them seemingly older, listening to music with shared earbuds, pierced all over, and smoking cigarettes.

Blanche told Valerie the story of her father seeing her with this crew for the first time. Hussein decided to surprise his daughter by picking her up after class. He drove past this crew of kids in his leased taxi cab. At first, he did not see his daughter when driving past her new slew of friends, saying a quick prayer to himself, thankful his daughter knew better than to hang out with such delinquents.

And just when he started looking for a spot to park his cab, he saw his daughter, for the first time, with her new strand of lavender hair and a cigarette burning in her mouth. He could not believe what he was seeing. He had to do a double take from the driver's seat. Hussein stopped his car short in the street and got out, leaving the driver's side door open; a line of cars stalled and honking their car horns behind him. He marched over to Samina, her new friends seeing her father before she did. Hussein grabbed her by the hair and yanked her, yelling obscenities in Urdu to her face, in front of her new friends.

She never forgot the look on their faces. She sank back into a deep embarrassment anytime a moment from that memory popped into her mind, like an intrusive thought. She remembered her friends' faces barely changing when her old man turned and started screaming, from the middle of the street, at them in front of his yellow cab, preaching to all who could hear him.

Back in the cab, Hussein berated Samina all the way home with insults in front of Kajal who was in the back seat. Calling his then thirteen-year-old daughter a *slut* and a *whore*; names she would never forget him calling her, even as she grew up and forgave him.

You're just like your mother, he spat, a disappointing burden.

Valerie sat listening to Blanche's story with a stillness and presence most people do not possess, allowing Blanche to focus on her thoughts without distraction. Valerie sipped her wine and sat with one hand on her leg, her eyes never diverting past Blanche's stare. Blanche continued telling her story without any pauses, lost in the story, never once thinking to ask Valerie a question about her own life.

After the incident with her father, Samina started skipping classes and stopped eating the food her mother cooked for her at home. Not eating was what got her parents' attention. They tried to feed her food they knew she liked, like potato chips, ice cream, and her mother's famous biryani. Anything they thought would go down their daughter's throat, so they could show her they loved her, nutrition was not the concern.

Some days were so bad Samina's mother had to sit on top of her in their bed and feed her mashed potatoes through a medicine dispenser they used to give Kajal antibiotics with. Still, Samina stayed stubborn and grew thin. She stopped seeing her friends. On the weekends, her parents would take her and Kajal over to visit family on Kings Highway. Some uncles of hers thought Blanche looked possessed. She had become so thin and pale; her uncles had grown afraid of her and deemed her cursed. They avoided eye contact with her and eventually stopped inviting them over for dinner. This added tension to the family. Hussein would fight with his brothers in their homes, in front of their wives and children, due to the disrespect they showed his family. The fights grew so intense that, at times, Samina remembers watching the veins ebb and flow from her father's neck.

Hussein wanted to get to the bottom of what was going on with his daughter. The insults from his brothers being the last straw. He knew Samina was not well. He was frustrated with her. Things had gotten out of hand, even for him. He never thought the scene he made in front of Samina's friends contributed to what was happening to his oldest daughter. He had forgotten all about it the very next day, after it happened. No weight of guilt sat on his chest; he thought he did the right thing.

Hussein saw Samina's condition as a test Allah gave him that he wanted to make right. His daughter's condition had worsened, so much so that he started to fear for the safety of both of his children. No longer trusting Samina to be alone with baby Kajal. He used to let Samina watch her in the living room, where the two would play and watch cartoons while he and his wife tried to find time in their bedroom to make a third. But after she stopped eating, he feared his oldest daughter could harm not just herself but his youngest daughter, too.

Seeing Samina outside in front of the school's parking lot, a cigarette burning in her mouth, made Hussein feel like he had lost control of his family. He started to become paranoid. The move to the States had been more difficult than he expected; New York was not the home that he had thought it would be. An insecurity burned inside him. Hussein wanted to move to America so that his daughters could have more than he ever had at home, but he no longer had an interest in engaging with the culture shock of Western tradition. He would if he could keep the lifestyle and traditions of his home country and give his daughters the opportunities that came with being an American. But he did not trust the people his daughters befriended or who taught them English and math. He did not trust those he drove in his cab or the owners of the homes his wife had cleaned. He brought his family to this country, but his dreams shattered shortly after moving, and he felt as if he had failed them, his children becoming a symbol of a future he did not see himself in.

Hussein did what he could to prevent his daughters from engaging with this new culture, hoping it would help prevent them from growing in a direction he did not like, afraid his daughters would be more influenced by the traditions of their new home then the one they came from. In his heart, he knew coming to this country was his decision, and their failure his fault, and there was no going back.

She heard the name *Blanche* from the play A *Streetcar Named Desire*. Ruksaana had given her cash, without her husband's knowledge, to go and see the play on a field trip with her English class. Her father would not have approved of her going. It was her first time seeing a show on Broadway. Samina stood in line in front of the theater with her fellow students, tucked quietly inside her hoody, keeping to herself. They were seeing a matineé show. She had never been to Times Square before; her family never left Brooklyn. The lights, the crowd, and the pace of the city's bustling center opened Blanche's eyes, revealing inside her an energy she was not before aware of. They waited outside the theater, eating their lunch.

Samina's class sat in the orchestra seats. She was in the front row; part of the stage obstructed her view. She could not see the far back of the stage and some parts of the middle. Walking into the theater was the second shock to her system that day. When she found where her seats were, a concoction of serotonin and adrenaline rushed through the brains of the students. Any sense of fatigue or dread was no longer there.

By the play's end, she hardly understood what it was about and even found parts of the play to be boring. But what she walked away with wasn't the story or the actors' performance, but the magical experience of seeing live theater.

Summer was just around the corner, and it was spent with her family, hardly going outside and never seeing those friends she made at school again, all of them changing and growing in their own directions. She could not face those who saw her father, berating her in the street. That loss of contact erased the memory of each other, and by the beginning of the new school year, they were again strangers. But there was a change forming inside Samina that no force could control. Things that once bothered her mattered less now, not really having a resolution to the heaviness she felt the year before. She began to feel the excitement of being a part of something bigger, that thing being, with the coming school year, one year older and somebody new. On her first day, she didn't see anyone she recognized; she saw only new faces. She felt safe starting again. When the first person asked her what her name was, the name rolled off her tongue effortlessly, and without thinking, she answered simply, *Blanche*.

Kajal only intended to sleep for an hour when she got home to her mother's apartment, but her sleep continued for a few hours more into the night. She woke to the sound of a fire truck leaving its station down the avenue. The truck's siren blaring as it pulled into the street and headed up the block. The dark sky disoriented her, confused by the time she thought it should be.

Kajal searched the bed for her phone, wanting to check the time; the panic that manifested was when one realized they had slept most of the day. Outside, the streetlights were turned on, and a breeze came in through her window. It wasn't open earlier, when she saw Dale's note and collapsed onto the bed; someone must have come inside while she was sleeping and opened it for her.

She no longer had a headache, but she did not feel good. Her mouth was dry, her stomach hurt, and she needed water. The events of the day prior felt as if they had happened years ago. Still, she had homework she needed to finish, which was due the following day. Today. This morning.

She shot out of bed and headed down the hallway. Behind his closed door, she heard Ayad playing video games inside his bedroom. It was two hours past midnight, the clock said. All Kajal wanted to do was lie back down and go to sleep. She stood in the hallway and held her head with her right hand, trying to orient herself. She saw tiny dots circling around her in the darkness, her blood rushing back inside her skull. She tried to take one step forward, and the hallway rotated slowly before her as if she were inside an amusement park's haunted mansion.

It was only when Kajal entered the living room that she remembered that Blanche had returned from her never-ending road trip. She wondered if her sister would be home for long, her intuition telling her she would not be. Kajal thought she might see her sister sleeping on the living room couch but remembered she had rented a hotel room with her husband. A light had been left on by the Possini wall mirror. It became apparent that only the usual cast of characters were present aside from Dale.

Kajal grabbed an empty pot from inside the oven, turned the knob from the sink, and watched as it swelled with water. She placed the pot of water on the stove, turned on the gas, and poured herself a drink.

She didn't hear her mother's approaching footsteps, believing, at first, the blurry image at the bottom of her glass to be that of an apparition. Kajal jumped in place, making her mother laugh.

Mama, you scared me. Appearing like a jinn, Kajal said in Urdu, sucking her teeth while moving the cup further away from her face.

You okay?

Yes. You?

Yes.

I have some work to do tonight, explained Kajal, giving off a small laugh. She laughed, not because she thought what she said was funny, but because laughing was a coping mechanism she used to deal with uncomfortable moments since her youth.

Tonight? The birds and I are up to pray, said Ruksaana.

The thought of doing schoolwork exhausted Kajal.

Ruksaana paused and asked where Dale was.

He's not coming home tonight, Mama.

No?

No.

Her mother stopped herself, not wanting to pry.

You'll see your sister tomorrow, yes?

I'll try.

Neither Kajal nor her mother said anything further. Both mother and daughter stood silently in the kitchen, waiting, wanting the other to say more.

Okay, good night, Beta.

Good night Mama. I love you.

I love you, too, three, four.

The next morning, Kajal finished a shift at the cafe, walked home, and took another nap. She was still exhausted from her outing with Kareena two nights before. She woke later in the afternoon with several text messages from Blanche on her phone, listing options for where they could meet for dinner. Blanche wanted to meet at a Cuban restaurant four blocks from their mother's apartment. But it was raining and cold outside, and the four blocks to the restaurant felt like twenty. Kajal didn't text her sister back, not right away. She took a shower first, brushed her teeth, and contemplated whether she wanted to go. But when she got out of the shower, her decision was made for her. There was a missed call on her phone and Kajal panicked, a reaction to the tumultuous relationship she had had with her sister. She texted Blanche back quickly to appease her. Confirming she'd meet her at the Cuban spot.

She put on her rain jacket and boots, said goodbye to her mother, and descended the twelfth-floor staircase. She entered the eleventh-floor hallway through the staircase entrance and headed towards the old man's apartment. She wanted to see those eyes again. To be looked at by those eyes again. She walked up to the old man's door and knocked.

Nothing happened. There was no response from the other side of the door. Before she left, Kajal had taken the rest of the biryani her mother made and wrapped it in tinfoil on a yellow glass plate. She waited and knocked three more times at the old man's door. There was no response; she couldn't wait any longer; her sister was waiting. Kajal placed the aluminum-wrapped plate on the floor in front of the old man's door, hoping when he came home, he'd see it.

Kajal made her way out of the apartment building. She opened her umbrella and headed north from 101st Street. She couldn't explain her nerves. It had been months since she had spent alone time with her sister. Blanche left for her trip soon after Kajal found out she was accepted into Columbia.

Walking to the restaurant, Kajal felt goosebumps ride up her arms, reacting to the cold weather and her fast-beating heart. She let a bus pass her by in the street, and she jaywalked the rest of the way and entered the doors to the restaurant.

It wasn't crowded inside. A small band was playing - what Kajal recognized to be Flamenco music – in a makeshift space at the back by the kitchen. There was no hostess at the front, but a waitress appeared and approached Kajal as she entered. The waitress directed her to an empty table by the windows near the front. But Kajal saw her sister sitting at a table, alone, eating tortilla chips from a small wooden bowl, alternating dips of the bitten chip into the green sauce and then the red.

When Kajal approached the table and saw her sister's face, her nerves dissipated. The two sisters looked almost identical, though a few years apart. If it wasn't for Blanche's West Coast transformation, her skin a little darker, her hair lighter, the two would look almost the same.

Blanche stood from her chair and hugged Kajal as she approached the table.

Thank you for coming, said Blanche, beaming, as she sat back down in her chair.

Kajal took off her rain jacket and gently closed her umbrella. Rogue raindrops slid off the umbrella's top, falling onto her chair. Kajal ordered herself a coke, and Blanche ordered one too. She much preferred a beer but was too uncomfortable to drink in front of her older sister, despite Blanche's own rule-breaking.

So, what did you want to talk about? Kajal asked forthrightly. She found it hard to ask her sister the question and make eye contact at the same time. Kajal took a sip from her drink and tried to hide the fact that she was nervous.

Oh, said Blanche, I guess I just really wanted to see you.

Kajal didn't say anything at first. She just stared down at her drink.

Mama didn't put you up to this?

No, what do you mean?

Nothing.

No, you meant something, she said again.

Nothing. You just want to talk now? When did you become the talking type?

Blanche did not know what Kajal meant by this. She was put off by her sister's tone but tried to stay calm. The last thing she wanted was for the dinner she planned with Kajal to turn into a fight. Blanche recognized her feelings and let them float past her. She was afraid if they fought, it would be the last time the two would speak.

I know you're mad at me for leaving. And I'm sorry.

I'm not mad.

Well, I'm sorry anyway.

I'm not mad.

Okay.

I got my own shit going on, Sam. I don't have time to waste thinking about whatever it is you and your new husband are doing.

You don't sound not mad.

Sorry.

What do you got going on? Blanche asked.

Kajal sighed and took a breath.

I mean it. I want to know.

I don't feel like talking about it. I don't know right now.

Okay.

I'm too in the middle of it, I guess.

Are you okay?

Define okay.

Mama's worried about you.

So, she did put you up to this.

No. I just know she's worried, that's all. Us meeting has nothing to do with her.

Mama won't talk about Papa. Did you know that? She doesn't feel like she has to. Neither does Ayad, said Kajal.

She misses him. They both do. People grieve in their own way, Kajal. You need to let them.

It just feels like it didn't happen. Like he was never here. We all moved on so fast.

I haven't moved on. Is that what you think? That I moved on?

Haven't you?

No. What makes you say that?

You left. You haven't been home in months.

It's not like that. It hasn't been easy, Kajal.

It hasn't been easy for anyone.

I get that.

You think it was fair of you to leave like you did? To get married without any of us there?

I thought you weren't mad about that?

I'm not mad. I'm disappointed. I'm angry.

That's the same thing, Kajal.

Well, then, maybe I am mad. What's it to you?

I said I was sorry. I shouldn't have done that. It was wrong of me. I didn't know better at the time.

Now you know better, huh?

Better than I did then. Yes. If I could do it all over again, I would. But I can't, and I'm sorry. What would you like me to do?

Do you think you've moved on?

I don't know. No. I don't know if that's possible.

You don't know if it's possible?

How could I move on? He was my father. How could I move on?

It makes everything worse. School. Home. People. Everything. It makes everything more complicated. I feel like I'm underwater, just below the surface. I can see the shapes and movements of everyone around me. I just lose the will to keep pushing up.

I can understand that.

Kajal started to cry. The tears surprised her. They welled up from behind her eyes and came out without permission. It frustrated her to show this kind of vulnerability in front of her older sister. She was afraid to be judged. Kajal banged her fist hard onto the table and took heavy breaths to stop the tears from coming. Seeing her sister cry made Blanche cry, too.

I miss him every day, Kajal.

Blanche grabbed Kajal's hand from across the table. It was the second time someone did that to her in the past twenty-four hours. Her sister's touch made Kajal think of Dale.

Suddenly, Kajal couldn't breathe; she could only produce small, thin, rapid breaths. She wheezed, in and out, in and out. No matter how hard she tried, she couldn't regulate her breathing.

Kajal? Blanche asked concerningly.

Blanche leaned over the table and grabbed Kajal's other arm, trying to get her to focus. The chips and soda fell onto the floor as she did this. The band, in the back of the restaurant, continued to play.

Kajal look at me. Breathe. Look at me. You have to breathe.

Kajal looked at her sister. Only thin breaths came to the service. Kajal tried to slow her breathing, but it was too hard. She felt as if she had no control. It had been a while since this last happened to her.

A thought passed through Kajal's mind as she fell to the floor: This was it. This was how she would die, just like her father, from a heart attack. For a moment, she felt relief.

Drink some water, said a voice she didn't recognize. You have to breathe.

Their waitress brought Kajal a glass of water. She passed the glass to Blanche, who took it, kneeling on the floor beside her sister. She didn't know until then the entire restaurant was watching.

Kajal, drink, commanded Blanche, her tone almost angry. She opened her sister's mouth and let the water drip down her throat.

Kajal coughed as the water entered her throat. Her breathing slowed, but her heart continued to beat fast. She felt lightheaded, exhausted.

And with the will to live faintly starting to reveal itself, Kajal grabbed the glass from her sister's hand and finished whatever was left inside it.

XI

The Bather

The mother took her baby out of the kitchen sink. She had just given him a bath. She infused the water with herbs like lemongrass and rosemary and heated the water to just the right temperature. She discovered, after becoming a mother, that her favorite scent in the world was how her baby smelled after a bath. She loved to take the time to wash each crevice of her newborn's body with soap and water, never missing a spot. The music she played in the background was Bruce Springsteen's *Born to Run*. *I want to know if love is wild, Babe, I want to know if love is real,* echoed through her husband's stereo speakers.

When the bath finished, the mother wrapped her son inside a white robe that was gifted to her by her mother for the baby almost a year ago. Steam from the baby's warm, soft body trailed through the air from the kitchen to the living room, as the young mother danced her way through the hallway, holding her young son, landing them both softly on the couch.

The highway's jammed with broken heroes on a last-chance power drive, played through the air. The boy bounced happily in his mother's arms, moving his arms and legs wide and freely. Dancing an Irish jig of his own to the music that was his mother's breath. The two sat down together. The boy lay horizontally on his mother's lap as she freed him of his robe. The air from the house sent a quick chill to the boy's now exposed, still wet, skin, creating goosebumps up and down his naked arms and naked legs.

The back door of the house opened. It was the woman's husband, the boy's father, coming home from work. He stepped inside the kitchen, put his bag down by the sink, walked the way to his wife and son, and kissed them both gently on the cheek. He stood over them both, looking down at his family, smiling, happy to be home.

The father asked, how's he doing?

Great, the mother answered, he just came out of a bath. He smells so clean and fresh now.

She moved her head closer to her son's skin. She had a smile on her face as she smelled her son and kissed the center of his exposed belly.

We should put clothes on him, no? He's going to get a cold like this, said her husband, I don't want him to get sick.

I know, but I just love him like this. Look. See how he feels.

With the tips of her fingernails, the young mother gently stroked the inner thigh of her son's leg. Never directing her eyes away from the boy's, she moved her fingernails up from the boy's thigh to the tip of his gender. The boy laughed from the feeling his mother's fingernails gave him, and he celebrated shooting his arms and legs out wide, straight and back, straight and back, projecting a curdled sound that came from the back of his throat.

Look how happy he is, the mother exclaimed, laughing, exuding the joy only a mother could. Look at those goosebumps. How cute is he?

With her fingertips, she made the move again, and like a fountain in Rome, the boy shot a spray of yellow liquid out into the air from his tiny tip. Gravity sent it back down onto his mother's face and lap. She reacted quickly, not thinking. Her facial expression frozen like a Dionysus mask, transitioning imperceptibly from one emotion to the next.

She stood up, trying to avoid getting any more of her son's urine onto her new clothes. Forgetting, in that brief moment, where the boy was placed on her lap. As she stood up, the boy fell onto the floor between her and her husband.

The boy's father screamed in horror. The mother stared in shock, horrified by what she'd just done. On the floor, the boy continued to pee himself. He lay face down on the ground, in a puddle of pee that started to visibly form underneath him, on top of the young parent's newly refurbished wooden floor.

Get the mop, the boy's father screamed, we just did this floor. Come on!

Oh, someday girl I don't know when. We're gonna get to that place where we really wanna go.

The husband lifted his son off the ground and quickly placed him inside his crib, down the hallway, never thinking to wipe his son free of the pee that had started to dry, cold on the boy's legs and lower stomach.

The father closed the bedroom door behind him and returned to the puddle in the living room. The boy's mother, already down on her knees, trying to wipe what was left of her son's urine with a towel.

It won't go away, she cried, it's warping the floor!

Did you wipe it, asked the father from the kitchen.

Yes, I'm wiping it now.

Where's the mop?

The mop?

Yes, the mop! God damn it!

I got a towel.

The father rushed over with the mop and pushed his wife aside. The strength of his push knocked her to the floor.

Tickets!

The young mother kneeling next to her husband. She screamed, I hate you, I hate you, I hate you, into her husband's ears, hitting his shoulders with her fist. The husband ignored his wife's crying as he mopped the section of the floor their son stained, moving his arms quickly, left to right.

Tickets!

The boy screamed in his crib, alone in the dark. Struggling to keep his head up, urine continued to flow out of him, forming a puddle in the center of the mattress he lay on.

Tickets!

Dale woke up at the Jamaica Avenue station, on the Long Island Rail Road, with a train line of urine going down his left pant leg and a man he did not know standing over him, asking him for his train ticket.

Tickets, please, Sir, commanded the train's ticket collector.

Dale woke from a deeper sleep than he'd ever thought he could get on a moving train, with the sun blasting through the window. He didn't sleep well the night before, waiting for Kajal to return. When he arrived at Ruksaana's apartment, he hoped speaking with Kajal would help him. He wanted her support to diminish the shame he felt towards the events at his job that led to him being fired. But as the night grew longer, as he tried to sleep, every noise he heard, every crack or footstep that made itself known to him, forced Dale to wake up, to check if it was her.

He felt like a child sitting on the train, trying not to put any focus on his leg, feeling the dampness on both sides of his hands as he searched his jean pockets for his ticket; the ticket collector was all too aware of the darker shade of blue running down the middle of Dale's pant leg.

Tickets, please, the man said agitated.

Dale searched his pockets blindly for the paper ticket, and when he found it and pulled it out for the man, it crumbled down into a small damp ball that formed from the inner depths of his inside pocket.

I'm not touching that.

I'm sorry?

I'm not touching that.

Dale unraveled the ticket for the man who clicked it twice, as it dangled in the air like a beaten flag from Dale's hand, and walked away aggressively down the aisle.

Dale was halfway home; at least another twenty minutes were left on the train ride to his parent's house. He touched the wet part of his leg with caution. He felt disgusting sitting on the train in his clothes and wanted nothing more than to remove himself from his jeans. Through his anger, he punched the plastic wall underneath his seat's window. The punch made a more audible sound than expected and it permeated throughout the train car.

He wanted to scream, but he couldn't. There were too many people around him. His anger ebbed and flowed like a pulse to various degrees within him, and when it ballooned, he had no choice but to suppress it. He was stuck. Stuck in life, stuck on this train car, and he was going home to a house he swore to himself he'd never again live in.

Behind him, he could see Manhattan. He was just there, he thought. The island acted as a visual reference for the distance between him and Kajal. If they had separated on good terms, gone down separate paths to just see each other again tomorrow, he wouldn't feel the violent ache he now had resting inside his stomach. Eleven years of a relationship gone. Eleven years of co-dependency to unlearn. I don't want you there, she said to him.

He could feel the separation from Kajal manifesting as a physical ache inside him, as if a giant manuscript were being torn from cover to cover inside his stomach. He wanted to hop off the train, get on one Manhattan-bound and run to Kajal, forgive her and be forgiven, and move on like they always had after an argument. But he knew that wouldn't happen today. It wouldn't wrap up nicely like the narrative he sought for in his brain. Running back to Kajal would only make them grow more distant. Space is what they needed. So, he stayed where he was, watched the train move slowly out of the station, and he sat in his filth and went home.

Carol came ten minutes after when he told her the train would arrive. He stood at the curbside, waiting. A few stragglers from the train walked past him into the street to their cars. He could see the headlights coming from down the road, the familiar sight of his family's car. The silhouette of his mother sitting in the driver's seat behind the glare. She stopped the car just before the municipal parking lot and flashed her lights to him. Dale got in the car and barely mumbled a hello.

Hello, she said to him. Do you want to talk?

Not now.

Are your pants wet?

No.

Then why is your leg like that?

Just drive, please.

The tears came when she put the car's gear into drive.

When they arrived home, Dale saw from the driveway the light from the TV reflected against the kitchen cabinets. He knew this meant his father was home. He closed his eyes in anger and slammed the passenger door shut. He hadn't expected to see his father this evening; knowing his dad was home meant he was well informed on the specifics of his oldest son's arrival, his mother never being able to keep a secret.

When he entered the house, his father's eyes stayed glued to the TV screen, his back lay against the cushioned sofa. Dale poked his head into the living room.

What's up, asked his father, staying as he lay on the couch.

Dale nodded his head, mumbled a hello, and continued past him, heading up the staircase to his old bedroom. It was all so natural, as if he had been staying at his parents' house for months.

When all the lights and sounds in the house were off, Dale stepped inside the shower. He felt like a guest in the house he grew up in. He'd taken all the clothes he needed to change from his bedroom to avoid walking out with just a towel wrapped around his waist. He didn't want to cross paths with either parent with his stomach or chest exposed, allowing them to see how his body had changed over the years.

He was critically aware of how he acted, careful not to offend or make anyone ashamed by his exposure. It was no different than staying at Kajal's mother's apartment. It had been a while since he last felt at home.

Stepping off the train, he felt the repercussions of every decision he made that led him here, becoming what the world ordained a failure. He had no job, no home, or lover to call his own. He wasn't convinced either parent wanted him there, either. They were just fulfilling their duties as good parents and having their front door open for their children whenever they needed to come through.

He could feel the inconvenience his arrival created when stepping inside their home with no known date to leave. His parents had gotten used to their children not living with them and may have come to prefer their solitude. Dale knew they would never admit this, but he could sense it in the tone at which they spoke and the body language they carried when around him in the house.

What he found out coming home, but did not know before arriving, was that his moving back home was not just a change he would have to adapt to, but his parents as well.

Dale turned off the showerhead, opened the sliding glass door, and grabbed a used towel, which hung from a hook on the bathroom door. The steam from the shower was so thick he could not see his reflection in the mirror. He brushed his teeth blindly and put on his clothes. Everyone had gone to bed. He walked through the hallway into the living room. All the lights in the house had been turned off. The furniture sat in their place in the dark, gently backlit from the streetlight from the living room window.

Dale walked into the living room and stood there, still, slightly dripping wet onto the newly refurbished wooden floor. It was a moment of stillness in a house that was never quiet, and though he could hardly see, he took advantage and stood still in the window's light.

Dale?

His father's voice came from the dark part of the living room. Dale had not seen him sitting there.

Yes? Dale answered.

What are you doing?

Nothing.

The following day, Dale had the house to himself. Both his parents left for work long before he woke up. There was a post-it note on the microwave from his father, asking him to eat yesterday's leftovers for breakfast. He considered it, took the note, placed it inside the trash bin, and made himself a pot of coffee.

It was the first day he hadn't somewhere to be. He wasn't used to having his options available to him. But since he no longer had an income and was, once again, living in the suburbs with his parents with no car, his options for the day were limited.

Dale sat down at the kitchen table, drinking his coffee, and watched two squirrels chase each other up a tree outside his parent's kitchen window.

He grabbed his laptop from upstairs and used it to look for work. He checked LinkedIn for jobs he felt he was suitable for. Though there was nothing that seemed of interest to him. Where did he see himself working in the future? What job did he want to do? He didn't want to sit in an office again. He looked for another twenty minutes and grew disheartened. Due to boredom, he went inside the bathroom to masturbate, and after, he felt no different. He cleaned up his mess from the toilet seat, left the bathroom, looked at the clock in the kitchen, and saw only an hour had gone by since he had woken up.

For years, he lived on the move, constantly moving from one task to the next. Always having somewhere to be. Something to finish. Standing in his parent's kitchen, he felt the world he knew had left him behind. That he had failed its test. He preferred a scheduled life because it was all he knew and he felt productive to always have a place to be and something to accomplish. It helped create the illusion that he was chasing after something, a goal, the perfect version of himself.

Even when he tried not to make plans, plans were made for him by other people. When he didn't know what he desired, he turned to his community to tell him. Now alone, he had every option at his disposal. He could go wherever he wanted to. He could move and live wherever he desired to go. Single, he could date other women if he wanted. But having these options made him feel the desire only to be still.

When he woke the following morning, he felt Kajal's distance again. He didn't remember going to sleep the night before. He drifted off, watching a cartoon on his laptop in bed. And woke to the sun's light present on every wall inside his old bedroom.

When his parents came home, he stayed in his room without greeting them. He ate dinner with them later that night in the dining room. The three of them sat and ate their food in silence, and after, Dale went back upstairs to his bedroom to lay down in the dark until there was nothing to do but sleep.

When he woke the following day, he wanted to text her. His anger had subsided significantly and he missed her. He looked at her Instagram, but she hadn't posted anything new. Frustrated, Dale deleted the app and threw his phone across his childhood bedroom.

He hadn't been outside since he left Kajal. After he made his coffee, he walked through the back door of his parent's house and exited through the white plastic fence that bordered the backyard. It all looked the same as it did when he was a child growing up here. The identical houses, the identical streets, the same trees growing older as he did each year. He held his coffee mug as the steam rose from underneath his chin. He walked outside barefoot to the front yard; each step was cold and wet, every strain of grass an ice pick under his feet. He continued to the curb lane in front of the house and stared at the road. A family of Monk Parakeets flew over his head, squawking loudly in their green feathers, flying to some faraway nest. His family's house sat on the southern point of a circular block, giving them two driveways and a more prominent front yard than the rest of the homes on the block. The road he stood in front of - where he remembered stickball in the street with his brother, fireworks on the fourth of July, blizzards that covered every inch of the lawn with snow - could take him to any state in the country he wanted to visit. He could drive to the most southern point of South America, up to Canada, and down to Mexico, from this road. But he wasn't going to any of those places. He was back home, stuck in the house where his story had started almost thirty years ago.

His mother came home after sunset. She'd gone out for drinks after work with coworkers in Manhattan but had done some grocery shopping on her way home. His father was working a double shift and planned to sleep at his office for his morning's early start. When his mother entered the house, Dale was sitting on the couch, his feet up, looking at his laptop. She came in with a few bags of groceries.

Can you help me, she asked him from the front door. There's more in the car, she said.

He went out and helped her without putting on a jacket. It was colder now. He grabbed whatever he thought was heaviest and hauled it back with both hands inside the house to set it down. He went out for one more trip to the car. His mother followed behind him. They looked in the trunk, and there was nothing besides a pack of water bottles that Dale would bring inside the house. He lifted the case of bottled water with both hands, his mother closed the trunk behind him, and they entered the house together, not saying a word.

The next day, he had to get out of the house. It had been almost a week since he last saw Kajal. He packed a small bag, punched in the code for the alarm to the house, and walked 20 minutes to the Rosedale station to catch the 11:45 AM railroad train to the city. He got off at Penn Station; the platform was packed with people. He looked in both directions of the platform and saw nothing but heads squished together, moving slowly towards an exit.

He waited his turn to squeeze onto an escalator. A tall white man dressed in a long beige raincoat, a fedora on his head, stood behind Dale mumbling, looking down at his phone, reading a message out loud as they lifted together onto the station's central platform. He bought a coffee and an everything bagel with lox cream cheese at a shop and ate it while walking down Seventh Avenue.

Dale woke up this morning wanting to see art. It had been a while since he had visited a museum. He was still determining which museum he wanted to visit. He knew his options and hadn't committed to visiting any particular place. He wanted the museum to call him. He put on his headphones, listened to the music of Django Reinhardt, walked the streets of Manhattan, and headed downtown.

He stopped at 23rd Street, in front of the old Chelsea Hotel. The old hotel had captured his attention. He had not planned to stop here. He crossed the street to the building and felt a kinship with the hotel, projecting, from his mind, all of the passing souls who once stepped foot inside the hotel's shuttered doors.

The block outside the hotel was packed with people. The street was congested with traffic, cars blaring horns and revving motors in both directions. He stared at the facade from the curb lane. Despite all the noise from the street, Dale managed to feel alone with the hotel. A face revealed itself to him on the front of the building. Once he saw the face's shape within the hotel's windows, it never diverted its eye contact. He passed under the scaffolding and walked underneath the red awning to the main entrance. Dale stood on the front steps of the hotel to see further inside, past the glass door. There was a long tea-green hallway beyond the hotel's main entrance. It looked dreary and exhausted, as if nobody stepped foot inside the lobby for years. He wondered how it could be, living in New York his whole life, and he was now just stopping to take notice of the old hotel lobby. His eyes trailed up the hallway's walls from the doorstep, stretching as far back as he could see, wishing he could go inside.

His phone vibrated inside his coat pocket. The phone's power pulling him away from the ghosts of the old Chelsea. Maybe it's Kajal, he thought and turned away from the entrance, eager to check his phone. The sound of the traffic became more apparent with each step further into the curb lane he took. Dale pulled out his cell phone and checked the phone's caller ID. If it was Kajal, he'd cancel his plans to see art and walk straight to Harlem from the Chelsea and knock on Ruksaana's front door with relief. But it was his mother calling him, and he could feel, as he stared down at his phone in the curb lane, the power of his disappointment. He clicked the button on the side of his phone, canceling the call, all of his problems rushing back to him. He cursed underneath his breath. He felt spotted in a moment where he did not want to be seen. He turned off his cell phone, stored it in his coat pocket, and walked east, away from the old hotel.

He made his way north to the Museum of Modern Art. He walked north up Sixth Avenue to 53rd Street. A queue ran outside the museum's doors, going down the block. He'd visited the MOMA more than any other museum in New York. In college, he had a professor who rendered the museum *The worst modern art museum in the world!* and each time Dale walked through its doors, the professor's line would ring true inside his head. There was art here Dale loved. Art that, when he was younger, inspired him to want to be an artist, and fall in love with art and travel to the cities where the artists whose work he saw there came from. It was these particular paintings Dale sought for now. He wanted something to take him out of his numbness. He wanted to feel his heart again.

On line, he looked through his wallet for his old school ID. He graduated almost six years ago but kept his ID for moments like this, hoping to pay the student discount.

He found his old ID warped and scratched at the back of his wallet. There was no marker to indicate what year Dale had been in school. He waited almost 20 minutes in line, and when it was his turn, he approached a woman who sat behind a desk and, with a smile, handed her his retired student ID card.

This you, questioned the woman.

Yeah.

Okay. What year did you graduate?

I didn't.

Normally, student ID's indicate what year the student is currently in school. It's how we can tell the students from the imposter's.

Well, I'm currently a student, said Dale. Shedding a small laugh.

No, you're not.

Okay, said Dale, maintaining some semblance of a polite smile.

I can see it's expired.

It's not a fake ID if that's what you're implying.

I'm not implying it's fake. I'm saying it's expired. I know you're not in school.

How?

You don't remember me?

Dale looked at the woman, trying to remember her face.

Clara. From the Metrograph, said Clara from behind the counter.

Clara? 400 Blows Clara?

Ugh, yeah...

Sorry.

It's a wig.

A what?

A wig. I'm wearing a blue wig right now?

I see that.

I wasn't, the first time we met.

Oh. Yes. Right. I remember you. Hello. The wig changed your face. I didn't recognize you.

Yes.

How are you?

Fine.

You're not in school, right?

No. You're right. I was lying. I'll take one grown-up ticket, please.

Were you trying to trick the MOMA, she said, laughing.

No, sorry. Just didn't want to pay full price, said Dale. He had almost mentioned that he lost his job but felt too embarrassed to reveal that information out loud and stopped short, leaving between him and Clara an uncomfortable pause.

Didn't you work for Google? Dale asked.

I did. I no longer do.

Right. And now you work for the MOMA?

Yes, part-time. I needed a little extra cash and got the gig from a temp agency. I'm working on my app, remember?

Right. Yes. Okay.

I have a lunch break coming soon. Would you want to walk around for a bit? I usually hang out on the fifth floor.

Fifth floor? Sure, I can meet you there. When?

I'm just waiting for my replacement.

Okay.

Are you sure you're okay? I thought you recognized me. I thought you were joking about the ID. I was just playing along...

No, sorry. It's the first time I've been to the city in a few days. I came to see a few older paintings I like here... To get out of my head.

Okay... It's okay if you want to be alone.

No, no. It's okay. I don't have an agenda. I'm just being nostalgic today. I'd love to hang out with you.

Okay, if you're sure.

Yes.

Clara typed something into her computer, and a paper ticket came from the small printer on her desk.

Here, said Clara, handing Dale a large paper rectangular ticket.

Great. Thanks. How much do I owe you?

Free. Friend discount.

Ha. Very clever, Clara.

See you in a bit!

See you.

He walked away feeling embarrassed and stepped off the elevator into the gallery space. When he left Clara the night of the screening, she had left his conscious mind after a few days, and he assumed they'd never see each other again. He did not expect to see her of all places, working the customer service line of the MOMA, wearing a wig...

The gallery on the fifth floor of the MOMA held both Van Gogh's *The Starry Night* and Picasso's *Les Demoiselles d'Avignon*. It was crowded, as expected. Everyone gravitated towards *The Starry Night* to take a selfie or a photo of the painting. He entered the gallery space, and contemplated how many people stood in front of the *Starry Night* each year compared to those who got to spend time with the painting and actually see it. Was it possible to like Van Gogh's *Starry Night* separate from its reputation as a famous work of art? Dale stood in front of Van Gogh's painting on several different occasions of his life. A younger version of Dale would have found it appropriate to show up just to take a selfie in front of the painting, while the person he was now, a more seasoned and older Dale, would only want to get lost in its paint, but it was too crowded to do so.

He made a mental note to walk by the painting later and see if it was possible to get a glance at it over the crowd on his way out. He saw another Van Gogh in the corner that he liked and approached it. It was a portrait of the artist's good friend Joseph Roulin, a big bearded pirate of a man, centered in front of a green floral background. Next, he went up to a Toulouse-Lautrec picture, portraying a well-dressed man who sat alone in a room on a decrepit chair.

Dale walked to the other side of the gallery and saw a few pieces he liked, but nothing stood out. Nothing stopped him. He wandered mindlessly for a bit, no longer alone with his thoughts. The anticipation of Clara was creeping up on him.

If she didn't come, he'd be okay with it. Her not coming would release him of the burden of having to make small talk with someone he barely knew. He had no interest in talking to people today. All he wanted from the day was to be inspired, get out of his head, and find something in the city that moved him. But he couldn't tell Clara that. He couldn't tell her he preferred to be alone because he was always alone. Nor did he know her well enough or owe her an explanation.

He walked along the east side of the gallery and came across a painting of a young man on the wall to his right. Dale stopped in front of the painting, noticing the features of the young man in the painting similar to that of his own. Dale touched the hem of his pants to ground himself, pinching the fabric between his thumb and middle finger, forcing himself not to continue on.

The young man in the painting was almost nude; he had a thin article of clothing that hung around his waist, and that was it. He held no attractive features. His brown hair was cut awkwardly in the front, and his pale gauntlet body showcased nothing heroic or attractive. He was plain, out of shape, and awkward. With the decrepit gray sky displayed behind him, Dale couldn't tell if it showed a forecasted sky or an approaching storm. The young man walked forward toward the viewer in a wet, overcast wasteland, where no person or animal could be seen in the distance behind him. The only thing evident about the young man was that he was pensive and entirely alone.

Dale took a moment from the painting to read its placard on the wall to its right. The piece was called *The Bather* by the artist Paul Cezanne. Dale noticed by how the room was curated that the piece was essential to the museum. The painting had a large frame, and with its placement and lighting in the gallery it was another great attraction at the MOMA, second in the gallery space to *The Starry Night.* But it got way less attention from the museum's visitors. Besides Dale, no one stood in front of the painting. The room was packed with people who walked past it, only glancing in the painting's direction on their way to take a selfie in front of a piece they knew already existed before they had arrived. *The Bather* was located on the opposite side of the room from *The Starry Night.* Dale couldn't help but see the irony of the scene. *The Bather* portrayed an ordinary man, considered an essential piece by the museum, and yet it was overlooked by the museum's patrons, Dale assumed, for exactly why it was deemed relevant.

Cezanne portrayed the young man in his painting as anxious, anonymous, and uncomfortable. It was his representation of the modern man, and those who stood in front of his painting could easily cast themselves in the role of its main subject, and yet no one around, aside from Dale, did so.

He wondered if Cezanne's painting was the reason for him leaving his parent's house today? Was there a lesson embedded somewhere inside the painting he could not yet understand? There was great pain in Dale's heart; had Kajal ever seen his self-worth? Was the reason they were together so long, he believing she loved him, the measurement of how much he valued himself? What happens when that love disappears? What made Cezanne's masterpiece less desirable than Van Gogh's? When does the ordinary leave the realm of ordinariness and become something more significant? Why had Dale never seen his self-worth?

He believed Kajal loved him. They were happy together, once. If art allows one to observe the undesirable in a safe space and think about the undesirable in ways we wouldn't, when coming face to face with it in our own lives, he wondered what Kajal would see if she saw herself reflected inside Cezanne's painting? Would she walk past it like the other's? Did she see her self-worth?

It is easy to turn away from the unwanted or from what we're afraid of. But Dale, being so self-absorbed, could not see anything else but himself inside Cezanne's painting and therefore was able to understand the piece, almost immediately. Because he felt so undesired. And what he resented was that nobody else had stopped in front of *The Bather* like he did. As if nobody else had felt the same way. Did everyone in the museum aside from Dale know their self-worth?

There was so much he couldn't see past, and what frustrated Dale was that he was no different. He also couldn't see the beauty in the young man in the painting. When Dale stopped before Cezanne's portrait, he didn't know why one would care for Cezanne's subject. He didn't stop because he thought the boy was beautiful. He stopped because he didn't know why anyone would care.

Dale judged the painting before looking at it, and when he did, he saw the painting as a mirror.

The patrons who entered the museum's fifth-floor walked past Dale, who stood in front of Cezanne's painting, to see a more famous piece by a man who had taken his own life not long after he had painted it. Van Gogh had also felt undesired. He, also, did not see his self worth, and, yet, no one thought that when staring at his most famous piece. No one cared for the truth. They only wanted to inherit what he saw, not how he felt that was symbiotic to the intrinsic need to create something both he and his audience thought was beautiful.

Van Gogh's *Starry Night* was the result of a moment when the artist saw perfection in his mind, which he both struggled to and seldom did. And was able to execute what he saw in his mind, that night, in the medium he chose, that best captured his artistic expression. The painting's subject is a fabric of his imagination perfectly rendered, but the moment that inspired him to create it was short lived. And Cezanne's masterpiece was one, due to its rendering of its subject's imperfection, which was universal and constant. But no one seemed to care.

Dale always wanted success but never knew how to attain it in a way that made sense to him. A corporate job in a fancy office was never going to be his way to financial freedom. He saw the road to success as one big scam out of his control. Why did he want it then? Why did the need for it never go away? He found making art as a way to better understand himself, and what he came to understand over time was that he was worthless. We only mattered as a whole, yet no one saw it that way. He saw everyone as little bubbles of ego fighting for a space in the spotlight without a specific means to be there. And yet, all he knew about himself was that he didn't want to be part of the whole. He wanted to be seen. He wanted to stand out, because he never did. Nor did he ever truly feel a part of a community. The only thing that mattered to him and that gave him a sense of belonging was when he documented the fragments of his life in his art. And his rendering of it, all he ever had control of.

It was the only thing he did that gave his life a purpose and an understanding of why he was another living, breathing, sentient being with a conscience. And being a part of someone else's dream took away the feeling of his autonomy and that feeling of being alive. He wanted to live this way, out of everyone else's business. He didn't care what anybody else did. He didn't want to be part of someone else's story. He wanted to be the story for once. He wanted to know that despite what his community showed him, there might have been something of value in him being himself because nothing in his life ever had. And being sent home with a broken heart, to be reminded of his failure, did not help him see things differently.

There was hope in Cezanne's painting, though. The painting's existence and the recognition it received allowed Dale to believe that there was a space for those who were lost, for those who were deemed ordinary. On its placard, the young man was described as *physically ungraceful* and *psychologically remote*. Dale took a step back from the painting after reading this, his heart broken for the boy, wanting to see the painting fully. If no one else would give it their attention, he would give it his all. Without art, he saw a future that lacked meaning, which scared him. And even if he didn't see it, he wanted to understand Cezanne's desire to portray a man with no direction, grace, poise, or courage.

Clara tapped him on the shoulder gently. Her touch made him jump slightly, returning him back from wherever the painting had sent him to.

Sorry, I have to go, he told her.

Oh okay.

Sorry.

Is everything alright?

It was nice bumping into you, Clara. I'm really sorry.

He smiled, touched the side of her shoulder, and left her standing in front of Cezanne's painting alone. He took the staircase down to the exit. An overwhelming amount of guilt swelled in his heart then, and he cried in the stairwell, racing to the lower levels of the museum, not knowing what he was running from. The image of her standing in front of the painting, watching him go, broke him. She didn't deserve the little he had to offer her, and there was no point in him wasting her time. Exiting the museum's front doors, he headed south towards Penn Station. The city had come to feel so small; he had no idea where else to go. He hoped to see Clara again. The chances of that happening, though, were slim. If there was a door for their friendship, it had just closed. He walked down Broadway, disgusted with himself. The sensation of guilt banged like a pulse throughout his entire body. He promised himself he would get better. He didn't know precisely what that entailed. All he knew was that he did not like the person he was, and at least knowing that was a start.

XII

The Apparition

Kajal rested a warm washcloth over her eyes. She was back inside her bedroom with a pounding headache. Blanche and Ruksaana spoke in hushed tones outside her bedroom door. Blanche described the scene that happened in the restaurant to her mother. Ruksaana had not understood, she said she couldn't breathe? Why not call 911?

They hadn't ordered any food. When her episode in the restaurant ended, Kajal became quite tired, barely able to keep her head up. She left the restaurant with her sister, embarrassed. The restaurant's waitstaff and its few patrons watched them leave. Blanche held onto her sister the entire walk home and laid her inside her bedroom. They were concerned about whether or not she should see a doctor. The term panic attack was tossed around between her mother and sister. Kajal just wanted to sleep. So they left her.

Kajal spent the following week disassociating. Every interaction she had with another person felt as if she were outside of herself; watching herself talk to them. The only people Kajal did speak to were with those she felt she had to; her mother, professors, a barista at a cafe. She didn't hang out with anybody for pleasure. She could not reproduce the feeling of pleasure. She masterbated profusely. She barely spoke a word that wasn't completely necessary, if it wasn't necessary the words could not find their shape or leave her mouth.

She woke one night with a dry mouth and got up for water. She peed and walked into the kitchen, and poured herself a glass to drink. Her brother wasn't home. Ruksaana was asleep in her bed. She could see snow falling outside the living room window.

She walked into the living room, sat on the couch with her glass of water, and drank it slowly. The moon's light hit her as she sat still, thoughtless, gazing at the spot on the wall where the moon's light hit.

In the corner of her right eye, a soft white light appeared. She turned her head towards its luminescence, which vanished as quickly as it had taken shape. She would have mistaken the apparition for a passing light had she not seen her father's face and his unmistakable eyes somewhere inside its luster.

He appeared in front of the door, stepping one foot at a time inside the apartment as if to avoid a hole in the linoleum only he could see. Once inside, he reenacted taking his shoes off, though Kajal saw his feet were bare. She could tell by the way he nodded his head and by how his mouth moved that Hussein was listening to somebody in the room, that Kajal could not see, talk to him. His eyes seemed to look past the rooms of the apartment as if he was staring off into another world, a different dimension. He nodded attentively and smiled at the invisible presence before him. It looked as if he were a guest in somebody else's home rather than a ghost who returned to haunt the apartment he had once lived in. He passed the living room's entrance and walked into the dining room. Whoever he was speaking to, from what Kajal could tell, they were getting along. He nodded politely towards their presence. Kajal saw him smiling. He sat down at the dining room table. The time on the living room's clock showed it was *2:18 AM*. Kajal sat on the couch, watching her father sit at the dining room table, alone, waiting. Her first instinct was to be still. Any fatigue she had left her eyes. Her heart started to beat fast inside her chest. Nervous, she knocked her glass of water onto the floor and cursed underneath her breath for the sound it made, though her father made no impression of having heard it.

Hussein bowed his head at the dinner table, admiring with a polite gaze what was placed before him. He turned his head upwards and smiled generously at the invisible presence, who then, Kajal assumed, walked away as she watched her father's limpid head turn as if watching someone leave.

Hussein started to use his hands as if to eat with. Kajal stood up from the couch and listened for any signs of movement coming from the hallway. Who had her father been speaking to? Whose house did he think he was in? Kajal realized, though she could see her father's actions, the words he spoke made no audible sound.

She walked towards the hallway's entrance and looked down towards her bedroom. She had not known what to expect. She saw her bedroom door open like she had left it. The hallway exuded a presence that was both quiet and still. All she could hear was her mother's soft snoring in her sleep from down the hall. Not sure if this was a dream or a symptom of some undiagnosed mental illness, Kajal turned back towards her father, who continued to eat with his hands, at the dining room table. She watched him until he finished, then he stood up from his chair; the chair stayed still as he mimed, pushing it out and then back in as he stood up.

His gaze then pointed in the direction of the hallway. She watched her father approach her. His energy was both soft and inquisitive. She stepped back until her shoulders touched with grace the apartment's front door. The apparition passed her and entered the hallway. She watched his lips mouth a word? A name? A question? Before heading down the hallway towards her bedroom, his feet softly touched the ground as he passed by his old bedroom, towards Kajal's room, in search of...something.

There was no fear inside of Kajal then, just a pending eagerness. She knew of people who have had these types of lucid dreams before, mostly stories told to her by Dale's mother of her own parents visiting her in her sleep. This was clearly a result of her missing her father, her brain playing tricks on her; an attempt to try and heal itself. Tomorrow morning, she would see her father's visit as merely that and continue on with her life and wait in anticipation for the next time he'd come.

Her father's ghost disappeared inside her bedroom, and she followed his illuminated path down the hallway. His face showed that of frustration. Hussein stood before her bedside window, his feet firmly planted on the ground now. Shocked, she watched him use his hands to open the window and put his head out through it to look out into the street. His form changed slightly when doing this. His movements then seemed more vivid, more real.

The apparition was dressed in casual clothes, what looked to be a plain two-piece pajama set. He had no skin or mass to his shape. From where she stood, her father had the appearance of an airy substance, the color of milk.

Hussein turned away from the window and looked in her direction. For a moment, she saw a reflection of recognition in his eyes, though it lasted for only a moment. His face the same as it was when he died, with his plump round head and thin black mustache.

If Hussein did see her, he ignored her and looked around the bedroom. His face now wore a more somber expression, different from the one he displayed when he first entered the apartment. He opened her dresser drawers, closing them after ruffling through her folded clothes.

She could see through his body the wall, window and bed behind him, swell in and out of focus, through his stomach as if he were a giant fish eye lens. He moved slowly around the bedroom, his milky form illuminating anything beneath him. For a moment, she was proud; if this was a recreation of her father's physical form, she was now reminded, due to the appearance of the apparition before her, that her father was once very much alive. Death hadn't taken him away from her, it had turned him into light.

He rushed out of the bedroom, giving Kajal no heads-up he was leaving. He passed through her, her reaction delayed, as she turned and panicked and hit her head hard on the wall behind her. Blood dripped from her nose onto the clean white fabric of her pajama shirt.

From the floor, she watched her father's form fade the closer he got to the door. She squeezed a droplet of blood in between her two fingers. What made him so angry? Hussein mimed picking up his shoes and putting them on his bare feet. He turned towards the living room and Kajal saw his face portray a look of extreme disappointment. A cold breeze entered her bedroom window, sending goosebumps down her spine. Hussein took one last look behind him and then turned towards the front entrance and faded into nothing as he stepped out through the front door the same way he had come.

When she woke, there was a blood stain from her nose on her white pillow sheet, and her dresser drawers were left wide open; remnants from last night's memory carried over into the new morning. Outside, it continued to snow.

The sound of movement came from the kitchen. Light and the sounds of city life came in through her bedroom window; she had memories of her father's ghost opening it. It was freezing inside her bedroom. How did she sleep the rest of the night with the window wide open like it was?

Kajal got out of bed, coughed, and shut the window. She stood where her father had in her dream and touched the window frame with her hands, just like he did. She could not separate from what felt real to her, to what she knew could not be true.

Her mother stood behind her in her bedroom doorway.

Hungry? Ruksaana asked her.

Kajal turned towards her mother.

You okay? Ruksaana asked. It's cold.

Yeah, bad dream, said Kajal.

Okay. Samina called, said Ruksaana. Why don't you eat and call her?

Without waiting for a response, Ruksaana turned down the hallway towards the kitchen, where paratha and eggs were cooking on the stove. Kajal turned back towards the window and looked out below her onto the city street, trying to imagine what her father's ghost was looking for.

Blanche called to tell Kajal the gravestone for their father had, finally, been placed. She spent several weeks after their father died trying to negotiate a price for the gravestone. It was planned after Hussein died for the whole family to gather together and watch the gravestone be placed into the ground, to celebrate the memory of their late father and husband. Kajal wanted to make it a ceremonial occasion and have people gather and eat food and listen to music while they ate and told stories of the past, sitting among the other graves. These were forgotten plans made a year ago. Blanche thought the process for the gravestone would take less time than it did.

Early on, Blanche was responsible for arranging her father's Janazah and burial arrangements. Two things she had never done before. But being the eldest daughter and the first-generation of immigrant parents, she didn't know who else would do it. She asked her uncle for help because she didn't know where to start. Her family had limited money, and after seeing what a gravestone cost, she quickly learned they couldn't afford a gravesite, let alone a gravestone. With her uncle's help, they raised money at the mosque her father had attended in Queens to help pay for the gravesite. But months had passed after the Janazah, and still no gravestone had been placed.

Each step further into the process of burying their father made mourning him more difficult. They had to wait to buy a gravestone, leaving his grave unmarked until one of her uncles connected her to a masonry, who was a friend of a friend.

Blanche had bargained for months on an already discounted price, with the acquainted masonry, for a generic stone to be put down. During that time, Blanche and her new husband would plan to wed and follow their heart's desire to travel West, leaving the unfinished business with her father's grave to be dealt with another time.

A year later, Blanche finally got the call that the gravestone had been put down while looking out the window of her hotel room in Brooklyn. A rain of guilt poured over her then as she realized she had forgotten all about it.

What Blanche did not know was that Ruksaana had started talking to distant relatives on the phone, who were also in New York, about specific *issues* she'd been having with her two daughters. Her intention was only to vent and talk shit on the phone to distant relatives she never sees about her children. Word about the gravestone had gotten out to cousins, aunts, and uncles, neither of whom Kajal or Blanche knew, or had seen in years. They only heard about these family members through their parent's stories shared over evening chai. It was not Ruksaana's intention to get other people involved to pay for her husband's afterlife inquiries. She knew it was her daughters' responsibility and honor. But when word got out to a cousin, a breeder of Bengal cats, he called Ruksaana on the phone and offered to pay. Unable to say no, Ruksaana gave her cousin the masonry's information, and he called to pay off the remaining installments.

Outside their building, the streets were covered with snow. After Kajal talked to Blanche, the excitement of seeing the gravestone had helped lift her out of whatever fog she'd been in from her episode inside the restaurant the week before. She asked her mom if she wanted to drive to Long Island to visit the cemetery.

I want to see it too, said Blanche, but it's not a good idea to drive out to Long Island in all this snow. Let's wait a few weeks for the weather to warm up.

Blanche couldn't go because she promised Henry she'd spend the day with his family. She told Kajal there was plenty of time to visit Papa's grave and suggested they all go together another day when it was safer. But when Kajal told Ruksaana about Blanche's hesitations about the drive, Ruksaana, who never drove a car in her life, said she didn't see an issue.

Kajal tried to wake her brother up so he could come along for the ride. The cemetery was a two-hour drive from their apartment in Harlem. If he went along with them, he'd make his mother happy without producing much effort and could sleep, the entire way, in the car.

Ayad got home late the previous night; Kajal had finally fallen asleep, and before entering his bedroom, he looked into Kajal's room and saw her lying in her bed uncovered with the snow coming in through the open window, not thinking to close it. Not yet tired, he smoked weed in his bedroom to relax, cooked a packet of instant ramen, and watched the snow cover the city until he felt compelled to lay his head down to rest. When he finally fell asleep, the clock showed it was *4 AM*.

Kajal tried to wake him for half an hour. During this time, she got herself ready, all the while trying to normalize the events that occurred in her dream the previous night. Each moment staying with her, never drifting, unlike with most dreams when the reality of the next morning separates you from the events brought on by your unconscious the night before.

Ruksaana would only leave after she made chai for the road and took an additional 20 minutes to do so. Kajal gave up on her brother and defrosted the car without him. She grabbed the windshield scraper and shovel from the closet and headed down the stairwell to the 11th floor.

Kajal walked through the 11th floor entrance. Outside the old man's apartment was the plate of food she left wrapped in aluminum foil, which the old man left untouched. It seemed he hadn't seen the food Kajal left for him or ignored it, as it sat on the floor, on the old man's beaten welcome mat, now with a few minor bite marks made on top of the aluminum. She bent down to pick up the plate, mad she hadn't thought of this happening, hating to have wasted her mother's precious cooking, something in her life that was sacred to her. Kajal peeled back the aluminum and screamed involuntarily, dropping the plate onto the floor as a sleeping mouse ran off the plate and up her arm, down onto the floor, and scurried away escaping underneath a closed door. Her scream echoed throughout the hallway, followed by the crashing sound of the plate.

Kajal picked up the shattered pieces of the yellow plate quickly, afraid someone would come out of their apartment and question what she was doing; not even knowing how to explain what she was doing to herself. She threw the chunks of the yellow plate into the floor's garbage chute and disappeared down the stairwell, running to the lower floor before anyone could see her.

The paving trucks had done most of the work for her. She wouldn't have a problem driving the car out of the lot, but still, there was a section in front of her car she needed to clear away. The snow had settled to a soft flurry then. The clouds scattered to reveal a blue sky, and the bright sun gave the impression of it being a warm day, though there was snow everywhere.

The car was caked in snow as well, and needed to be cleared. She brushed her hand along the car's windshield and used the scraper to scratch off the ice.

She had taken one step forward and slipped and hit her head along the adjacent car's trunk. A lump had started to form at the back of her head. Kajal cursed under her breath, and tears she tried to suppress fell from her eyes. She stood up, fearing a possible concussion, and slammed her fist down hard against the trunk of her car. She walked to the driver's side door and tried to open it. A headache had started to form inside her skull. She needed two pain-killers and a bottle of water.

Kajal pulled the handle to the car's door back. It zinged out of her hand quickly, folding into place. It made a popping sound she didn't like. The door was frozen shut. She tried again, pulling harder this time, putting one foot on the car, and pulled the door open on the third try. She turned on the heat of the car and cleared the snow that had piled in front of it.

When she saw her mother walk out of the building, the car was half cleared. She took a break from shoveling, leaning the shovel against the car's hood to catch her breath. Ruksaana's limp had aged her. Seeing her outside the apartment building was the first time Kajal had thought of her mother's death. Kajal wanted to ask Ruksaana if she needed help but was afraid to embarrass her, so she waved from the car instead, to which Ruksaana responded with just a head nod, concentrating primarily on her footing along the unsalted icy path.

They were on the road minutes later. The streets were salted and decent enough to drive on. Kajal drove her car cautiously towards the FDR highway. With the trees and facades of the pre-war buildings of Harlem now graced with snow, the city looked still and quiet; the only visible moving object on the road was the vehicle Kajal was driving.

It had been a while since she was behind the wheel of a car. There hadn't been much of a reason to escape the city because of school. But once on the road, she had become highly aware of the car's size. She was excited to drive after talking with her sister on the phone, treating this news regarding her father's gravestone as motivation for a much-needed family road trip. But once behind the wheel and on the icy weather-beaten streets of Manhattan, she felt as if this might have been a mistake and the car too big for the road on which she drove. She tried to hide any signs of nervousness from her mother, who sat comfortably in the backseat of the car, lounging over the whole seat, without concern, eating powdered flavored tortilla chips out of a purple polyethylene bag; occasionally reaching over and putting one in Kajal's mouth as she drove. Ruksaana had been busy explaining the saga of her niece, Alveena, who lived in Karachi and was looking for an American boy to marry.

What if I suggest Ayad? Asked Ruksaana

For who, Alveena? Let the girl finish med school and decide on her own. If that's what she wanted, why not directly ask you about Ayad?

Because that's inappropriate. You can't just go around asking for what you want.

Kajal kept her hands ten-and-two, listening to her mother. She took some deep breaths while looking at the GPS occasionally for guidance. Driving reminded Kajal of her father. He was the one who had taught her how to drive when she was young. She was ordained the official passenger seat driver, helping her father with *Mapquest* instructions on family road trips to Canada and late-night drives home from visiting family. Feeling distant from his oldest daughter, and his wife unable to read the English instructions on the print-outs and street signs, Kajal was the frontrunner for the job.

Ruksaana had shifted to telling the story of when Hussein first came to America. When he married his first wife, who had helped get him citizenship. She had dumped him not long after he got his passport. He had paid the woman two thousand dollars, which took him a lifetime to save up, to be his wife. After the divorce, he was left to fend for himself and was sleeping on his friends couches, until he finally could support himself and he got himself a place to live; a small one bedroom apartment in the Bronx.

Ruksaana told the story of how her late husband had spent a few years driving a taxi and after working a few odd jobs he had saved enough to invest in a few taxi medallions in New York. This was the first time in his life Hussein had money. He had met Ruksaana, on trips back and forth from Pakistan. He brought her along a few times to impress her. She had never been tó the states before then. The trips would become a common occurrence, and they fell in love. He enjoyed spoiling her with vacations to the Caribbean and buying her expensive jewelry and large bottles of perfumes.

You guys went on vacation together? Kajal asked her mother from the driver's seat, the view of Manhattan now in the distance.

Yes. All the time. So many vacations!

Ruksaana told Kajal her father was an impressive man when he met her. His hard days, it seemed, were behind him. They did not know then what the future entailed.

Hussein had Ravi Shankar's phone number. Ate at four-star restaurants in cities like Paris, San Sebastian, and New York. He discussed policy with sitting politicians in New York and held rallies for leaders in Pakistan, meeting these high-up officials in places like the Carlyle or the Four Seasons. He was living the American dream; from rags to riches. This lifestyle her father lived was not something Kajal or her siblings would see in their lifetime. But know about only through stories told to them over chai.

Before he married Ruksaana, Hussein helped build a hospital in Pakistan from the ground up. It was at the hospital where they met. He considered the hospital a passion project of his, something he had always wanted for his community ever since he was a child. Interested in business, health policy, and community service from a young age. The hospital was a dream he thought impossible as a boy, running around the streets of Karachi with his brothers. It made him proud to be able to give back to his community in this way. An accomplishment that justified his ever leaving home in the first place and having dealt with the discomfort when he first came to the States; sleeping in bus terminals, racism, white people, couch surfing among friends, losing friends who stabbed him in the back and threw him back out into the streets, then becoming lifelong enemies.

Like Kajal, he had always wanted to serve his community. Healthcare in Pakistan was abysmal unless you were rich. He took pride in helping his community back home and giving it a good hospital in a poorer neighborhood in Karachi where he grew up. With his position on the board and administration, he was able to oversee the physicians and doctors who were hired, making sure they were educated and well trained and not corrupt. He was rare in that he actually wanted to help his people. He felt in charge. The hospital was his vision. His life had meaning then. He had lived in New York for only a few years, always working, networking, and investing what he earned. In those years, what he earned was poured back into the hospital in the form of new hospital beds, upgraded MRI machines, and proper facilities.

Kajal was a good audience for these stories her mother told, even when Hussein was alive, and the one to tell them. She'd always listened attentively, looking past their plot holes and contradictions. She did not challenge him like her sister did with the real-life facts they knew and witnessed. Her mother, now the successor of these stories, was also one to embellish on the details. Kajal never knew or found it relevant to ask how her father saved the money he needed, working the few odd jobs he did when first arriving in the States, to buy not just one medallion but three, when she knew he came from a poor family in Karachi.

Hussein was a man of many stories. Kajal's uncles and aunts always had a story to tell her about her father after he died, and Kajal listened, interested in knowing more about her father's past, him being one to be secretive and skim over the details. On the rare occasion he did let a juicy detail slip in a story he was telling, Kajal and her siblings wouldn't let him move on without asking him to elaborate, like the time he told them he had helped on occasion a particular gang in Pakistan! This had raised his children's eyebrows. Or, like when he told them, he kept a gun on his person when he was young!

What gangs? Blanche had asked him. Did you ever kill anyone? Kajal quickly followed up with. The questions took their father out of whatever nostalgic trance his oration put him in, and forced him to give away details from his past he would rather not explain to his adolescent children. When he realized he said too much, he stumbled over his words and tried to retract what he had said by way of mumbling under his breath, hoping to change the subject.

Because of how uncomfortable it made him to talk, Kajal learned not to interrupt her father with any questions when he was telling them a story, because asking him would always cut the story short. She just sat and listened to him talk, making sure he was happy and not challenging him even if she knew the details of the story to be questionable.

If any of Hussein's children wanted to learn anything new about their father, he would have to be the one to tell them, and in his own way. This was why, when he died, Kajal and her siblings felt there was a considerable part of their father they did not know.

In the stories told, he had lost a great deal of his wealth by investing it into his family, dividing his net worth among his brothers, a decision influenced by his mother so that all of her children could be equal and invest in their futures and spoil their wives and children and make ends meet. Hussein felt it was his duty, as the oldest male child, to help support his family. His brother's promised to give Hussein the money back once they made it and got their own houses and families to spoil. Hussein recommended that his siblings invest the money he gave them or take positions at the hospital for work so they could make their own way. But they didn't take his advice and gambled all that he gave them on either booze or bad real estate, to salvage their debt.

The end of the hospital was what led Hussein to financial ruin. It fell apart due to corrupt investors whose vision for the hospital swayed in the opposing direction. He decided to put what he had left into the hospital, trying to keep it afloat, holding onto his dream a bit longer. Hussein and Ruksaana had been married for over a year by this point. Not ready to give up, they had to sell their home and fire doctors, friends of his, good doctors, whom he had personally hired, to cushion some of the hospital's spending. They needed more staff. The emergency room swelled with sick people. They had to turn people away, people who were dying, to another hospital that was well over two hours away. He needed help finding new investors to replace the ones that had left. The hospital fell apart. Hussein lost all of his money. The remaining doctors had to leave to find work, and eventually, the hallways grew quiet. There were no more patients. The electricity had gone out. Homeless people started to use the abandoned rooms as free real estate and steal the equipment that was left behind to barter for cash. But according to folklore, the hospital where Hussein put his heart and soul still stands today as a ruin, somewhere in Pakistan, as a reminder of his failed legacy.

When was the last time anyone visited the hospital, asked Kajal, heading east on the Long Island Expressway. The GPS on her phone said it would be another 50 miles until they arrived.

A long time. I haven't been since we left Pakistan, said Ruksaana in Urdu, nostalgically.

I'm curious what it looks like now.

Just an abandoned building, I guess. Samina was born there.

Really?

Yes, I used to leave her with the younger staff to babysit.

Wow, I wonder if she remembers?

Maybe, said Ruksaana.

When deciding to take out the loans necessary to pay Columbia's rather sizable tuition, she only had her father's face in mind. If it weren't for him, she wouldn't have done it. She wanted to live the dream her father always preached to his children about when they were younger. She wanted to showcase her father's life by becoming his success story and giving thanks for his sacrifice for his children when he left his home country for their benefit many years before she was born. When moving to America, he didn't worry about the identity his children would take growing up in a foreign country. That fear would come later.

Kajal felt the touch of a hand on her knee. Thinking it was her mother's, she turned to acknowledge her mother with a smile but saw her father sitting beside her.

Kajal swerved unexpectedly into the opposing lane. Her father was staring at her from the passenger seat of her car. She swerved back and stopped the car abruptly on the side of the road.

What's going on? What's going on? Ruksaana said in a panic.

Kajal looked up from the driver's seat. He was no longer there.

I slipped. I slipped, she lied, hyperventilating.

Are you okay, beta?

Yes. Yes.

We're lucky no one else was on the road.

Kajal could feel her chest tighten. The desire to destroy herself made the appearance like a spark that could cause the likes of a forest fire. She had almost killed herself and her mother. Her sister was right; she should have known better than to be on the road during such hazardous conditions. Who was around to help them if something were to happen?

There was no promise of the pain she felt to go away. She feared this was how living the rest of her life would feel, that there was once a happy version of her but now there was only the person grief had transformed her into.

She started to hyperventilate again. She couldn't breathe. From the backseat, Ruksaana touched her shoulder. Her mother's touch made the car they were in somehow feel smaller.

Beta! Beta! What's wrong?

She felt his presence again. She didn't look up. He was sitting beside her. She could feel the hem of his shirt touching her leg. She looked outside her window, trying to focus on the objects outside her car, trying to bring back her breath. It scared her to look. She could feel his presence swell like a giant lung sitting beside her; his cold presence contrasted with her mother's warmth. She questioned if this was her mind playing tricks on her. If this was her mind's way of inflicting pain without producing physical harm. She made a choice and turned to look toward the apparition. She saw his face then. Her mother's voice disappeared in the background like an echo. It didn't resemble the face he had last night, the one she recognized. What had happened to his eyes? To his nose? His mouth?

She didn't yell, afraid to cause a scene, or scare her mother more than she already had. He said her name. The voice that came out of him was unfamiliar to her, similar to that of a distorted growl. He said her name once more, and the light from her eyes dissipated. Her mother screamed in her ear as Kajal sank deeper into the driver's seat and slumped her head against the driver's side window.

The GPS said they were 14 minutes from the cemetery. Kajal woke up to her mother sitting in the passenger seat, pouring water from a bottle down her throat.

Ruksaana screamed, Beta! Beta! Wake up!

She had only been out for a minute. No car had driven past them the entire time they had been on the side of the road. It was a mistake to have come all this way, Kajal thought.

Kajal woke to the sounds of her mother crying. Kajal hugged her and apologized in her arms.

I'm sorry. I don't know what's wrong. I don't know what's wrong.

When she finally calmed down, they both took a moment of silence to gather their thoughts. Ruksaana suggested they head back. Kajal wanted to go forward. They argued, and Kajal won. She drove her car back onto the cracked asphalt and headed forward. There was no traffic.

They drove through a neighborhood that was unfamiliar to them. She had become nervous about seeing her father's headstone. Would he be waiting there for her?

She exited the highway into a little town south of Oyster Bay, where the cemetery was located. The drive consisted of one long road to the next, except here, you could see fences that protected the privacy of the backyards of houses, all of which looked like nobody was inside.

The last time she had seen her father's physical body was before they closed the coffin, for the last time, at the mosque where her father's Janazah had taken place. Then they drove out to Long Island, to the cemetery. That was the last time she had been on this road.

There was a plant nursery close by that she remembered visiting. When they came to it, Kajal steered the car slowly into the opposing lane and parked outside the shop. The sky had cleared, but the clouds were still fragmented. There was a crisp saltiness in the air produced by the sea that reminded them that they were not home.

Kajal sat back in her seat, still weak. She took a breath and moved her legs out of the car. Ruksaana followed her, taking a second bottle of water with her and offering it to Kajal to drink. But she declined.

Ruksaana wanted roses. They found a display on a table by the front right as they walked in. Ruksaana grabbed one of the bouquets and strolled the aisles for a bit. They passed pots of lavender and eucalyptus, which hung from the ceiling. She ducked her head under the pots, following her mother in the garden, ignoring how light her head felt sitting on her shoulders.

Ruksaana wanted to pay, but Kajal insisted and pulled out cash from the tips she made at her cafe job. The cemetery was just up the road. She drove the car not 10 minutes to the gate of the cemetery, which was opened. It was fucked up, she thought, but the neighborhood her father was buried in was the nicest one she had known him to live in.

They drove onto the cemetery's premises and continued towards a small house, which Kajal knew, from when she was here last, was the groundskeeper's office. It was also a space where visitors could pray or use the facilities. It looked closed as they drove past it, both silent, directing their eyes across the grounds they had left more than a year ago.

The cemetery looked vast and endless, covered in snow. Neither Kajal nor Ruksaana could see a single headstone before them; it was just a large white pasture.

She could not remember where her father's grave had been located. Dale was the one who drove here last after they left the mosque and came here for the burial. She drove forward slowly, thinking about where the gravesite could be.

They drove past a family who seemed to be the only people besides them visiting the cemetery today. The family consisted of a young man, somewhere in his mid-30s, with a young female toddler. Both were dressed warmly, wearing heavy jackets, pink mittens for the girl, and a scarf tied tightly around both their necks.

Kajal did not get a chance to see the young man's face as they drove past, but she caught the eye of the toddler, who stood on the ground next to who Kajal assumed was her father. In the rearview mirror, the young man wiped the snow off the grave he stood in front of and tied a string, attached to a mylar balloon to a rock that read *Happy Birthday*.

A heavy wind hit the car. She could feel the car shake as she drove the necessary speed limit of five miles per hour down the smooth gray pavement with blind optimism. She saw a barren tree that looked familiar and drove towards it. Everything looked the same. There was no landmark or marker to indicate the section her father's body was buried in.

She put the car in park. A gust of wind hit the car for the second time, making the car sway left to right.

You go, said Ruksaana and handed Kajal the bouquet of roses that sat on her lap.

Surprised, she obeyed her mother's orders and stepped onto the icy pavement. With the bouquet of roses in her hand, she felt like Hamlet with a skull. She could hear the soft pop sound made by her boots as she stepped into the snow, walking over the line where the mildly paved road ended and the snow began. She walked further onto the grounds. Unknowingly, she stepped on the tops of graves, none of which she knew to be her father's. He was not this close to the road, she remembered. She said his name out loud as if she knew his ghost would answer her. She saw the apparition in the distance then and walked towards it. His face was familiar again and now wearing a calm expression, not like it had been in the car. It was so quiet in the cemetery. The wind ebbed and flowed around her.

Kajal looked back at the car. Committing only half her body to turn. She could no longer see her mother, just the haze of the car's silhouette. She walked further, heading closer to the apparition, and stopped a few feet before him. She bent down onto her knees. Kajal felt her heart sink into her stomach, and she began to cry. The apparition stood still before her. She began to wipe the snow away at the ground beneath her. The corner of the new headstone protruded out from behind the snow's thick crust. It had turned into an icy shield overnight, and she used her fist to smash most of it away until she could read the letters engraved on the stone.

It read: *Syed Hussein Imam Raza. Born 1949 – 2019.*

Her father's name was written in stone before her. It was official.

Kajal cleared the snow off the best she could. The ground was too thick to place the roses right side up like she would have wanted to. Instead, she laid down the bouquet on its side before the stone.

She looked out into the white pasture, kissed her gloved hands, and swiped her fingers across her father's name.

You are so deeply loved, she said out loud.

Tears fell down her face. Kajal said a quick prayer and headed back towards the car. Before heading inside, she clapped her hands hard to warm them and watched the snow fall, like powder, onto the road.

Once inside, she closed the door behind her, the heat from the car relief on her cold skin.

Did you find him? Ruksaana asked her.

Yes. It's beautiful. Papa would be very proud.

Inshallah, her mother said, now smiling. Inshallah.

XIII

Death by Capitalism

Dale walked the 20 minutes from the train station to his parent's house. It started to snow on his walk home. He would stay inside his parent's house for the next three days, never leaving, walking from room to room until his father asked for his help in shoveling the sidewalk, clearing the snow from the blizzard between both driveways. Guilt ruminated from his short interaction with Clara. He wanted to talk to his mother about how he was feeling, not having anyone else to speak to. But speaking to her about what caused him anxiety, only left him most times feeling worse.

When Dale would open up to his mother, she'd indulge in her own curiosities about his life and ask questions Dale found irrelevant. It wasn't just how he left Clara, he felt bad about. It was the realization, when walking to Penn Station, with nowhere to go but home, that he missed an opportunity to participate in a bid for connection, and his abrupt exit embarrassed him.

He wasn't religious but it was the residue of religion, stained on the periphery of the community that raised him, that he felt was responsible for him viewing his trip to the city as a pilgrimage, to seek out a new direction to take with his life. And he realized too late, it might not have been *The Bather* he came to the city for, but quite possibly for Clara.

With this view, he feared he had missed an opportunity to participate in something he did not understand, nor had he the foresight to see, out of fear of what lies ahead through a door he had not sought out to find. This brought on a major feeling of self-contempt and a wave of self-hatred. He mourned the possibility of what could have been and resented himself for choosing what he was already familiar with.

To avoid any unnecessary conflict with his mother, he kept to himself and dealt with his feelings alone, wishing he had some way to contact Clara to apologize; hoping to reach out again and see if he could reopen the door he closed. He went on Instagram and searched her name but found no profile with a picture that matched the Clara he knew.

He found a Clara Desmoines in his search but the account was private and the image was that of a young child, who could have been Clara when she was younger, using a picture from her youth for her profile. But he was not sure and he did not friend request her to find out. He remembered she had given him her card and he went into his phone's wallet and opened Clara's card and saw a phone number and dialed it, and as it began to ring he quickly hung up.

The accumulation of snow outside had made being inside the house feel smaller. Dale woke just before

5 AM in the upstairs bedroom of his parent's house. The heat was strong in the house; the bedroom was hot. He woke in a sweat and in need of water. He removed the weighted blanket from over him. A gift from his mother, who said it should help things. Dale slid off the bed and slowly descended the staircase to the living room. He was relieved to find the whole first floor dark and barren. He tiptoed across the living room to the kitchen, grabbed a glass from out of the renovated pantry, and poured himself water from the tap located on the front side of the refrigerator.

The refrigerator in his parent's kitchen was brand new. It greeted Dale good morning by illuminating its LED screen light next to the molded plastic door handle, which displayed the day's date and impending cold temperatures.

Dale squinted through the brightly illuminated screen, with tired eyes, until his glass was full. Beneath the day's date and temperature were mock photos of a family, not of Dale's family, but another family huddled together on a lawn in front of a house similar to the one Dale's parents lived in. Each member of the stimulated family smiling happily, with a middle-aged Golden Retriever dog – a breed of dog Dale's family never owned – lying at their feet. He stared at the photos, having never recognized them until now.

The photos, meant to be replaced, were left on the refrigerator's LED screen, Dale figured, to act as a vision board for the life his parents aspired to lead. Whether they believed they were living the life they imagined for themselves, he did not dare to ask.

He stepped back and sipped his water as the light from the LED screen darkened.

He preferred the dark this early in the morning. Not fully awake, he directed his attention to the new French-style windows above the marble sink, and took notice of the sunrise, which revealed itself behind the houses just beyond his parent's plastic fence. All of them, he noticed, were covered with snow. He had the impulse to put his shoes on, grab his parent's car keys, and run out with the pajamas he had on to a beach, not 20 minutes away, to see what he could of the day's first light. This was something he could do with Kajal if she were here. If she were here, he'd have the energy to do it.

Dale put his half-finished glass of water on the counter, knowing he wasn't going anywhere but back upstairs to his bedroom to sleep. He turned the knob from the sink, allowing a soft flow of water to come out of its faucet. He cupped his hands together, caught what he could of the water, and gently splashed some onto his face.

You're up? Asked Carol, who was standing in the hallway behind him.

He turned his head towards her, the water left running from the faucet. He wasn't surprised his mother was up this early, but he hadn't heard her coming.

He nodded his head the obvious yes and slurred his first word of the day. She had not heard his response but did not repeat her question, having already known the answer.

Carol asked gently, can't sleep?

It was hot.

Hot? Should I turn down the heat?

No. It's fine.

I'm freezing in my room.

Why are you up now, asked Dale, unable to hide his tone.

I had to go to the bathroom.

Okay.

I'm off today.

Why?

I have PTO I need to use. Plus, I have all this gift wrapping I have to do for Christmas.

Is dad home today, too?

No. He left for work already.

Dale couldn't imagine his father utilizing the same space he did in the kitchen before him. Before his mother arrived, it felt as if he was the first to utilize the space in the kitchen that morning. He directed his gaze through the dining room window and imagined his father walking the dark, snowy suburban landscape all the way to the bus stop Dale knew he took to work.

In this weather?

The snow was supposed to slow down. He never doesn't have work, though. You know that. Why are you asking? Asked Carol, raising her eyebrow, a tactic Dale couldn't see. She paused to let him respond.

No reason.

Dale wanted to go back upstairs but was hesitant to make any movements that suggested this.

Do you think Kajal will be coming here for Christmas? She asked him.

Why are you asking me that now?

Because your father and I bought gifts for her and we want to know if she is coming, that's all.

Does it look like she'll be coming over for Christmas, Ma?

She comes over every year.

Not every year do we break up.

Is it a break or a breakup, Dale?

What's the difference?

I don't know. I thought that's what you said she said it was.

I don't know what it is. We're not talking.

Are you and I not going to talk about it?

What is there to talk about?

Are you okay?

I don't want to live anymore. But I'm okay.

That's not okay to say to me, Dale. That's not what a mother wants to hear from her son.

Well, ask questions you want the answers to then.

Don't be rude, Dale!

The pitch of his mother's voice made it intolerable for him to stay inside the kitchen any longer. He stormed past Carol in the dark. She tried to stop him, grabbing his arms and tugging them towards her side. Her touch surprised him. He was shocked by how much he wanted it.

Talk to me, she said, her body blocking the only available space to his bedroom.

All she wanted to say was *It'll be okay* or *I love you* but he never gave her the chance and she didn't know the simple words to use. There was no room to think, and he wasn't thinking, and he pushed past her, knocking her a few inches towards the other direction down the hallway. The peace and quiet he felt in the kitchen just moments before, now gone.

Carol stumbled in the dark, almost falling over, but she caught herself on the closet door handle, hitting her head on the wall, crying out loud, after criss crossing her legs a few times over each other, the whole time afraid she was going to fall down.

Dale climbed the steps to his bedroom fast, afraid to look behind him. Everything had happened so quickly. He didn't want to admit to himself what happened, what he knew he did, and was too far away emotionally to apologize and too far past the moment to prevent it from happening. Something stopped him from climbing back down the staircase to check on his mother after seeing her in his peripheral vision stumble in the opposite direction away from his hands, in the dark. He felt detached from his surroundings then.

He stood at the top of the staircase, frozen with guilt, disgusted with himself and for whom he reminded himself of. The events of his past recurring in the small walls he grew up in with new characters. As he climbed the staircase he had this fear that she might be right behind him. In his mind he mixed events from his past with his present. Remembering the sound of footsteps running up the staircase behind him, the staircase of his youth, the staircase he stood at the top of now, that he had climbed a thousand times when he was young, out of fear, to avoid a baby-boomer-beating. But she didn't chase after him now. Not at the age he was; she was too tired. Though Dale wished she had, this time with a bat to beat him with until he couldn't think, feel, or breathe.

He slammed his bedroom door shut and paced quickly, back and forth, around the room, hyperventilating. His face bright red, his mouth widening. Unable to keep still. It was coming out. Dale grabbed a pillow from off his bed and screamed into it. At the top of his lungs, he bellowed and screeched, punching the mattress that lay underneath him with the full force of his fist. The sound of his voice, though muffled, could be heard in every room throughout the house. Carol heard him from the hallway, where she stood up in shock. In shock, not because of how her oldest son had touched her but by how she no longer recognized him. His face was different. His attitude was wrong.

She slowly started to move away from the space in the hallway. She migrated towards the kitchen sink and turned on the faucet to let the sound of running water transition her to some place else and kill whatever vibe her son had set.

Upstairs, Dale continued screaming into his pillowcase, lying belly-down on his bed, until he could taste blood from the back of his throat. The sound of his hoarse voice ebbed, and he lay still, unable to close his eyes. He stayed like that until the darkness of the night sky faded, and the usual flock of Monk Parakeets came squawking past his bedroom window to notify him and the rest of the neighborhood that the day had finally begun.

Dale, then, tentatively made his second trip down the staircase to the first floor of the house, stepping foot inside the living room. Sunlight poured through each window of the house, allowing the scene that took place earlier to disappear within the morning's light. If the moment were to repeat itself, there would be no shadows to project thoughts on or a blank face to push past, only a real person to confront. There was no sign of his mother, though. He was alone as far as he could tell, not relieved by his solitude like he was earlier. He looked out through the kitchen windows. His instincts had proven to be correct. On the second driveway, located on the backside of the house, he saw that his mother's car was gone.

Carol just wanted to drive. She wasn't mad at Dale, not really. But she did need to get out of the house and away from him, at least for a little while. She could sympathize with her son. She's had her heart broken and understood his anger. He was sensitive like she was. He got it from her. But she wouldn't let him get away with taking his feelings out on her, not like that. Carol knew Dale wanted her to console him. To tell him everything was going to be okay. And pushing past her was his way of showing he resented her for not doing so. And Carol knew that, but Dale should know he wasn't a child anymore and had to manage his feelings like an adult and she wasn't going to let him have it easy. She wasn't going to let him feel good. Not today. Not after that.

Carol did blame herself, though. She blamed herself for staying married to a man that would teach her son to behave that way. She should have left his father long ago, before the kids grew up. When there was still a chance to unlearn their father's bad habits. But despite knowing any better, she stayed, afraid to be a single mother with two children, a lifestyle that didn't fit the narrative she sought for herself when she was a young girl.

Carol chose to keep her family together despite the hardships that came with it. Not willing to lose certain privileges, like owning a home with a backyard, something that reminded her of her late father, who was so proud of her for achieving his version of the American dream. She didn't want to let it go. Her house was something she took pride in and could not afford without her husband's additional paycheck.

Her children had more than she had growing up, minus a happy home. The alternative lifestyle of being a single mother with two children wasn't ideal for her. She wasn't interested in holding grudges or going backwards; only forward was she going, and she was taking the mess she accumulated over the years with her. She was too old to start new again.

Carol stopped at a red light a block away from her house. She'd been driving through the quiet streets of her neighborhood since sunrise, talking to herself inside her car; trying to self-soothe. She left the house with what she had on: a purple bathrobe and, underneath, a pair of light gray pajamas. When the traffic light changed, Carol drove onto the main road and turned left.

She was good at feeling her feelings and letting them go. Always seeing the other person's perspective after some time had passed and never holding a grudge for long or remembering what the fuss was about after the argument was over. Holding grudges was how you got cancer, she would tell herself. In difficult moments, she would reach out to a friend or make a pros and cons list about whether or not to leave or stay, but despite the results, she always chose to keep her family together. It seemed better to let the hardships come and die down, and when they died, everything seemed normal, again. And why make a fuss and leave when everything was good? When everyone was happy again?

Throughout the years, as her children grew older, she learned to deal with her problems independently; as long as everyone else was happy, she could manage.

When the kids were younger and lived in the house, fights with her husband got out of hand. In the three years they dated before getting married, he never laid a hand on her. Then they had children, and the reality of the storybook image of the life she wanted, the life she thought marriage would bring her, slowly unveiled its true form over time.

The hope of living life as a happy family was intercepted by her first interactions with male violence, anger, and rage. The acrobatic ritual of fresh-bought groceries thrown across the kitchen table, plates smashed against the walls, picture frames covering the dents in the drywall. This practice of band-aiding their wounds would become routine in their home, as well as the bruises and cuts on their children's arms and legs.

Dale could remember walking on scattered bits of eggshells along the old tiled kitchen floor. The new vinyl flooring that now replaced those tiles were forever stained in his mind by the color of egg yoke and the smell of sulfuric acid.

For Dale, the renovations in his parents' home were to cover up the past. The memories of what happened here, though, could never be expunged from his mind. And Carol knew that too, it's why she didn't have it in her to be upset with Dale for too long. She blamed herself for the way he was.

Carol regretted lying to her now-dead parents all those years ago about how things were at home. Covering the bruises on her children's arms and backs from toys thrown at them by their father from across the rooms of their home. A series of her crying in cars, strangers approaching her window. Her kids in the backseat, watching strange people ask their mother through locked doors if she was okay and in need of any help.

But no matter how bad things got, the blacks and blues would fade to yellows, and the evidence would heal, and the way things were at home would crystalize and become normal. Until the cycle would repeat again and the fights would start and she'd make plans to leave, until her kids would beg her to stay, or come back home and she would. She would always come back and he'd apologize and things would calm down, to once again settle.

She and the kids became accustomed to her husband's rage, and even when happy, she was cautious when around him. Carol assumed, like her, that her children learned to avoid unnecessary conflict with their father or specific words or phrases that might flare his insecurities. Learning how to walk on eggshells in their home like she did. Until they'd, of course, slip, as children do, and the fights would happen again. And in her weakest moments, being young herself, she'd blame her kids for begging her to stay when she threatened her husband she'd leave him. And now everyone was grown, and she felt it was too late to change. She feared whatever spirit of anger her husband possessed was now inside Dale. And she blamed herself. She had passed down the family curse.

Carol turned right at a corner and passed a municipal parking lot temporarily dedicated to selling Christmas trees. She continued east on the boulevard. Letting the adjacent cars pass her as she maintained a speed below the legal limit. In the distance, she saw the twin-tailed Siren logo of a popular coffee chain waving to her from on top of a tall multi-tenant sign. Carol continued forward towards the sign, signaling to the few cars on the road behind her that she would eventually be changing lanes.

At the drive-thru, there was a longer line than usual. She slowly crept her car over the coffee shop's entry ramp and contemplated for a moment parking but decided against it. She was still a little tired from the morning with Dale, and it was cold out. She put her car in park. Her car shook from the whistling wind that brushed outside the door of her car's front seat. She parked behind the last car in the queue and let out a heavy sigh.

She hadn't slept well since Dale moved back home. They had different sleeping schedules, and she had not yet grown accustomed to the sounds he would make on the floor above hers. Sounds she used to sleep through when he was a child, having had an empty nest now for a few years. Her younger son, Cal, had moved back home to live with them, on and off, a few times over the years, too. After he dropped out of college, he took a ride on the Metro North train to upstate New York, where he spent a good deal of his time partying with his friends, who were continuing with their education. Carol was always unsure why, if his friends could continue with school, why couldn't Cal? He would only come home for a week or two when his friends were on holiday from school, and he could no longer stay in their dorm rooms or sleep on their couches or in their beds. He'd come home and spend his time in his parent's house sleeping, in his old bedroom, like Dale was now, and wake up late in the afternoons when his parents were gone and leave before they'd come home to go do god knows what until early the next day.

Cal had been away, living in Prague for almost a year. He followed a girl, a poet, who studied English at Brooklyn College, who had plans to move to the Czech Republic for a semester and drink pilsner beer and play Kepler while staring at the Astronomical Clock.

Cal had met the poet at a barn fire upstate, not too far from the Bard campus, where a lot of Cal's friends had been going for undergrad. Cal and the poet got lost in conversation one night about Kierkegaard and the Beatles and he played for her his rendition of *Here Comes the Sun* on an old Fender acoustic. All before everyone was escorted off the premises by the police for vandalism, the poet, cuffed and taken away, had fallen for Cal. When she told him she was leaving for Prague at the end of the month, he asked if he could go with her and meant it. This charmed the poet, and she agreed to him joining and Cal left with her, without telling his parents, to the Czech Republic to start his short career as an expat.

Cal and the poet were supposed to be coming home for Christmas this year, and Carol wondered if the snow would affect their travel plans. It would be Cal's first time back home since he left over a year ago. But since hearing news of his proposed arrival on a brief and choppy Skype call from a loud pub in Prague, Carol had not heard another word about it. Cal wasn't the best communicator with his parents, so when and where they would be landing and on what date, or if they were still coming home, was news to her. But since everyone gets so annoyed when Carol asks questions, she would make a point not to ask and stay quiet and make peace with whatever ended up happening.

A car's horn came blaring behind her, bringing Carol back into the present state. She was lost in thought and had not been aware of the gap that had formed between her car and the one in front of her. She gave the same look she gave to Dale in the morning, to the driver behind her, through her car's windshield mirror, and slowly crept forward until the gap between her car and the one in front of her closed.

She put her car in park again and glanced at the drive-thru menu briefly. She looked to see if there was anything new on the menu she might like. Still, she decided to go with her usual skinny vanilla latte with skim milk. She made the order to a distorted male voice from the intercom outside her driver seat window and moved a few inches ahead.

There were only a few cars ahead of her, to the window. A Cumulonimbus cloud appeared above the coffee shop, giving the impression it would rain. There was no sign of the sunrise she saw earlier this morning. She wouldn't mind a rainy day to keep her inside the house to finish wrapping the Christmas gifts she'd bought.

Kajal's face popped into Carol's mind as she inched her car closer to its destination. More specifically, it was the situation between Kajal and her son that was now on her mind. Dale had told her very little about what was going on between them, and she wished she could talk more about it with him, but he always seemed uncomfortable to reveal more than he already had. He was very protective of Kajal. Every time Carol tried to bring up their situation, every word out of his mouth was met with aggression. If the problem was going to be solved, she would have to take matters into her own hands.

Carol grabbed her phone off the small tripod that was suction cupped to the car's dashboard to quickly scroll through her phone's primary contacts. The phone's ringtone came out through the car's stereo speakers loudly, making Carol jump in her seat, not expecting its violent, piercing sound.

The phone rang a few times until there was a crack and then a pause, and then Kajal's groggy voice came out through the car's stereo speakers, loud.

Back at home, Dale had grown hysterical. He was desperate for an outlet for his energy. He spent the morning pacing around the house. He couldn't sit still. He tried to meditate but could not find peace inside his home, inside his mind, inside his body. He attempted to go outside, but once he set foot into the inches of snow that accumulated in his parent's backyard, he lost interest and went back in.

He wanted to exchange words with a real person. He spent the hours his mother was gone talking to himself, to people who weren't there. He had a conversation with Clara, apologizing for his behavior. He held conversations with his old boss, calling her names, cursing out everyone who worked at S.R.P. He spoke to Kajal and told her what he had done to his mother, the whole time trying to convince himself he was right until he asked her if he was a good person and she could not respond and the realness of the conversation faded and he was no longer able to talk to those inside his head and he found himself, once again, alone.

He opened one window and then all of them, trying to free the house of his scent. His odor wreaked, and he could feel himself rotting underneath the t-shirt he slept in and wore all day. He played music loudly from his father's stereo speakers, raising the volume to levels that distorted the words of the song meant to entertain. He forced open his parents' renovated pantry, his anger making it unable to touch things gently and a jar of red pepper flakes fell and shattered to the floor. Not recognizing the fallen pepper flakes he knocked more things out of the closet. He grabbed the flour his mother used to make bread with and the bags of sugar and threw them to the ground. He grabbed from the risers organizing his parents' dishes, and threw them through the cloud of white powder that formed from the flour and watched each one crash and break through it and scatter into little pieces all over the newly furbished kitchen floor. He knocked everything in sight over with his bare hands. If it was in a reachable distance he thrashed in its direction and knocked it over. He thrashed around the kitchen to the distorted music, like he was in a mosh pit at a punk show and opened the refrigerator door and grabbed the container of milk and threw it against the wall. He took out the eggs and threw them across the room. The yolk dripped down the walls like they did in his memories. He slammed the refrigerator door shut hard and it greeted him good morning. On hearing the refrigerator's synthetic, cheery tone, he slammed his fist hard into the L.E.D. screen cracking the artificial family, breaking them in half.

Dale grabbed his chest and felt his heart's palpitating pulse corrode his arteries. He picked up a pen and started writing words down on a notepad. Ideas in his mind that he held for years but never wrote, now writing them down in scratchy ink inside a warped pad that collected years of old ideas.

He wrote quickly on the page. A stream of consciousness that could only come out of Dale appeared before him. Words of self-sabotage. Pictures, bold letters, and underlining thoughts. Spirals of exaggerated paragraphs. He wrote until he felt his present state on the page.

Behind him, Carol's car pulled into the driveway. When she exited her car, in the distance, she could hear the sounds of the distorted speakers interrupting the early, quiet light of the morning. She locked her car. The lousy mood she drove out of already on its way back as she inched forward, through the snow to the entrance of her backyard; the gate held open by the thickness of the snow.

In her hand, she held her vanilla skim latte and entered the backyard. She opened the sliding doors to her home, entered the kitchen, and couldn't speak. She saw the mess. Egg yolk running down the walls. Dishes broken on the new vinyl flooring. It felt as if she was entering a scene from her past. She walked past Dale, who did not seem to notice her. He continued, hunched over his notepad, writing, sitting at the dining room table, lost in thought.

Carol walked to the stereo speakers in the living room, turned down the volume to a significant, almost inaudible level, and sat down on the couch in a daze, drinking her now cold, sweetened coffee.

XIV

Time Alone

Kajal never expected to get a call from Dale's mother. She couldn't remember the last time she and Carol spoke, but it was on the day she and Dale moved out of their apartment in Brooklyn, and Dale's parents came to help them trek their furniture out to their garage in Long Island where it still resides. A time of her life she had forgotten, as if it were a memory she had inherited from another life.

When Carol called Kajal she was lying in her bedroom asleep. She could smell her mother's cooking from inside the kitchen. Her phone vibrating under her pillow. With her eyes closed, she reached under her pillow and found her phone.

She answered the call groggily without looking at the caller id and said Hello, into the phone's receiver half asleep.

Hi, honey. How are you? It's Carol speaking.

Kajal shot up in bed like she'd been given a shot of adrenaline to recover from an overdose. She didn't know what the call was about and had regretted having picked up the phone, not able to shake the feeling she was in trouble.

Yes. Hi Carol. It's nice to hear from you. It's been so long.

I know. I know. How are you? I'm just waiting for my coffee.

Coffee? Okay. I can use some coffee. It's still early, she said laughing uncomfortably.

A thought ran through Kajal's mind that Carol had not been up to speed on the situation between her and her son.

Yeah. I was up early this morning. I'm exhausted now. It's still early, I guess. School going okay?

Yes, it is early, she said. But, yeah, school is okay. Hard. I'm almost done with the semester. Nervous about my grades, though. But I'll be fine, I'm sure.

Oh, I'm sure you did well, honey. You always did well in school.

Awh, thank you for saying that. I appreciate that, Carol.

Of course. It's true. Wouldn't say it if it wasn't. Mom, good?

Yeah. She's good. She's good. She misses you, she lied. She asked recently if she would be invited to your place for dinner soon.

Kajal squinted her eyes and punched her bed with her clenched fist.

Carol laughed, Well, she knows she's always welcomed here. Once this winter's over, maybe we'll do something.

Of course. We drove to the cemetery the other day. We weren't too far from you guys. They put my father's headstone down finally.

Wow, that just happened? I remember you saying to Dale there was an issue with the headstone. I'm surprised it took as long as it did. I feel like you were talking about it last year.

Yeah, we were. It took a long time.

Well, how did it go? That could be a tricky thing for some people.

It was tough, but I'm glad it's finished. I'm glad it's over with.

How'd it look? Did everything work out?

Yeah. It was not the best day to go out there with how the weather's been, but I'm glad we saw it. We couldn't wait. We had to get out of the house too. We've been going crazy inside.

Oh, same here. I think that's the reason for half of our problems. At least those of us who live on the east coast, anyway. Being stuck inside our homes because of the weather, plus whatever life brings into it. Crazy way to live. Half of my friends are moving to Florida. I may join them.

I'm sure you'd love it there.

Yeah. That's for sure.

We'll have to go back another time. We didn't stay long, so... but it was nice to see.

I couldn't imagine driving all that way with how the weather's been. How long is that ride for you? It was two hours from my house I remember.

Yeah, it was almost three for us. But my mother likes to wander. There wasn't traffic but it was scary with the roads. All that snow.

I bet. It's just gross this weather. Like, enough already. Was it dangerous to drive out there?

It was not a good idea to drive. Let's just say that.

I bet it wasn't. Glad you all are okay and that you got to see it. Did your mother give you a hard time about going?

No! She wanted to go. She wanted to get out of the house as much as me. It was my sister who was hesitant.

I see. I would have told you not to go, too.

How is Doug doing?

Doug is Doug, you know.

Yeah. Are you not at home waiting for your coffee?

No, not at home. I'm sitting in my car, talking to myself. You know me. Getting a coffee at the drive-thru here. Decided to call you, so...

Well, it's nice to hear from you, Carol. I might have to make a cup of coffee for myself. I'm still tired.

Oh jeez. Did I wake you, Kajal?

No. It's okay. It's good you called. I wouldn't have woken up this early otherwise. I have some schoolwork I need to finish.

Jeez, how embarrassing. I'm so stuck inside my head sometimes I lose my manners. I wish I could go back to sleep. But once I'm up, I'm up, you know? Can't help it. I had a rendezvous with Dale this morning. I guess a part of it is my fault. Once the mind gets going... I really shouldn't have called you. It's way too early. I didn't realize how early it was, still. Sorry, I wasn't paying attention.

No, it's okay, Carol. Really. I'm...glad...you... called.

Ouch! Hot! Thank you!

What? Said Kajal, sharing a small laugh.

Oh, sorry. I was talking to the guy at the window here. Just got my coffee. A vanilla skim latté! You have to treat yourself once in a while, Kajal. It's important.

Yes, I agree.

Hold on a second, dear.

Okay.

Kajal heard Carol thank someone and then fumble with her phone in the background.

Alright, I'm back. How we lookin?

Good?

Hold another second dear.

Okay...

I just need to close my windows here...

Okay. Said Kajal, giggling uncomfortably

So long to you... Mr. Coffee, man. Alright, I'm back on the road. Damn, this coffee's hot. Ouch!

Good.

But it's delicious, though. Wow.

Glad to hear.

Honey, can I ask you a question? It's the reason I'm calling.

Sure. Okay. Go ahead.

Are you coming over for Christmas this year? We bought a few things for you, and I wanted to know so I can plan. If you're not, it's fine.

Hmm, Christmas. I'm not sure yet. I know my family has plans to celebrate this year...

Oh, you are? Good. Good.

I know we don't every year, but...

I see.

But, yeah, I'm not sure yet. I would have to talk with Dale first...

Have you spoken with Dale at all recently?

Uhmm, it has been a few weeks, actually. Just been busy here.

Okay, I see. School is hard.

Yeah, it is. How is Dale?

Uhm, hard to say, honey. I don't think he's too good, to be honest. He doesn't really speak to anyone. It's hard to talk to him, as you know. He just hangs out in his room alone. Grumpy as usual.

Is he working?

No. I doubt he's even looking for a job the way he's been acting. That place was horrible to him, though. I'm glad he's not working there anymore. He hated working there. But what do I know? No one tells me anything, and if I say something they're mad at me, you know? It's good he doesn't work there anymore. That's all I know.

Yeah... I always told him to leave.

So did I! He feels like there's nothing out there for him besides being a writer. He feels like he's not qualified for anything else.

Yeah. But he has to look. He won't find a job if he's not looking for one.

Yes, you're right. He'll find a job, though. I just feel bad he's not making any money. I know it's hard for him. He's the responsible one of my two sons if you can believe it. He'll be fine. I'm sure. He'll pull through. He has too.

Yeah.

You know, if there's anything you want to talk to me about, I'm always here. Just because you guys are going through your own thing doesn't mean we have to stop talking.

I appreciate that, Carol. Thank you.

I know what it's like to lose a dad. I lost mine when I was your age, and I had two kids then and a husband. I know it's not easy. And I know what grieving and showing up for other people feels like. It's a hard thing to balance.

Thank you for saying that. It's hard to find people who understand. No one I know does, even at home.

Yes, well, I understand, and I know it's not easy.

Thank you for saying that, Carol. It means a lot. Truly.

You'll get through. You just have to give it time. I still miss my father, Kajal. The pain never goes away, but it will change, and you'll learn how to live with it. It does become more manageable, and I know that's hard to hear now because you probably don't want to. But it does get easier. But your grief is not all you have left of your father. Not a day goes by, honey, that I don't think about my own dad. I miss him at every life milestone. I never would have thought my father wouldn't have a relationship with my sons. For the short time he was with them, he loved them, and then he was taken away from us. It seemed impossible to comprehend that life could be so unfair. It still is, in a way. But I'm not holding any grudges. I couldn't do that to myself. That's how you get cancer.

Yeah. I understand what you're saying. I'm trying to get there.

And they're always with us, Kajal. They're always watching. I believe that.

Yes...Thank you.

At least, I hope so. We could all use a little bit of guidance every now and then. I know I could. Have you dreamed of your father yet?

She wanted to tell Carol about her father's visits in the night. She wanted to tell someone, because she hadn't told anyone what she saw in the car driving to the cemetery. What her father's face looked like then. She wanted to tell Carol everything but couldn't find the words without sounding insane.

No, I haven't had any dreams of him yet, said Kajal.

Yeah, sometimes they do that. A visit, I like to think of it as. It's been a while since I last dreamt of my own parents. They might be spending all their time with Dale. Who knows? Or maybe they have better things to do than look down on us living our silly lives.

I'm sure your parents are watching over you.

Look at me being negative. I'm sorry. I called to try and help, and I hurt your feelings. I'm sorry.

No, you didn't. Not at all.

Well, anyway. What do I know? As my mother used to say, *Such is life*.

Yes. Said Kajal. I remember.

You and Dale will find your way, too, and it'll be fine if you don't. You both have your own lives to live, and that's what's most important.

Thank you for saying that.

But he does miss you. I know that.

Well, despite what you may think, I miss him too.

I'm sure. You two have been together forever.

Yes. A long time.

Yeah.

Yeah.

Well, anyway, I love you Kajal. We consider you part of our family. So. Call anytime. Kajal heard Carol's voice break when she said this, and thought she might be crying.

Awh, thank you for saying that, Carol. I...love... you...too.

Okay, honey. I'll leave you alone now. I'm sure I'll talk to you soon.

For sure. I'll talk to you soon. Thank you for calling. You're not an inconvenience!

Thank you. Appreciate you saying that, sweety. Miss having you at the house, so... I just wanted to give you a call.

Miss you too! It was nice to hear your voice.

You too, honey. Okay. Bye-bye now.

Bye bye.

Kajal hung up the phone. The conversation had left her feeling lighter. She was relieved to have whatever it was removed from her chest. A feeling she could only describe as a heaviness. She didn't know how long it would last and thinking about it ending even started to make the heaviness come back. It was a miraculous feeling to feel better for a moment, even if the feeling would only last a moment. She appreciated Carol calling her and having had the opportunity to connect with someone she felt did understand where she was coming from. Why was it so hard to come to this moment that felt so simple?

Later that evening, Kareena met with Kajal before her redeye flight back home to London. She was flying home to spend the holidays with her family. The semester was near end and Kareena had sent Kajal a slew of text messages through out the week she had not answered.

Kajal did not know what she would say to Kareena when she saw her. In her response, she apologized and suggested they meet for a coffee to catch up. There was too much happening in her life for her to process her feelings properly, from that night with Kareena and Marc. She felt if Kareena never talked to her again she would be fine with it.

Kareena suggested they meet at a café by the school, one they had never visited before together and was only convenient for Kareena to get to since it was right around the corner from her apartment. But wanting to get out of her mother's place, Kajal did not mind the trek.

Kareena had on what Kajal noticed to be a very expensive long beige raincoat, a black Kate Spade purse hung over her shoulder, and a pair of octagonal-shaped sunglasses with large frames that covered the majority of her face. If she hadn't known Kareena, she would have mistaken her for Lady Gaga. Compared to how Kareena looked, Kajal was underdressed, in her Kirkland pullover and jeans. She didn't put as much effort into her outfit as Kareena did for their coffee date. She was too tired, too busy, too sad to care. But still, that didn't stop her insecurities from percolating, which she knew would make it difficult for her to sit comfortably across the table from her friend, be present, drink coffee, and bond organically with her like she would have wanted.

I'm thinking seriously about taking a semester off, said Kareena as she took a bite of what looked to be a stale crumb cake.

Why? Asked Kajal, realizing, after taking her first sip of coffee, that she had also forgotten to brush her teeth.

I don't know. I'm getting quite fed up with New York. I think I want to find another place to live for a while. I've forgotten why I've come here. I'm young, you know? I can always go back to school.

I get that. I wish I could do that too. But it took so much for me to go back to school, said Kajal. I kind of, now, just want to get it over with. It's hard not having a real job.

Yeah. I keep telling myself I have time. Maybe, when I'm ready, I can finish school somewhere else, like back home in London.

Through Columbia?

Maybe. It's not the school I have a problem with. I just want to be out in the world, you know? I don't think I can be in one place for too long. I've been thinking a lot about Japan, too. Last night, I watched a movie about this girl who lived in Tokyo, and I just saw myself as her, you know? And after, I went down this internet spiral of everything Japanese: photos, films, books, Airbnb's where I could stay for a month and feel the place out. I even found myself looking at airplane tickets for after Christmas. I almost booked a $2000 one-way flight there, leaving tomorrow from JFK, but I stopped myself knowing my parents would be pissed if I didn't spend the holidays with them. But I'd rather spend my holiday in Japan and be alone there for a month, then see my family, if i'm being honest.

I've never been to Japan, said Kajal looking down at her coffee.

Am I boring you?

No. Not at all. Why? Asked Kajal, embarrassed she had revealed too much of how she was feeling.

Like, I hear myself talking, and I'm afraid I sound completely mental or something.

No, I get it. You want to get out of your life. You need a reset. Grad school is hard.

Yeah. I guess. But it seems pretentious to talk about travel these days. Like, I hate when other people do it. But, also, like, it's where I'm at. This is what happens when you live alone. You're the first person I've spoken to all day.

I get it. You don't sound pretentious. Really.

If I take a semester off, I'll still have my apartment here.

Oh, nice. You're keeping the apartment?

Yeah, it's my parent's place. We've had it for a few years now. Ever since my father started doing business in the States.

Lovely, said Kajal, raising her eyebrows as she sipped her now lukewarm coffee.

There was an unjustified anger rising inside of Kajal. The space she took away from her friend made her see her in a new light. Why had Kareena wanted to meet with her? Why had they ever become friends? There was this constant feeling that Kareena kept trying to show off her life to her and would feel bad about it, then do something nice to make up for having said anything at all.

Can I open up to you about something? Asked Kareena.

Sure, of course, said Kajal.

With this question, she had become anxious. She didn't know what Kareena would say about their night together with Marc. She didn't want to talk about it now. She needed time to process her feelings alone and then, maybe, she would be able to talk to Kareena seriously about what they did together. And waiting impatiently for Kareena to speak, Kajal had the urge to run out of the coffee shop. Run back home to her mother's apartment, lay down in her bed and hide from the world.

The real reason I may take a semester off is because my father was diagnosed with lung cancer. I haven't told anybody this, not even the school.

Oh, no Kareena. I'm so sorry.

It's okay. Thank you. It just happened. He smoked all his life so it makes sense but he starts chemo soon.

Wow, I'm so sorry. I can't imagine. What stage is he...

I don't know. I didn't ask.

There was a silence but Kajal showed so much empathy through her face, it was like a new way of communicating. There were no words necessary.

I'm so sorry, Kareena. How are you doing?

I don't know. Like I feel like I should know what to tell you.

No, you don't.

Like, I don't feel anything strangely. I don't think it's hit me yet. I just don't care about school anymore. I know that. I don't have the bandwidth for it. I just want to run away, if im being honest. It would be nice to go to Japan. I felt so free in my body letting my brain explore the possibilities of going there. It made me so happy, I forgot what was happening.

Yeah, I totally understand why you would feel that way. To get away from everything.

I don't want to go home but I feel like I have to for my mother. She doesn't want me to come but she isn't doing well. My father doesn't know that I know yet, my mother accidentally told me.

How?

She kept it too herself for too long. It just broke out of her.

I'm so sorry Kareena. Really. That's so hard. People do get better. Our bodies want to heal themselves.

Yeah, sure. Of course. I think it's just the not knowing. I've truly never been in this situation before. I didn't know how frightening it could be.

Yeah, said Kajal and she grabbed Kareena's hand from across the table and carressed it with such love and care that Kareena felt from her such a warmth she had not known from a friend.

You can stay at my place while I'm gone, said Kareena, I can leave you the key.

Okay. Sure. Is that what you want?

I think it would comfort me to know you were there, said Kareena.

Okay. I think I can do that.

Only if you want to. Nobody will be there, at least not for the rest of December or January. I still have to decide whether or not I'm taking the semester, but I trust you. And my parents would feel comfortable having someone I know watch the place.

Yeah. Sure. I can do that. It wouldn't be a problem. Im not going anywhere.

Are you sure? You don't have to if you don't want to. Don't take pity on me.

No, im not. I can do it. It'll be good for me, I think.

Kajal removed her hand from Kareena's and slid it across the table and took a sip of her coffee.

What will you do about the rest of the semester?

I got a referral to finish at home. Told all my professors I have anxiety.

Okay. I can help you with any school stuff too. In case you need me for anything.

Kareena smiled and said, Thank you. I appreciate that.

And no one else would be there, you said?

Not until I come back, of course.

Okay. Sure. And you're sure about this?

Of course. You'd be doing me a huge favor. As long as you don't mind meeting me later tonight, I can leave you the key. Maybe you could even lock up for me?

Sure. Yes. Of course. Whatever works best.

Thank you. You're a good friend, Kajal.

Kajal smiled but said nothing. It didn't matter what her feelings were to her. It didn't matter what she had to say. To Kajal, there was no choice but to show up for her friend. Someone was asking for her help and she felt obligated to do so. The unarticulated though would grow like a cancer of it's own untreated.

Kajal didn't stay at Kareena's right away. After getting the keys from Kareena, Kajal saw her out and took a moment alone inside the apartment. She sat on the couch and observed the variety of plants hanging on the walls contrasted against Kareena's neutral-toned living room. Kajal walked into the bathroom, peed, and tried Kareena's Japanese heated toilet seat. She peeked through the medicine cabinet which had just a few products lined up in cylindrical glass containers. She went into Kareena's bedroom and looked through the top dresser drawer and found a vibrator with elaborate offshoots that looked like a sculpture one would find in a modern art museum, and touched the ends of the contraption with the tips of her fingers.

When the opportunity for Kajal to be alone revealed itself, she realized she didn't want it. Not right away, at least. In the past, if Dale and Kajal got the opportunity to house sit, they both would immediately move in and play house: cooking, drinking wine, doing laundry, and having sex. She was not used to being alone, and when the opportunity revealed itself she did not see the point of it.

She did not like the idea of being alone inside someone else's empty apartment by herself.

She was different from Dale in this way. In time, she would see this as something she would have to work on, finding it important to spend quality time with oneself. But she was raised with the mindset that if doing something made her uncomfortable, it was okay for her not to do it, even if it was good for her.

One evening, she returned from the store with her mother, and an ambulance was outside their apartment building. They walked past their car up through the building ramp, and three men dressed as paramedic's rolled out a body on a stretcher outside the building's back entrance. The body was placed inside a black rugged leather bag, and one could only tell by the imprints of a head and feet that the bag was not empty.

Kajal gasped when she realized what was in front of her, not noticing the body at first, lost in conversation with her mother. She had dropped the plastic bags she'd been holding onto the snowy ground beneath her and grabbed her mother's arm in shock. The three men rolled the stretcher to the parked ambulance outside in the curb lane. One of the uniformed men told Kajal and her mother to stand back as they wheeled the body past them, closer to the ambulance, before collapsing the stretcher to the ground, picking it up aggressively, and placing it inside the back of the ambulance, before closing its doors and driving away.

Kajal asked a woman who'd been watching if she happened to know who it was the ambulance had taken. The lady responded, saying she didn't know the man personally but that they had taken the body out of an apartment on the 11th floor.

XV

Regretting Choices

Dale had not known about Carol cold-calling Kajal. She would have told him if he had not destroyed her kitchen.

He sat on his bed listening to Doug and Carol fight through the night. It was just like how things were before he met Kajal. It was like nothing had changed. He felt as if he was twelve years old again.

Before Doug had come home, Dale helped Carol clean whatever he could of the kitchen. He apologized profusely to Carol, but she wouldn't listen. She was hurt. Dale watched his mother sweep the flour and sugar off the floor, crying as she did it. It broke him to see her suppress her tears. Her crying had cleared his senses. Like only now after he had hurt someone who mattered to him, did he have the foresight to make rational choices.

When he saw Doug crossing the street to their house, he ran up the staircase and never came back down, until the next morning.

For the damages made, Dale gave his mother what was left in his savings account: a tight 5,000 dollars, all the money he had saved from his first job to his time at S.R.P.

Though Carol would give it all back to him in time, she wanted him to sweat. She wanted him to feel the repercussions of his actions. She didn't want to punish him, he was an adult, he was no longer a boy. But she no longer knew the boy she raised. Dale wanted her to tell him how to be, how to act and she did not know what else to tell him. She had told him everything his whole life. She tried her best for years to teach her children how to be decent human beings, the best she knew how, and she felt as if she had failed them. When she first entered her house and saw Dale scribbling notes at the kitchen table, she did not know what to think. She saw her life flash before her eyes, not knowing what to make out of the life she lived. What was the purpose in all of this? To feel such pain and disappointment. To feel like you have failed yourself and the ones you love. She didn't know if having children was the right thing for her and her husband to have done, and Carol found that out when it was too late. Her children were now adults. She and her husband had participated in making monsters. And they could not undo what they had done.

She didn't know, in retrospect, what she could have done differently other than to not have stayed with her husband. But there was never a time when leaving him wouldn't have broken her heart and the idea of that pain even, was too much to bear. Just thinking about leaving hurt her. But staying only leads her to another type of pain. She didn't know what to make of that. Every choice she had to make hurt her in some way and it was either to be hurt now or hurt later. But what had led to the idea of leaving had caused her pain, and made her not want to stay, but who was to say that there was something better out there for her? She knew Dale and Doug loved her, and she them, and there was never a doubt in her mind, if she left, if she ever walked away from them, to never see her family again, she may never feel that love she felt for them with anyone else. In what version of her life, could happiness take precedent? Leaving would only lead to a life of fighting the guilt from having left a love that she might not ever be open to receiving again. It was as if things were bad from the beginning and there was no way to undo the things that were done and life was happening just as it was supposed to.

Following their heart had led them to where they were and it felt unfair. No one was exactly happy. No one had a relationship they were happy in and no one knew what to do about it.

XVI

Peace Piece

Her excuse to her mother for leaving was that she had a group meeting she had forgotten about for a project that didn't exist with people who were not currently in New York. Her mother would think her crazy if she told her the truth. But the truth was she couldn't stand being in the building any longer. Before she left, she ate a small meal with her mother and packed a light bag of clothes, including her toothbrush, a few notebooks, a face scrub, a body moisturizer, her 12-inch Macbook laptop, a phone charger, and walked out the front door as if she were soon to return.

Her plan for her first morning alone in Kareena's apartment was to do nothing. She planned not to get out of bed until noon, hoping to make up for the sleep she had lost since the start of the school year. She hadn't slept like that since she was a teenager and was excited to not have any kind of distraction. She was excited to do nothing for a change.

Kajal convinced herself when she was younger, after reading *Little Women*, that sleeping past *10:00 AM* was a waste of a day. But after this year, and the exhaustion of finishing her first semester of grad school, she wasn't intrigued by the outside world anymore. She didn't care if the sun was up or down or who was doing what. All she wanted was to rest, and to recover.

Something unknown to Kajal, had woken her up. She was in Kareena's bed. She looked at the clock and sighed; it was only 7 AM. She tried to go back to sleep but couldn't; her thoughts ruminating. She had a physical exhaustion that kept her body down, wanting to lay still, but her mind was wandering, keeping her up. Kajal gave in and got out of bed. She'd have another night to catch up on her sleep, planning to stay longer at Kareena's apartment than she had originally planned; she had come to like the solitude. She made coffee from the touchscreen Nespresso machine, and scrolled through Kareena's record collection, half-awake. She put on a Bill Evan's record she found, imagining Dale would've picked this one. She had always liked his taste in music.

When she walked into the living room, she opened the curtains to the windows and looked out. A wave of uneasiness she could not explain passed through her.

Outside, only one or two small piles of grayed snow were left melting on the curbside as if the snow had been gone for days.

It was difficult for Kajal to see the street barren of snow, like it was. When she entered the building the night before, she took one last look behind her to find the street and the parked cars covered with a soft white bed of snow. The only thing that disturbed the snow's consistency were the boot marks she left trailing up the block from which she came. It felt like the city was her playground, quiet and secluded, existing only for her to leave her mark.

But within just a few hours, that consistent white bed disappeared and it felt to Kajal that some time-lapse had occurred and she experienced a moment of panic, afraid she had in fact slept too long, and that the stress from the year induced her into a coma that she was just now waking up from, leaving her grasping for any sense of familiarity or belonging.

She allowed this scenario to run through her mind a moment longer and then took a deep breath. With some distance, she rendered the scenario absurd. With the year she had, she honestly considered that grad school had been the thing that fucked her up the most, even more than her father's passing. Knowing there must be some logical explanation for the snow's absence or maybe it was only in a dream that the world outside was covered in snow, to wake up to find it barren.

She turned from the window, walked over to the Nespresso machine and tried to put this uneasy feeling past her. She made another cup and watched each drop drip into the black pool inside her ceramic blue mug.

Bill Evans played like an echo in the background. Kajal's eyes were heavy; she could use another hour or two more of sleep but was aware at the same time a restlessness that lingered. She leaned on the counter and rested her head on her palms, trying to calm herself, trying to focus her attention on the music coming from the living room.

The name of the Bill Evans piece playing was called *Peace Piece*. Kajal listened to Bill Evans sparingly. She wasn't too much into jazz music, but when she listened, she'd always find herself inside a headspace she liked. Dale used to play Evans inside the apartment they shared together in Brooklyn. He'd play the record *Waltz For Debby* on Sunday mornings, and together, the two would sit on the couch and drink coffee and watch the one beam of sunlight that came in through the window of their garden-floor apartment in synchronized silence.

Kareena had a display of only a few records to choose from. Since the apartment belonged to her family, she assumed Kareena was not the one responsible for curating the display of records available. Among the small record collection were mostly jazz records and a few rock records. She chose Bill Evans simply because he was the only name she recognized. And though she was not the biggest fan of jazz music, the music of Bill Evans helped her concentrate on simple, synchromatic tasks, like chopping vegetables, or when she cleaned the apartment, or folded laundry. The music's purpose was to help keep her focused on what her mind sometimes did not have the bandwidth for without some type of tether to keep her concentrated. But no matter the task, every time she listened to one of Bill Evan's records, she'd find herself inside the same daydream:

In the front row of an old low-lit jazz club, alone at a small round marble table, Kajal sits wearing a beautiful golden dress, drinking a cocktail whose volume of liquid never seems to diminish from it's glass. There is some semblance of an audience, but they're barely visible in her peripheral view. All she can see are their hands, feet, arms, legs, lips, mouth, cheeks; never the full body of the person. They give off the presence of a laugh track in a sitcom; its sound lacks the tangibility of real laughter but provokes a substance that is both ephemeral and empty. In front of Kajal, Bill Evans sits on a stage performing; it is unclear what year it is but it's clear to Kajal, even in the dream, it's not in the present time. His hands always moving in a fast forward motion like in a VHS tape, moving up and down along the piano's scale, producing sound waves that sync with the invisible band behind him. His stoic face seems concentrated to Kajal. She calls out to him but he never loses his focus. His body leaning over the keys, his bottom just hovering over the black bench that sits beneath him. She sees his knees bent forward, aching, sweat running down his forehead, landing in a pool of liquid that sits before her on the old tiled stage she sits in front of.

A silence followed that of the soft pop sound of the needle leaving the record's edge, kicking Kajal out of her day dream. She sighed and opened her eyes; she was back in Kareena's kitchen.

She lifted her head up off the counter, walked to where the record player was, turned the vinyl over and continued the record.

She watched as the record slowly began to spin on the turntable, as the needle moved over to the waxed vinyl surface, and made another soft pop sound that signaled the music to start again. She grabbed her cup of coffee, laid down on the couch and closed her eyes. She took a deep breath, in through her nose and out through her mouth, focusing on the music, following images that appeared in her mind until she, again, drifted off.

She was unsure how much time had passed when a slew of knocks came rapidly from the front door. She sat up quickly, irritated, her coffee cup nearly tipping over as she slid her feet off the couch, bellowing a grunt only one could hear if they were inside her head. She was not in the mood to interact with anyone, let alone anyone inside of Kareena's apartment building where everyone to her was a stranger.

Kajal marched towards the front door, starting to get the uneasy feeling she had forgotten something off the short list of instructions Kareena dictated to her before leaving the café. She checked her phone to see if there were any messages from Kareena, saying a visitor would be on their way, but there wasn't any information she could find. When the second slew of knocks came, Kajal couldn't decide whether to make her presence known or not. Her intuition told her to say nothing and she cautiously approached the apartment's front door, trying not to make any sounds that would pass over the apartment's front door's threshold.

Kajal looked out through the front door's peephole to find the head of a boy quickly descending the staircase. The boy wore an old overseas cap, similar to the shape of an old train conductor's hat or that of a paper hat given to a child as a souvenir from a local pizzeria. Over his shoulder he wore an old gray corduroy jacket and had on thin black weatherbeaten shoes.

For a moment, based off of his fast rigid movements, it seemed as if the boy were not real but instead made out of plastic.

The boy descended the staircase quickly, hopping from one step to the next. She opened the door slowly and walked onto the old Persian-style rug in the hallway, leaned her head over the banister, and watched the boy's right arm quickly glide along the spiral staircase all the way down to the lobby's tiled floor.

When he reached the end, the boy's hand vanished from the banister, and she saw his thin frame for a moment as he leaped off the last few steps, two feet into the air, and disappeared past the landing. His feet made a sound as they touched the tiled floor that echoed from the bottom of the boy's shoes to the top of the banister where Kajal stood over watching.

She heard the front door to the building open and knew the boy had left when she heard the familiar sound of the front door slamming shut, followed by the hallway's familiar silence.

Kajal waited at the top of the staircase and stayed still until she was sure the boy had left. She turned around and noticed a package on the floor leaning against the wall, on the right side of the apartment's main entrance. Kajal went to the package and picked it up. It was not addressed to anyone specific. There was no return address, just the address to the building written aggressively in black Sharpie marker along the front of what looked to be a 12x12 inch-sized box. Kajal picked up the package. She thought it might be heavy, but it wasn't. It felt almost hollow inside and weightless in her hands. The package exuded the energy of a sardonic joke. It did not travel gently. The package was beaten up at the corners as if it were punched in and dented, like it had traveled from one side of the world to the other, in the back of cars, delivery trucks, and airplanes, constantly moving and shifting among the other packages in its company that were also making their journey to some unknown destination.

Though the package had the building's correct address, there was nothing to indicate that it was for this specific apartment, Kareena, or anyone in her family. She had the impulse to abandon the package at another door or walk it back down the spiral staircase and leave it in the designated space in the lobby, where the other mail and packages were left, a space Kajal was sure the boy must have seen on his way up to Kareena's apartment. But since it wasn't addressed to anyone specific, she didn't know what else to do with the package but took it back inside with her.

Kajal left the package on the table in the living room. She took a picture of it with her phone, leaving the front side of the package facing upwards, showcasing for Kareena the tumultuous handwriting written on the front. She sent a question mark to Kareena following her photo of the package. She almost opened the package herself but decided against it. She would at least wait and see what Kareena texted back. She checked her phone a few minutes later, anxious for a response. Nothing. Anxious, Kajal dropped her phone onto the table and sat down on the couch, bored and restless, finding herself now filled with energy. She stared at the ground in Kareena's living room, wanting to depart from her body like a cicada, leave her shriveled skin on the couch and move on to the next unoccupied space.

She knew she wanted to do something but was indecisive about what she wanted at the moment. She was hungry but didn't want to eat. She wanted to sleep but couldn't rest. She wanted to fuck but didn't know who with.

She shifted her head slightly. A cloud moved from its position in front of the sun, allowing light to hit the building's block suddenly. She walked over to the window, looked outside, and stood in the light that now shined into the living room. She didn't recognize it then, but what was left of the snow, the small gray piles she saw melting in the curb lane that morning, were gone, and for the first time that day, she thought about going outside.

She hadn't seen the magnolia tree before then and noted that it was the only living tree on the block. It was full and beautiful, sitting in its sanctioned-off spot on the sidewalk, sitting in the sunlight like an actor onstage in a play. The tree's beauty had taken Kajal by surprise. She knew the magnolia tree only blooms in the springtime and winter was well underway. But the tree on Kareena's block was bright pink, and each flower opened, taking its energy from the sun like a famished child.

She had come to feel slightly faint standing by the window and thought she might need a glass of water. She went to the sink in the kitchen, poured herself a glass from the tap, and drank it slowly like it were medicine prescribed to her by a doctor.

Like the sudden absence of the snow, there was something uneasy about the sudden appearance of the magnolia tree, with it's fullness and beauty that now appeared outside on the block in front of Kareena's apartment.

She noticed a slight breeze had gently shaken the tree's flowers, and she wondered if it was still cold out and how she should appropriately dress if she were to go outside. There was nothing for her to do inside the apartment, and outside, with how the light showed against the tree, was perfect.

Kajal grabbed a pair of scissors from the kitchen and went inside the living room to open the package. The box was haphazardly taped by the two creases in its center. The package was almost opened anyway, she thought. She could carefully rip it open with her bare hands. But with the scissors, she cut the tape in the center, where the last line of the address showed, and made sure to cut only the box and not whatever object may be inside it.

The object in the box was a glistening golden dress. She moved the package to the floor and ran her fingers along the fabric and felt the metallic embroidery that lay stitched in between the dress's thin fibers.

Despite the package's lightweight, the dress was solid and heavy in her hands, and from what Kajal could tell, it was made out of a thick golden silk with paillettes that transformed in golden hues as she turned it in the light. There was no tag to show a brand name or size. There was no mark or signature to show who might have been the dress's proprietor.

Kajal carefully lifted the dress out of its package; it was folded into thirds. And when she stood up from the couch, she let the dress fall to the floor, holding it against her shoulders until the fabric flowed out, stopping at her knees.

Kajal ran through the corridor to the bedroom to look at herself in front of Kareena's standing view mirror, holding the dress. Kajal did not think she would put the dress on, but after seeing it held against her body, she could not help but fantasize what the dress might look like on her honeyed colored skin. She lifted her leg up from behind her, posing in front of the mirror, and then she lowered her hand and held the dress tightly against her stomach, as she turned slightly to see her lower backside.

It's beautiful, she said out loud.

She pictured the woman who she thought the dress might be for, standing before her in the mirror. In her mind's eye, she couldn't help but see a sketch of a white woman standing before her with long red hair and voluptuous breasts. This image of a woman based on an old cartoon character from a movie she had seen years ago as a child.

She was frustrated that it was this type of woman she saw in the mirror, who she felt deserved to wear the dress and not someone who looked more like herself. Was this how she saw women, too? Was her image of a woman influenced by some character she had seen in a cartoon from years ago?

Kajal forced herself to see only her body standing before her. She focused on the dress, leaning against her skin. She could feel the dress wanting to speak to her. She loved the juxtaposition of the dresses golden color against her brown skin, and now excited laid the dress down gently on the bed behind her.

Kajal undressed in front of the mirror. She let her clothes fall to the floor and lay scattered at her feet. She looked at herself naked in the mirror and ran her hands alongside her breast, stomach, and waist, coming back to meet at the flap of skin that hung off the front of her belly. Kajal sighed with disappointment, wishing secretly she could shed this skin, like her clothes, transfer it to the floor, and walk to the closet to try on another-sized vessel.

She changed into a pair of clean underwear, picked the dress up from off the bed, and held it against her naked body. Kajal turned from the mirror and laid the dress down again on the bed. Careful not to pull or rip the fabric, Kajal got down on her knees as if she were to recite a prayer and lifted the dress's bottom-up softly, poked her head in, and pulled herself up by the bed's comforter, and crawled into the golden dress, pushing herself up through it, like a butterfly emerging from its chrysalis.

When she got her head out through the neckline, Kajal stood up by the bedside and pulled the rest of the dress down alongside her waist. It was tighter than she would have liked, but it fit. Kajal looked at herself in the mirror again. She turned to show herself her front side and back, the image not what she had imagined. It was better. It was real.

An older couple were chatting in the hallway, just a few feet from the apartment's front door entrance. Kajal watching through the peephole, listening to their conversation, waiting for them to return to their apartments and clear the hallway. The dress did not instill any new confidence inside Kajal, and now, wearing shoes and a handbag borrowed from Kareena's closet, she wanted to leave the building unnoticed.

Kajal looked at the clock. It was already a quarter past five. The hours between now and the morning were lost to her. When she was able to leave the apartment unnoticed, she grabbed a shawl to cover her shoulders and closed the door to the apartment behind her and sneaked down the stairwell.

She walked down Broadway in the crisp cold and watched people eat through the restaurant's windows and grew hungry. They looked warm sitting at their tables. Their faces showed no sense of concern or anxiety. They could afford the food they were enjoying without consequence, without feeling they overpaid, or wished they had made the dish at home for less money, like she would have.

Kajal chose what looked to be a garden level bar, away from the crowd. She happily left the noise and stares of Broadway and walked south from the sidewalk, down a staircase into a bar.

There was a chalkboard sign outside the bar's entrance that read *Jazz Band on Sundays*, as she approached the bar's entrance, the music transitioned from the 808 synthetic beats from cars to the metal waves of a wind instrument reverberating the remnants of an exhale. The band was playing a piece written by the band leader, a saxophonist born and raised in Harlem.

Kajal was directed to a seat at the back by a hurried hostess. A man, who was seated at a table by the front, lost track of the band when Kajal walked past him in her golden dress. He kept his eyes on her as she gracefully settled into the bar stool at the back of the club.

The hostess didn't ask Kajal if she needed a space for one seat or two. Because of the band, every seat in the club was filled, and the only available seat for Kajal was the one bar stool left at the back of the club.

She knew before attempting to sit on the stool that it would be too tall for her. Her legs wouldn't reach the bottom, and because of the dress, a good portion of her legs would be exposed, and she'd have to spend every moment of her time there trying not to flash the band from the bar.

There was an unexpected silence, followed by an applause. The band finished their piece, and the energy in the room ebbed for a moment, and before the band could begin again, the crowd grew impatient and continued with their conversations.

Kajal climbed her way up towards the stool's flat surface, positioned her legs away from the band, and ordered a drink. She felt it was a mistake to be there, after all. She felt uncomfortable sitting at the bar alone and grew embarrassed being at the club, feeling like an outsider there.

Kajal sipped her cocktail. She had followed her instincts without questioning their motive, and they had led her here.

The bartender placed a second drink before her as the band began to play their rendition of *Peace Piece* by Bill Evans. Kajal put the rim of the glass to her lips and turned to give the band her full attention. The recognition of the Bill Evan's piece relaxed her and hearing it play made her feel the bar to be exactly where she was supposed to be.

She never heard the piece played live before and the familiarity of the music comforted her in a foreign space, along with the warmth that came from the gin of her cocktail.

If she and Dale were on good terms she would have texted him to join her. She only planned to stay for one or two more sets and then leave. She didn't feel comfortable staying at a bar alone for long without company, though was grateful for the comfort that came with the familiarity of the music.

Kajal went to drink the last sip of her cocktail when she felt a slight touch of someone's coat brush alongside her hand. Though unintentional, the touch of the coat made her aware of the tight space around her and when she looked at the person sitting next to her, she saw an older Japanese man sitting at the bar with a drink, making eye contact with her and smiling. She smiled back to be polite, but the act had caused her body to turn towards the man more than she would have wanted to. Kajal made eye contact with him to make sure his gaze was intentional, and when he did not look away or deflect his eyes, she knew his gaze was on purpose, and he stayed put and continued smiling in her direction.

The man wore a black suit, a button-down white shirt, and a tie. She knew him to be around her father's age though he had energy in his face, and his skin the proper color of someone out in the world, and not bedridden for days with no exposure to light. The old man, not being white, made Kajal wonder if his gaze was perverted or if he was someone not attuned to the rules of the Western world.

Hello, Kajal said to the man, surprising herself.

She realized the man being her father's age made her more comfortable with speaking to him directly and accepting of whatever reason he had decided to pay her any mind.

Hi, my apologies for staring. You just look so familiar to me. Your dress...

The old man had a deep English accent, which surprised Kajal.

What about my dress?

It's beautiful. I've seen one before, just like it.

Well, I'm sure there's another one of its kind out there somewhere.

You look very beautiful in it. No one here has dressed as nicely as you have tonight. Have you noticed that? Everyone here is dressed for the park. You and I are the only ones who have dressed with any kind of fashion sense.

I hadn't noticed that, actually.

My name's Samson.

Hi, Samson.

Can I ask you what your name is, my dear?

Carol.

Carol? You don't look like a Carol.

You don't look like a Samson.

I see. Well, then, nice to meet you, Carol. Can I say, Carol, that you look beautiful in your dress?

You did. Thank you.

To me, you look like you were shot out from a different decade. It's very attractive to me. I don't like the present times much and you don't look like you belong here.

I was born in New York.

Oh, sorry. That's not what I meant. I meant a different decade. Another time. I was not born here, also, as you can probably tell.

What decade do you think I'm from then?

I'm not sure, dear. I was hoping you could tell me that yourself.

Okay, Kajal laughed. She couldn't help it, but she was charmed by the old man.

I don't meet many people who give me that feeling, you know? Once you walked into the bar, my attention was taken away from the band and given to you. I couldn't take my eyes off you.

Sorry for distracting you, then.

Oh, don't worry! I much prefer to look at you than watch them perform. I've seen the band play many times. Tonight, I feel something about them is off, don't you think?

I think they're fine. I don't know much about jazz music. But I know the piece they're playing now.

You like Bill Evans?

I do.

I knew him, you know. Well, I didn't know him, but I've seen him play many times before.

That must have been very nice for you.

Yes, there was a period where you couldn't walk into a jazz club in New York and not see Bill Evans either watching or playing a set. You could see any of the big-name musicians from that time play. Coltrane. Davis. Mingus. They were always hanging around. It was a very exciting time to be alive.

I'm sure it was.

Yes. Being a celebrity was a different thing back then. The paparazzi ruined that.

What a shame.

Would you have wanted to see Bill Evans perform?

Of course. Why wouldn't I? Too bad I was born twelve years after his death.

How old are you?

I'm sure you could do the math.

This made Samson laugh, and he paused from speaking and took a sip of his drink.

What if I told you, you could see him? Samson asked this putting his drink back down onto the bar.

Kajal paused before answering, as if she might have misheard him.

What do you mean? Asked Kajal.

What if I told you that you could see Bill Evans play?

Kajal stared at the man, confused. She was half smiling.

I don't understand.

Samson laughed and ate the olives from his martini glass.

Do you mind if I ask again where you bought your dress from, Carol?

It was a gift, said Kajal.

A gift? Hmm.

Samson smiled and didn't say anything else, not wanting to pry further. He could tell he was starting to lose Kajal with the direction his questions were going.

On stage, the band finished their rendition of *Peace Piece* and the audience applauded them. After the applause had settled the band took a small bow and slowly left the stage without stating a reason for their departure.

They're leaving, said Kajal. She had not intended to say these words out loud and have Samson hear her and she felt a wave of embarrassment pass through her.

Yes, they have a flight to catch tonight. They were doing the manager a favor by being here, which is why they played poorly, I think. They're typically much better, I tell you. I know the manager, too, and he's not the type of guy to hold a grudge, but we'll see after tonight. The band and him have had a good working relationship, but I heard they owed the manager a favor, which I assumed was why they were forced to play here before beginning their tour.

They're going on tour?

Yes! They're starting a whole tour tomorrow in Europe, so I'm sure this is the last place they'd want to be. I know the minute they get off the plane, they'll have to go to a club and perform jetlagged. It takes work to live the life of a musician. It's actually quite exhausting.

Yes, I can imagine, said Kajal.

But, of course, they get to play music for a living and travel the world. Not so bad.

No, not so bad.

The two sat quietly for a moment together. Kajal took the last sip of her drink, quietly planning her escape from the club back to Kareena's apartment.

Could I buy you another drink, Carol?

No, that's okay. Thank you. I should being going.

Are you sure? I swear nothing of it. I don't get out much. I wouldn't mind buying you a drink if it meant we could talk for a little while longer.

You seem like you get out plenty.

What makes you say that?

How you dress. You know the band and the manager. You've seen Bill Evans play. You seem very cultured to me.

This made Samson laugh. I see why you would think that, said Samson. I'm an old man, Carol, but I don't get out much like I used to. I used to spend my days traveling, you know? But now, not so much. The world is different. It's not what it used to be. And I like getting to know people but I'm shy. How about you?

Yes, I'm shy.

Have you traveled at all?

I haven't traveled that much. I'm in grad school now.

Ah, good for you. An education is a beautiful thing. But like me, you've also dressed up tonight and if I were to judge you based on your looks, as you did me, I would say you are also a well traveled and cultured person. But you're saying you don't get out much?

No, not really. I haven't traveled that much. I've been to Europe a few times but that's it. Does how a person dresses show how cultured they are?

Samson took a moment to think about his answer.

People who travel outside of their hometowns often take things from the places they've been to. They go to another city or country and exchange a piece of themselves with an offering from that new city and bring it with them wherever they go. You look to me like you've been to a few places.

No, I wouldn't say I have.

Your eyes wear a sort of heaviness. They're beautiful, but there is a sadness behind them.

I think I'm just tired.

I see. He paused. Are you sure you don't want another drink, Carol?

I'm sure, thank you.

Samson took a moment to redirect his eyes from Kajal to the club's ceiling, thinking carefully again of his words. The club's patrons had started to clear out after the band had left the stage. Only a few people remained seated, finishing their food and cocktails. A waiter started to flip the barren seats over onto the cleared tables.

Did you intend to come to this club tonight, Carol?

I didn't. I found it while I was walking around, said Kajal.

I see. Does it make you think of anything specific?

What does?

The club.

No, not really.

You know, you can travel in other ways. You don't have to buy a plane ticket to go somewhere.

Maybe.

Like coming here, for instance, coming to this jazz club tonight, for me, transports me to Paris. I miss Paris. I miss it daily, yet I don't like to fly anymore. So, I come here when I feel nostalgic for a city I no longer get to see.

I understand that feeling.

To elaborate, I don't feel like the two of us are in New York having a conversation right now. In my heart, I believe you to be a woman I met in a jazz club in Paris in the 14th arrondissement thirty-five years ago. You look exactly like her. The features you share with this woman are uncanny. Which is why I feel so drawn to you. I think because you look like her, it gave me the confidence to come up to you and offer to buy you a drink. I'm normally a very shy person and keep to myself but with you I couldn't help but come over and say hello.

You said you like to get to know people.

I do.

But you consider yourself a shy person?

I am shy, but I also like people. I contain multitudes, my dear.

Yeah, you don't seem shy to me.

I appreciate that but I am. Really. I came up to you tonight because of my lady friend I mentioned, who you remind me of, who is sadly no longer with us. She died fifteen years ago in a car accident. And I know I'm not in Paris. I'm in Harlem, in a bar with a beautiful young woman who is old enough to be my granddaughter. And as much as I don't want to see the woman I fell so madly in love with all those years ago when I look at you, I can't help but do so and refuse to believe you're not her in some way.

But I'm not her.

I hear you, but in my heart I won't believe you aren't her until I've stepped out of this club tonight and have walked out into the street to probably be transported somewhere else on my way back home.

Kajal stayed quiet, not knowing how to respond to the old man. Samson kept his gaze on her, his posture relaxed and present. His face showed no readable sign for Kajal to interpret.

I've scared you.

No.

Then what are you thinking about?

I'm wondering what happens afterwards?

What happens when?

When you leave.

I become incredibly depressed. I go back home to my apartment and my cats. I take off my suit, go to bed, and wake up the next day with the craving to leave again. But I probably won't go out for a few days afterwards to be honest.

I feel like everybody nowadays wants to be somewhere different from where they are, said Kajal. No one I know seems to be happy.

Where would you rather be tonight?

I don't know.

You don't have anywhere you'd rather be than sitting next to an old man like me talking to you? This is where you want to be the most?

I don't know, maybe with my dad.

That's nice. That's not what I expected you to say. Have you not seen him in a while?

No. Not in some time.

Well, I'm sure you will see him soon.

Yes. Maybe.

Samson smiled.

I wish I had a daughter like you. My daughter's didn't want me around them much. But I don't think I was the best father to them.

Maybe you should tell them that.

I would. I've tried. They won't let me.

Kajal paused before asking her next question.

Can I ask you something?

Sure, anything, said Samson, whose face lit up when Kajal asked him this.

Did you see the snowfall yesterday?

Snow? When was there snow?

Yesterday. There was a heavy snowstorm a few days ago. Snow covered the entire city and now, as of this morning, it's all gone. When I woke up, there was no snow anywhere, and when I went to bed last night, snow covered the entire city. Even walking here, I couldn't even find slush on the sidewalk.

I don't believe I did see any snow yesterday. But you're saying you did?

Yes. I did.

Samson took a moment to himself.

Oh, I remember! No, I don't believe I saw any snow yesterday. If my memory serves me correctly, I was watching a bullfight at a bar somewhere uptown that reminds me of my time spent in Madrid!

Samson's joke brought a frown to Kajal's face. Samson cracked himself up at his joke and had to stop himself from laughing. But once he saw Kajal's face, he calmed down and apologized.

I'm sorry, I upset you.

You didn't upset me.

I did. I can tell. I just didn't expect that from myself. I'm rarely comfortable enough to make a joke and it felt good to laugh. I can feel how good it was in my stomach. It made me happy to say it but it saddens me it upset you.

It didn't, Kajal said, slightly annoyed.

Let me make it up to you. Let me buy you another drink.

No, I should be going.

I ruined it. You were going to stay longer, but I ruined it with my stupid joke. You liked me for a moment, didn't you? But my joke ruined the moment.

No, it's not that. I guess I just don't feel like laughing much lately. Things don't make much sense to me anymore. I feel like everything is changing.

What do you mean?

I don't know how to explain it.

Everything is always changing.

Yes, I guess I am just coming to terms with that.

I would never want to be young again. The things you kids worry about. Laughing is a beautiful thing, Carol. You should never suppress your laughter. I know what it's like to hear that when you feel the opposite, but sometimes we need to hear things we don't want to. And I feel it is my obligation as your elder to tell you to remember to laugh. Can you do that for me? Can you remember to laugh?

Kajal smiled at Samson, and said, Yes, I will. Thank you for the reminder.

Good, you have a beautiful smile by the way.

Thank you. But I should be going now. It's late.

Yes, you can go. I'll get your drinks for you.

Oh, no. You don't have to do that.

No, I want to. Think of it as my apology for my bad joke.

Are you sure?

Yes, please. I'm gonna get another drink before I go. I'll get your bill. Please let me do so. Make an old man happy.

Kajal thanked Samson and leapt off the stool. Samson stayed at the bar and signaled to the bartender to order another martini. As the bartender made his drink, he watched Kajal walk up the staircase to exit and disappear into the night.

Outside, it began to rain. Kajal didn't try to take cover or make any attempt to hurry back home. She embraced the rain falling down on her. And the dress. And her shoes. And her makeup. And let it do whatever damage it would as punishment for taking the dress out from its box.

When she arrived on Kareena's block, she noticed the magnolia tree. She had forgotten all about it when she left the apartment. It was covered entirely by the moon's light.

She couldn't see the tree's flowers or the beauty or the color any more. The tree's pedals that once had life were now shriveled and dying.

If the tree had a face, she'd be staring right at it. When she turned to go back inside, a single flower, the first of the leaves to fall, left from the highest branch and floated the distance between the tree's designated spot on the sidewalk, just missing Kajal's shoulder.

XVII

Merry Christmas from the President

Kajal didn't want to be alone anymore. She texted Dale the night of Christmas Eve and he woke Christmas morning to her message, saying she would come to his family's house for Christmas. She took until the last minute to text Dale because she knew in her mind she would go, because of Carol, and how Carol made her feel. And because she made the decision to go, she did not feel it necessary to text Dale and let him know she was coming until it was most necessary.

She had been drinking wine, watching a movie in Kareena's living room when she texted Dale. The buzz from the wine made it possible for her to reach out. Kajal did not think much time had passed since they had last spoken, busy with wrapping things up for the semester. But for Dale it had felt like a year had gone by. Each day he fought the urge to reach out to Kajal or look at her Instagram. He did not have the ability she had to compartmentalize the confusion he felt towards their separation. It was the not knowing what had changed regarding her feelings for Dale, for not including him in whatever she was going through, that hurt Dale the most. He did not have any answers or understanding for their separation. And it was the residual feelings from this lack of communication that sat with him like a void in his stomach, making him feel ill each day since he moved back home.

Before Dale read Kajal's text message, he was in the midst of a nightmare. In the dream, he was falling down a well. He had yet to learn how he had come across the well or how he had fallen into it. He had no cultural significance to a well. He wasn't sure if he had ever seen one up close in his life, so why he was dreaming of one he did not know. He had heard once, you could never dream of a face you have not seen in real life. Even if you interact with someone in your dreams who is no longer alive, or you met only once in passing, it allows you the opportunity to meet them again in your sleep. But there was no well in Dale's life he knew of that did not come from a book or a film he had seen. The well in his dream came from someone else's but he did not know whose. All he remembered when he came to, was that he was falling quickly down an endless shaft, and coming closer and closer to its bottom. And when in his dream he hit his head, he woke up.

When he woke up, he looked at his cell phone. He could not believe it when he saw Kajal's name on the front of his phone's screen with a pending text message, waiting for him to read it. He swiped right on the screen and read the message which stated in a diplomatic tone: *Your mom invited me over for Christmas. Can you pick me up from the train station?*

He was confused at first, but relieved to hear from Kajal. His mother had invited her over for Christmas?

He texted her back: *Sure. What time?* Ignoring the impulse to ask any more questions, and becoming more aware of the almond scent that protruded from the kitchen, underneath his closed door.

Kajal wanted to chat with Dale first before she arrived at his parent's house. Not long after he sent his message to her, she responded asking if she could call him. Dale suggested they talk when she gets there, but Kajal called him while he was still in bed. The call was the first he heard of her voice in weeks. The number appeared as an unknown caller, and the pitch in the voice of the caller was unfamiliar to him. He thought the call was from a telemarketer trying to spam him. He had almost hung up, but she said his name - *Dale* - in a broken tone that was familiar enough for him to recognize.

On the phone, Kajal seemed skeptical or slightly hesitant to come over. Like, even she didn't know why she was calling him. There was no big reveal in the conversation. Just an exchange of a few words to solidify the plans for the evening. Dale would pick her up at the LIRR station at 2PM and drop her off later that night, back at the station. Dale did not say this to Kajal, but he thought if things went well and she stayed later than expected, he'd drive her back home into the city.

Kajal did manage on their brief phone call to curate a list of boundaries for them to abide by. They could not sleep together. This was the big one. They could not kiss. They promised each other that neither she nor Dale would stay at each other's place's, no matter how well the day went. Dale promised he would stay sober enough to properly drive her to wherever she wanted to go.

Dale crawled out of bed and went down the staircase to the living room, and found his father alone in the kitchen wearing a Santa hat, a reindeer apron tied around his waist, standing in front of the stove, holding a spatula.

Dale stared at his father speechless for a few moments, before uttering the words *Good morning* to him, and looking past him to see if there was any coffee made.

Doug had not commented on the damages Dale made to the kitchen, as Dale expected he wouldn't. Doug blamed Dale's mother for the damages. She had made him the person he was, of course. Carol was more upset with Dale than Doug was, but still, they had not talked about what had happened.

Your mother went to pick up your brother and his new girlfriend from the airport, said Doug.

So, they are coming, asked Dale.

Yeah. Cal texted her last night or this morning. Whatever the hell time it was. Said he'd be arriving around 11.

What's his girlfriend's name again?

No idea, said Doug and then flipped one of the keto flapjacks over on its other side on the frying pan.

Dale took a mug out from the cabinet and poured himself a large cup of coffee. Aside from the cracked LED screen on the refrigerator, everything looked relatively the same as when he first arrived. Dale looked at his father, as he sipped his coffee. His father hadn't made eye contact with him since he entered the kitchen that morning, but that was relatively normal of him to do. Dale sipped his coffee first in the kitchen observing his father inspect the pancakes frying on the stove. Then he opened the screen door to the backyard and stepped outside. He closed the door quickly behind him, trying to stop the brisk chill from entering the warm house. A fast breeze made its way up Dale's arms and legs, making him shiver, and he held onto his coffee mug tight so that it wouldn't fall.

He looked at the street, past the white gated fence, and sipped his warm coffee. It was always the same view with a different sky. The street was empty as if no other family lived on the block. This Christmas morning, the sky was cloudy above Dale, and the steam from his coffee mug blew erratically in the wind. In that moment, Dale did not feel the anxiety he had felt all month; he was excited to celebrate the holiday he had come, in his older age, to be nostalgic for. He was happy Kajal was coming over though had no idea what to expect when she finally arrived. But he was excited to see her and that excitement eliminated the dread he'd been experiencing all month since he moved back home with his parents.

Gazing at the sky Dale's mind shifted to a calmness. And, though he did not know why, Dale realized he was happy.

Later, Dale was getting dressed when he heard his mother's car come up through the front driveway. Dale climbed down the staircase for the second time that morning to greet his brother and new girlfriend, who were now standing, chatting inside the kitchen. Dale realized as he climbed down the staircase he had not seen his brother in over a year.

Cal was taller than Dale now. Dale's little brother was not little anymore. He was sun-kissed from the other side of the ocean. The grit and color on his brother's skin showed Cal's adventures abroad that Dale could not have had here, at home.

He heard their foreign voices first before turning the corner and seeing the back of his brother's head, which was angled downward so that he could speak to his mother properly. Nobody noticed Dale when he entered the living room. His family continued their chatter, introducing their new selves into each other's old lives. Dale walked through the living room to greet them.

Cal's girlfriend, the poet, noticed Dale first. She nudged Cal with her eyes, telling him to turn and greet his brother.

Hey man, Dale said with a smile, opening his arms for a hug.

This is Kit, by the way, said Cal.

Nice to meet you, Dale, grinned Kit.

Hi, smiled Dale and shook her hand.

It's a full house, Carol shouted teary-eyed, making Dale and Cal uncomfortable.

I have to piss, said Cal, changing the subject and running towards the hallway, the bathroom still where it used to be?

Of course, said Carol, sucking her teeth. She was excited to have her family home. How was the flight, she turned and asked Kit.

As good as it could get, said Kit. We visited some friends in Milan and then flew to New York from there. But we had to stop for 12 hours in Germany for some reason. We would have been here a day earlier if it wasn't for a cancellation, but there were no other flights due to the holidays.

You must be exhausted, said Carol.

Yeah, I wouldn't mind a nap and a shower, said Kit laughing. We've practically been living in airports for the past twenty-four hours.

You can sleep in Cal's old bedroom, if you'd like, until everyone arrives.

Cool. Cool. Cool. Cool. Cool.

Carol took Kit down the hallway, where Cal had fled to. Dale looked at the clock. He would need to leave to pick up Kajal soon from the train station. He wanted to text her but didn't want to hear from her that she had changed her mind by deciding not to come. It would ruin his mood for the rest of the day if he read a message like that from Kajal. If she wasn't coming, he thought, she'd tell him that herself. If he didn't say anything, he thought, things for the day would go as planned.

Dale watched his father stack the keto pancakes he made onto a single plate by the stove and place them at the center of the dining room table, and took a moment to himself to marvel in awe at what he had created. In that moment, Dale recognized another mask he and his father both shared and it was that of a creative spirit. He saw in his father that of a creator.

Dale got to the train station early and parked in front of the station's municipal parking lot. The morning rush had come and gone. He recognized the familiar shape, size, and height of the singular body that walked the platform alone to the staircase. He saw no details of her face, what mood she was in, or what she was wearing, but he knew that walk. He knew it was her.

Dale wore his favorite green wool sweater along with a pair of brown Brooks Brother pants, which he saved for only special occasions. It was an outfit Kajal splurged on buying him when they were young, when neither of them had any money. And he knew it might make her happy to see him wear the outfit; hoping it would help provoke a good first impression.

Kajal opened the passenger side door and got in.

Hey, said Dale, smiling.

Hey, said Kajal, looking down at her feet with a shy face that exuded a sadness that made Dale nervous.

He didn't know what words to use that were appropriate to say to her. He felt such an emotional distance in that moment from Kajal that it shocked him. It was foreign for him to feel this distant from her. He never felt like a stranger around Kajal, even in the first moment they met. When they first met, it felt like they knew each other for a thousand years. He was afraid that showing too much emotion would make her run away and catch the next train back to the city. But still his tears fell. As he cried, she stayed seated next to him, silent. She showed no sign of leaving but grew impatient. There were no words Dale could utter, just bottled-up feelings that needed release. He cried, and she sat still in the car beside him, quiet.

She was uncomfortable by the emotion he was showing her. She felt it to be unfair somehow. She was hoping he would help her get through the day and not make it about them. But Dale didn't know how to be around Kajal and not make it about them. She felt irritated by his emotions because she didn't understand them. She could not hold what she was holding inside of her and give space for his feelings too.

I'm sorry, said Dale, finally breaking the silence as he wiped his tears with the sleeve of his wool sweater.

Here, said Kajal. She took a piece of tissue paper out from her purse and handed it to Dale.

Dale slowly reached over the center console of his mother's car to kiss Kajal, who kissed him back. It was a friendly kiss, almost platonic, between old lovers.

Let's not go to your parent's house right away, okay, requested Kajal.

Where do you want to go, then?

I don't know. I just don't think I can go there right now. Okay? I'm sorry.

Dale didn't want to argue with her. He felt any opposing view he expressed would make this house of cards come crumbling down. Quietly, he put the car in drive, and he drove down a random street and then down another one until he found himself on the highway going east, further into Long Island.

They didn't say a word to each other for a long time. There were no tears anymore, just bottled-up feelings for different reasons until a sedated silence came over them, and then it was calm in the car. From the residue of the silence, for the first time, things between them felt normal.

Dale didn't know how far he'd gone out. He didn't read the signs coming here. He just intuited where the water was and drove his best, hoping not to turn to ask Kajal to look at her phone for directions. They found themselves at an unfamiliar beach. Kajal had always liked the ocean. She couldn't swim, but she did her best thinking by the sea. He drove the car into a sanctioned-off spot in another municipal parking lot adjacent to the beach, and put the car in park. Both were afraid to speak, not wanting to break the peace that had been created between them.

Secretly, Dale had grown disappointed about not being with his family. He found it selfish of Kajal to take him away from his family on a holiday he had wanted to celebrate with them. If he had taken her away from her family on a religious holiday she would have resented him forever.

Kajal stepped out of the car first and walked to the wooden split-rail fence where sand started to appear on the white concrete path leading to the beach's entry-way. In an attempt to shift her thoughts, Kajal read the list of rules for the beach to have something to look at as she waited for Dale to catch up.

Dale stepped out of the car. With the boost of oxygen he felt from the ocean air he immediately felt lighter and could think more clearly.

There was no one on the beach besides them. They walked together where the sea broke, and both avoided getting their feet wet in the cold crashing waves. There were houses up the hill, past the sand dunes that separated the beach from the town. They both talked about what they thought the insides of the houses looked like, and each made up scenarios for what they thought was going on inside each one.

Maybe they're just waking up now to gifts under the tree!

Can you imagine living in a house like that? On a hill, on the beach, overlooking the ocean.

Maybe one day we will. I always wanted the best for us.

I know you did. You always had big dreams for us. I always respected that about you. I loved how you cared for us.

It was easy because I loved you.

Dale quietly allowed his fingers to brush past Kajal's. They were happy. He relaxed and started to make her laugh. He loved her laugh. Behind them, waves crashed along the beaches' groyne, making sounds similar to that of lightning. Dale asked about Kajal's mother. Kajal asked about Dale's writing. All the while, seagulls were flying above their heads, with live fish in their mouths, to be taken to a nest somewhere safe, far deep along the shore, to feed their young.

She stopped speaking and touched his arm and he turned his body slightly towards her. She fluttered her eyelashes. He didn't want to make a move towards her and make her angry with him. He felt that he had finally come to a place with her they both wanted. It had been a long time since both felt safe around the other. He didn't want to ruin that. Not today. And, yet, the attention she gave him confused him and made him want to take a risk, because, he felt, she wanted him to do so. He wondered, though, where this attention was when she had entered the car, when she sat across from him at the diner, so detached. They were already breaking the rules they had made on the phone earlier that morning. He was so happy to touch her, though, and be touched by her. He loved her. He knew that. He had always known that but had forgotten, not just over the last few weeks but the last couple of years of their relationship. Before the years they lived together in their first apartment in Brooklyn. Before she went to grad school. Before her father passed away. Dale had taken Kajal for granted, not knowing life without her, and now he knew what life was without her and he didn't want to live life that way. He knew what Kajal's absence felt like in his life now and he knew they were growing apart, and no longer the children that fell in love so long ago and he regretted not being wise enough to understand that without her having to tell him. He wished he had the foresight to know what she could not say. He wished he could make her life easier, and do for her what was difficult for them both, by taking on whatever burden that came for her away off her shoulders. He wished he had the strength to walk away to let her grieve, instead of fighting her to upkeep whatever it was, that he could not articulate in words, that he needed from her.

He kissed her lips. Blood rushed to their brains as their tongues explored the insides of each other's mouths, the two only wanting to go deeper inside of the other. He took Kajal's hand and placed it over the bulge that had now swelled inside his pants and he told her he wanted her on the sand dunes, and she pushed him away, stopping him. Her eyelids fluttered as if she were about to pass out.

Stop, she said to herself.

What?

Hold on. Hold on. I need to sit.

Kajal sat hard on her bottom on the sand, laughing. Dale sat down beside her. They were confused but happy.

What is it, he asked her, grinning.

Nothing, she said, trying to catch her breath.

He was so happy he pushed his body deeper into the sand not knowing another way to express his joy, forgetting the clothes he had on, and the distance that had ever formed between them. He screeched a sound from between his clenched teeth. He wanted to scream his joy towards the sky. He wanted this feeling to last forever.

Kajal stayed sitting upright. Her breath finally caught up with her, and she was calm and done with her laughing. She focused her eyes on a fading cargo ship in the distance and imagined herself on it, alone, riding with the exports, wanting to be free. She wanted to be shipped like a package to some faraway unknown place.

Dale drove his mother's car back into her driveway and put the car in park. The couple sat still for a moment longer in silence. Both were hesitant to go inside the house, embarrassed, assuming everyone would be discussing why they were delayed to partake in the Christmas evening festivities. Dale had not told his mother he would not be returning immediately after picking up Kajal. While they were driving back to the house, Carol texted him, and then called him but he didn't respond to either, hesitant to explain himself.

The presents sat untouched under the Christmas tree, waiting for Dale and Kajal to come and help open them. But there was no semblance of a celebration going on. No music nor any rushing around in the kitchen, with empty bottles of wine on the counter to be dumped for recycling. Dale and Kajal entered the house, and it felt like they were ghosts visiting a new world and the world they knew had left them behind.

They walked inside the house together and found everybody standing in front of the TV inside the living room, watching the news. A female news anchor spoke fervently to the camera.

No one turned their heads to check and see who'd come inside. Dale saw Kit was crying as she stood beside Cal, wiping tears from her eyes.

Hey, guys, said Dale, breaking the silence. He dropped the car keys on the dining room table, hoping the sound would get their attention.

What's up, he tried again.

Hey, said Carol, finally noticing them. She walked over to Dale and Kajal from the living room and hugged them both.

Merry Christmas, said Kajal, smiling.

Hi Kajal, honey, said Carol, it's nice to see you, turning her attention back to the TV. I'm glad you came.

What's everyone watching? Asked Dale.

Oh, it's nothing.

Hey Cal, said Kajal.

What's up?

How is living abroad? Asked Kajal with a smile, happy to see him.

Good. Good. It's cool, you know? I like Prague, actually.

Everything alright? Asked Dale, nodding his head in the direction of Kit.

Oh, yeah. She's fine.

I'm sorry we never came out to visit you, said Kajal. Grad school's been a bit much.

Yeah. For sure. Maybe you still can, unless this thing gets us, said Cal nodding his head in the direction of the television.

Don't say that, said Carol.

What's happening?

You haven't heard?

They're talking about some virus on the TV. It's all everyone's been talking about this morning. Apparently, it's in New York now, too. Might have been for some time.

A virus?

Yeah, they have a person in quarantine up in Westchester somewhere. People are saying the president should implement a lockdown or whatever.

The president of what?

America.

Because of one person? That's ridiculous, no?

It's not just one person, said Kit from the living room.

They think more than one person, has it?

Thousands. They think thousands of people could have it. Apparently, the hospitals are crazy right now.

Really, asked Kajal. It's strange no one at Columbia reported this.

The news reported it, but it didn't become a big story until now. Apparently, the president's cabinet had been breached months ago.

It's been here for a while, they think.

And they waited until the last minute to say something?

Why talk about it now on Christmas of all days, I wonder.

We were just in Italy, said Kit, walking over to Dale and Kajal, who were still in the dining room. Everything seemed out of order, but I thought it was because of the holiday. Apparently, they're recording close to 50 deaths in Rome within the past 48 hours, and they think it's linked to the virus.

I mean, 50 people died in Rome? Is that terribly unusual, asked Cal. I mean, how many people die in New York each day?

But not from the same thing and within that short period of time? Forty-eight hours isn't a very long span of time.

And more people are showing up to the hospitals in New York with similar symptoms?

Yes.

What are the symptoms?

According to the news, the guy, now in quarantine, had symptoms similar to that of the flu. But it's not the flu, apparently.

So, how do you know if you have it?

You don't.

I'm sure being on a plane didn't help him.

It's the flu, they're saying. It's just like the flu except you can't breathe or something like that, parroted Doug. They think the guy had an infection. No one knows what they're talking about.

They want the president to implement a lockdown because they don't know how to differentiate the virus that's spreading here from the one in other countries. The president's saying he's not concerned.

Well, that's concerning.

What if they cancel flights and we can't get home? Asked Kit.

That'll never happen, said Cal. Don't be ridiculous.

You can always stay here! We have plenty of space, screamed Carol.

They're saying the guy is in a coma now, said Doug, after hearing an update from the female news anchor on the television. They don't know if he is gonna make the night.

It's that serious?

The guy in Westchester?

Yeah.

Wow, that's so sad.

Merry Christmas everyone!

Why are we watching this? Turn something else on.

What if we all have it?

That would be a great way to end the night! *Died of the flu.*

Does anyone want a glass of wine? Why don't we open some presents!

He has a wife and two children.

That's terrible.

My father died in a hospital. Why didn't the news channels report his death? Asked Carol.

How do they know he won't die because of the disease and not some other secondary illness, asked Kajal.

They don't know. They don't know anything. But that's why they're talking about lockdowns because they think it might be linked to whatever that's spreading abroad. Because of the symptoms the guy had. They would only take these precautions if they were sure.

Who would take precautions? The president is a moron.

It's probably not that big of a deal, said Cal. If it's just like the flu, the flu kills thousands of people each year. If it's in New York, everybody should just wash their hands. I don't see what the big deal is.

The guy came from Italy on vacation, exclaimed Kit.

Yeah, see? We came from Italy. We're not experiencing any symptoms of a disease. We were in the airport for hours. We're not sick.

Yeah, not now.

What do you mean?

Symptoms take two or three days to show themselves, said Doug.

Well, how many days has it been?

So what if there is a virus? It's not like the world is gonna shut down or something.

It may.

I doubt it. When has anything like that ever happened before? That's an absurd thing to say.

What about the plague? The Spanish flu?

In our lifetime, Kit. Technology and medicine are way more advanced than they were back then. There's no way the government would let something like the plague ever happen to us. Even with this president. We're living in a more advanced time!

I think we're fucked, said Kit. It's the end of things as we know it.

Can we just mind our words everybody? Asked Carol, to the group. It is still a holiday.

Yeah, everybody! No cursing until tomorrow.

Always sarcastic.

They're saying the virus originated in a meat market somewhere in Asia. Apparently, it's been known for quite some time now. But they had no lockdowns implemented and it spread to different cities from people flying in and out of the country, said Doug. They're mentioning specifically Italy.

Of course they are.

What if this is the end of world?

It could be, said Dale. I feel more calm than I expected.

Nothing's going to happen guys. It should be illegal to show this kind of stuff on a holiday. Ruining everyone's good mood. It comes one day a year. And it's one guy, not everybody in America. I bet if he was black, no one would care.

I think he is black.

We should all just relax and enjoy ourselves, said Carol, turning off the television.

Let's open some gifts, huh? Carol continued. I think we've all had enough. Whatever will happen will happen. At least we have each other. Here, Kajal, this one's for you. Carol picked up a wrapped box from under the tree and handed it to her. Whatever happens we'll get through it together.

Can we turn back on the television, asked Kit, we should stay informed. I want to see what happens to the guy and his family.

That's not going to help anything, hun. It's not an episode of CSI.

Did they say precisely what the symptoms were the guy was experiencing? Asked Kajal.

I mean just general symptoms at first, like a fever and cough.

We should leave, Kit whispered to Cal.

Why, asked Cal, irritated.

We could have it, Cal. We could be infecting everyone here.

I don't think you are, honey, reassured Carol whispering from behind her. We should all just relax and listen to music!

Doug indulged his wife and turned on a Christmas radio station from his stereo system in the living room. The scent of premade sugar cookies exuded out from the oven, and a timer went off. Carol picked up another wrapped box, and gave it to Dale, who reached over the other wrapped gifts on the floor to take it from her.

The cookies are ready, said Carol.

Thanks, said Dale, grabbing his gift.

Kit, here's a gift for you, said Carol who continued to hand out presents.

Doug, could you get the cookies from the oven?

Does anyone want an espresso?

Put the cookies on the ceramic platter in the cabinet, the one with the pink nutcracker on it!

Kajal turned to Dale.

What about my mom, whispered Kajal.

What do you mean?

What if there really is a virus? I wouldn't want anyone to give it to her.

I mean, we're not showing any symptoms. I'm sure it'll be fine. No one knows now what is going to happen

Kajal was afraid to tell Dale what she'd been seeing around her mother's apartment, on the drive to the cemetery, worried it might in some way be linked to whatever was spreading.

You can call your mom if you want, Dale continued, see how she's doing? Would that make you feel better? Ask her if she's heard the news, tell her to be careful. Make sure your brother knows too so that he doesn't go out and give it to her.

Right, said Kajal.

It'll be fine, Kajal, said Dale.

Yeah.

What could possibly go wrong?

Past midnight, Dale drove Kajal back to Kareena's apartment. When they arrived in Manhattan, it was too late for her to send Dale back home to Long Island alone. She still cared for Dale. She wanted, still, to take care of him.

Why don't you park and come upstairs, offered Kajal.

Is that a good idea? I can drive home. I'm fine.

No, come up. It's too late. You can sleep on the couch. There's enough room in the apartment for the two of us.

Dale was happy she asked but disappointed she was committed to maintaining some semblance of the boundaries set from the morning, though they had broken them by kissing on the beach. With Dale's family, it felt like things had settled into their old ways. She started to speak to him like they were a couple, again. Like, she was in love with him again. Like, the past few weeks had not happened.

He didn't want to challenge her and drove his parent's car down the block and parked it on the corner in a spot just out of reach of a fire hydrant. He stepped out of his car and locked it. It was cold out. The street was beautifully lit by the tall street lights. A small flurry of snow began.

He walked up the block to her. Kajal was standing in front of a magnolia tree, waiting for him. She was looking at the tree and holding her jacket's collar tight around her neck to protect herself from the cold. Her face looked sad, he noticed. Dale followed Kajal's gaze and looked at the tree. Her interest in the tree made him interested. He noticed the tree's flowers were brown and shriveled.

Everything alright, he asked her.

Yeah, said Kajal and then she turned her back from the tree and walked up the steps to the apartment building's main entrance.

The couple entered the apartment together. Kajal turned on the lights. Dale noticed how much of a mess the apartment was. Dale knew it was very unlike Kajal to live in a cluttered space with clothes on the floor and shelves with plants that had vines that carried their length down onto the floor. There was hardly any room to walk around the apartment without stepping on something as you passed it. He couldn't believe Kajal would be staying here alone. She hated clutter and mess. Even at parties, she was the one to clean up the dishes, ending the night in the kitchen alone, scrubbing everyone's dirty plates and silverware.

Kajal disappeared into the bathroom for a moment, and Dale walked into the living room to see the couch where he was supposedly spending the night. He removed a golden dress that was lying unfolded on the middle cushion of the sofa and moved it to the arm of the couch to rest. Though it wasn't perfect, he was still glad to be out of his parents' house and with Kajal.

Kajal came out of the bathroom. Dale could see how tired she was then. She had washed her face with soap and water but missed some of the mascara under her eyelids and could see it crawling down her cheeks, making it look like she had been crying.

So, this is where you've been staying, asked Dale.

Yeah. Why, asked Kajal, opening her eyes momentarily to answer Dale's question.

It's big. Messy.

I'm gonna go to sleep.

Okay.

You can sleep on the couch.

Yeah, I think I found it.

Okay. Goodnight. Thanks for the ride home.

You okay?

Yeah, said Kajal without ever turning around to face him.

Dale watched her disappear down the hallway and felt their distance again. It was a constant push and pull with her. He could never keep up with her ever changing emotions.

He was slightly disappointed she had not asked him to join her in bed after thinking the day had gone so well. Something was different in her persona; the moods she embodied at the beach and at his parents' house were gone, and she gave no effort to indulge him in explaining why. It was like she didn't care about how she was messing with his heart.

He turned off all the ceiling lights but left on a small lamp by the bookshelf in the living room, walked up to the window, and looked at the magnolia tree outside on the sidewalk. He didn't think much of the tree, but how it was positioned in its sanctioned corner on the sidewalk made him feel as if it was looking straight at him.

He noticed the slight flurry of snow he saw falling earlier had thickened, and he watched it fall and cover every inch of the sidewalk.

Dale slipped his shoes off and took off his belt, and pulled down his pants and laid down on the couch. He had forgotten to turn off the lamp. He wasn't tired but stayed put, wanting the lamp to turn itself off. Feeling lazy, he decided to stay where he was on the couch, ignore the light, and look up at the ceiling, hoping to drift fast asleep, but his mind was racing with thoughts rendered by the hour-long drive to the city.

A noise came from inside the kitchen. It was a sound similar to a pot or pan moving inside the steel sink. Dale sat up on the couch to see. If the sound was made during the daytime or in a familiar space, he wouldn't have given it a second thought. But he could see the kitchen's dark entrance and was afraid it was a mouse that would find itself inside the living room when he was sleeping. He felt his mind playing tricks on him, and he sensed the presence of someone inside the kitchen, moving around in the dark.

Dale knew Kajal had not walked past him. As far as he knew, she was fast asleep inside Kareena's bedroom unless he had drifted into a light sleep, and she walked past him, unnoticed.

He said Kajal's name out loud to make sure.

Dale stood up from the couch and waited to hear another sound come before entering.

He took a few cautious steps toward the kitchen, passing the tall windows in the living room. He poked his head inside the kitchen and saw a still life of a regular everyday kitchen, caked in shadow, except for the single light that shined onto the stove from the streetlight outside on the sidewalk.

Dale stepped forward and put his whole body inside the kitchen and stood there for a moment, fitting into the still life, becoming an inanimate object in the shadows, like the dirty dishes Kajal left inside the sink.

There was nothing there.

Dale stepped out of the kitchen, and looked across the living room.

A presence was standing by the window. Dale stared at the old man first in shock, then in utter confusion. This was not a stranger in the apartment, but someone he knew well.

Hussein's ghost turned his attention away from the light and looked at Dale. Dale noticed Hussein's milky white form in the living room and tried to understand what he was seeing. Hussein moved his lips, trying to speak, but no audible sound would come out. He stopped and tried again to talk, but Dale could not hear him. There was a light, a bright light that came from the outside. Dale couldn't have seen its source or what it was, or where it was coming from, but at that moment, every flower on the magnolia tree was back and whole, in its bright pink colors as Kajal first saw it on her first morning waking up inside the apartment.

Hussein tried to force sound out of his mouth. It was clear he wanted to communicate with Dale, but nothing more than a hoarse whisper left his throat. The apparition tried again, with more force this time. It looked to Dale like it hurt him to speak. Dale could see tears coming out of his eyes. The veins in his neck bulged from the tension of trying to force out words. Hussein's eyes widened, and his mouth was large. Dale could almost put his entire head inside the circumference of the apparition's mouth. He could see it's teeth fall in a straight line all the way back to his throat.

If Dale could hear whatever words Hussein was attempting to say, all he would hear was the rupture of a voice screaming.

The veins in Hussein's neck softened, his eyes deflated back inside his skull, and the light from the tree behind him dimmed and the leaves again were brown and shrivelled.

He took one step towards Dale, trying to get closer, reaching out his hand. Dale took one step back, afraid. He fell onto the kitchen floor, hit his head and passed out, finally falling asleep.

XVIII
March 2020

He never left. They never talked about him leaving or staying or their time apart. He just stayed and neither of them spoke about it. They rang in the new year together, staying in from the cold and fell asleep before midnight. Dale was angry at Kajal, but kept that to himself. He did not feel safe enough to bring up the topic of their separation, though when he felt weak he would try; always afraid bringing up their past would cause a fight or send him home packing. Any conversation Kajal was uncomfortable having, she'd shut down. And he dealt with it because he was more comfortable living on eggshells around Kajal then living back at home. She was his best option.

Kajal woke up one morning wrapped in Kareena's blanket, tired, and with her throat aching. She checked her phone, scrolling through Instagram. The virus was trending. Europe was trending. Twenty more deaths were reported during the night. The man in quarantine now long dead.

Kajal coughed and tried to get out whatever was stuck inside her throat. Maybe if she swallowed enough spit the mucus will go down, she thought. She coughed again, got out of bed, and put on her pajamas. There was barely enough light to see in front of her.

Kajal switched on the flashlight setting on her phone, and used it to guide her to the bathroom. Kajal put down the toilet seat and sat to pee. She scrolled through Instagram again and stayed on the bowl longer than she had intended to, distracted by what stories were trending regarding the virus. Friends of hers stuck in airports, flying back to their home countries to be with their families. Schools were shutting down across the country. Kajal looked at her school's email address for news regarding updates for next semester but there was no news yet.

Kajal flushed and washed her hands and then washed her face with a face scrub she found, and spit out another wad of green mucus into the sink. It was then she remembered Dale had separated himself from her to sleep on the couch, to try and not get sick.

The events of the year quickly unfolded in her mind like that of a flashback scene in a superhero comic book. It was a year ago this month she had buried her father.

Kajal let out a deep sigh over the bathroom sink. She didn't have the stamina to get into any serious conversation with Dale. All he wanted to do was talk about their relationship. Which was the last thing Kajal wanted to talk about. There were bigger things going on in the world. She found him selfish for wanting to talk about them, while people less fortunate were dying from a disease that had no cure; and she was afraid now she may have it. She could see Dale was upset and hurt by how he felt she treated him over the past few months. She eventually told him she had been unfaithful but that it was nothing serious. That it was only a kiss between her and Kareena. She left out Marc and the fucking that happened on the bed both her and Dale now sleep on together. He was hurt but because it was another woman and not another man he eventually forgave her.

Though she was complicit in the indecision in Dale staying with her, she felt resentment towards Dale for not sticking to their word and for both of them not being strong enough to go their separate ways after Christmas.

Kajal flushed the toilet again, stepped out of the bathroom and walked down the hallway, through the corridor, into the living room. There was a fatigue pending inside her, that made the walk from the bathroom to the living room seem longer than it was.

Slightly out of breath, Kajal walked up to the couch to find Dale in his white t-shirt and boxer shorts, asleep in the same position he had always slept in when they lived together. Kajal stood over him. Dale's legs were curled like he was kneeling, each of his hands placed on the other, laying gently in front of his mouth. She wouldn't have been able to tell that he was breathing if it were not for the subtle ebb and flow coming from behind his white t-shirt.

She noticed the hair on his legs and how it had thickened over the years. Thick, wiry hair scattered, with a consistent pattern, throughout both of Dale's long white legs. Somewhere inside these changes she recognized the 17 year old she fell in love with.

Kajal walked into the kitchen and turned on the stove light that gave the small room a welcoming glow. She grabbed a teapot and filled it with water, turned on the stove, removed a tea bag from the cabinet, placed it gently inside the mug, and waited for the tea kettle to whistle. There was a stir from inside the living room. Dale shifted positions on the couch. Kajal looked up from her tea mug and saw Dale's foot extending over the arm of the couch, hanging mid-air like a piece of fruit at the end of the longest branch on a beautiful tree.

The teakettle began to whistle, and Kajal silenced it before the sound woke up Dale. She poured the boiling water inside the mug with a tea bag, she squeezed a few drops of lemon juice from an already cut piece, added honey, and sat down in the armchair in the living room next to Dale.

Kajal could feel a stream of cold liquid running down her leg. She jumped in place, staying within the confines of the armchair. She had fallen asleep for what felt like a moment or two, but an hour had passed. The mug with her tea had fallen over and was now lying pathetically on her thigh, followed by the shadow of a damp circle growing within the fabric of her pajama pants.

She stood up quickly, walked over to the kitchen, grabbed a towel, and squeezed the dry fabric over the soaked portion of her pant leg. A flush from the bathroom was heard, followed by the sound of a door opening. Dale appeared at the side entrance of the kitchen. He found Kajal bent over, focused on dabbing the fresh towel on her leg.

Spilled your tea, he asked.

Yeah, said Kajal, annoyed that he had to mention it, and she turned her head upwards to look at him.

How did you sleep? Asked Kajal.

She heard her own voice. It had come out hoarse and bare and it surprised her. She was hesitant to speak more, afraid to allow Dale to hear what she sounded like.

Alright, I guess. I woke up a few times in the night, said Dale.

Sorry about that.

It's alright. How are you feeling?

Im alright, she said coughing.

You don't sound alright, said Dale. I should have grabbed it from you.

What? Asked Kajal.

Your mug. But I had to pee.

It's okay. It's my fault.

I knew it might fall, though.

It's okay.

Your voice doesn't sound too good, Kajal.

My throat hurts.

Do you feel sick?

Definitely seems so, she said, annoyed.

Well, how are you feeling?

Heavy chested. Headache. My throat is soar.

It worsened overnight?

Yeah.

Dale paused, stopping himself from saying something he might regret.

Do you need any help with the floor? asked Dale, changing the subject.

What?

The tea.

Dale grabbed the roll of paper towels from the counter, trying to be overly helpful, hoping Kajal would notice. He walked over to the armchair to clean up any tea that might have spilled onto the floor.

Only a little bit, he said, bending down to clean up whatever was there. All good, he continued, standing up.

Kajal coughed up another wad of green mucus and spat it out into the tea mug she was using. Gross, she said. She walked to the kitchen faucet, disgusted with herself, and coughed again, trying to subdue the volume of her cough with the sound of running water. But Dale could hear how bad her congestion was from the living room, and the sound of running water did nothing to hide it.

That doesn't sound too good, he said.

Twenty more deaths were reported because of the virus.

You don't have whatever they had, Kajal, reassured Dale.

You should go. You're going to get sick.

Is that what you want me to do? You want me to leave?

What's the alternative? We both die.

Stop being ridiculous.

Kajal had to cough again but tried to suppress it but it didn't work. Her face turned red from the force of the cough, and she had to arch her body over the kitchen counter to let it out, the cough prevented her from standing up straight. The only thing Dale could do was stand beside her and watch. He put his hand on her back to help, to show support, but she shrugged him away due to the discomfort of his touch. On top of the coughing, Dale's presence only made her feel claustrophobic, and Dale touching her then only made things worse.

I'm sorry. I just don't feel like being touched right now, she said.

Maybe I'll make you some more tea?

No. I just want to shower, said Kajal, wiping phlegm off the side of her mouth and washing it away in the sink.

Okay, he said.

You should consider leaving. Seriously. You're gonna get sick.

How do I know I'm not already sick, questioned Dale.

She couldn't argue with him. Kajal walked towards the bathroom without responding. In the bathroom, she turned on the showerhead and waited for the water to heat. Within seconds, steam filled the walls of the bathroom, and Kajal undressed. She stepped inside the shower, and let the hot water hit her chest and run over her nose, allowing any excess snot to run down her body and into the drain.

There was a knock on the door, and Dale stepped inside before Kajal could respond. She covered herself with her hands in reaction to Dale entering, though she was already covered by the shower curtain.

I'm just leaving this here for you, said Dale, it's on the sink.

Okay. Thank you, said Kajal in a near helpless tone.

She was surprised to feel exposed when he entered without her granting him permission. If Dale tried to come into the shower with her, she wouldn't have allowed it. But a part of her wanted him in the shower with her. To hold each other in the steam and catch up on their days like they used to.

Kajal heard the door close shut, and her heart sank. She moved the curtain aside to see what was behind it and saw a fresh cup of tea on the bathroom sink and a small plate holding a chocolate dipped biscotti.

Later, Kajal walked out of the bathroom with her towel wrapped tightly around her torso. Dale cleaned up the kitchen a bit and straightened the living room. Kajal thought he looked handsome, cleaning. For a moment, she forgot this was not their apartment, that this was not their life, and that this was not their year.

Hey, said Dale.

Hey.

How are you feeling?

The shower was nice. Thanks for the tea.

Sure.

The two said nothing for a moment.

I know now is not a good time, began Dale, unable to control himself.

From the kitchen, a notification for an email dinged on Kajal's phone.

Hold on a minute, said Kajal, interrupting Dale as he was about to speak further. She ran into the kitchen and grabbed her phone from the top of the counter where it was charging.

Sorry, you were saying, continued Kajal, coming back into the living room, keeping her eyes focused on her cell phone's screen and using her index finger to scroll through her email.

I was just wondering if I should...

Hold on, she interrupted again.

What is it, Kajal, said Dale, slightly annoyed.

An email from the school. Hold on... sorry.

What? What is it, asked Dale, seeing her face he had grown worried. He stood up from the arm of the couch he'd been sitting on and walked closer to where Kajal was standing, now distraught. She finished reading the email before responding. Dale grew anxious as he waited, the look on her face; nervous something had happened to her mother or to one of her friend's. As he waited for Kajal to find her words, Dale prepared for the worst.

Kajal, what happened?

They canceled all indoor classes for next semester.

What? What do you mean?

It's all virtual. For the foreseeable future.

What is virtual?

There are no indoor classes next semester. Everything's online for school.

What does that mean, exactly? I'm sorry. I'm not understanding. Is that such a bad thing? I think that's happening everywhere no?

I can't go to campus anymore for class.

Okay, so what?

You don't understand, said Kajal. You never understand.

Kajal had to take the phone away from her face to cough. Her face turned red from the force of it and for a moment, it looked as if she couldn't breathe.

Oh my god, said Kajal, coming out of a coughing fit. When her body finally allowed her to take a moment to breathe, she fell over her leg and stumbled backwards.

Kajal! Dale screamed. He went to catch her but she caught herself. But feeling lightheaded she sat down on the couch and rested her head in her arms.

Why don't you rest, Kajal? It's not that big of a deal about the school. The world is changing. This is only a small part of it.

You always need help understanding me. You never understood me. What a fucking waste, said Kajal, hyperventilating, sitting down on the couch now.

What's a waste? What are you so upset about?

Something had erupted from inside of her then. She threw her phone across the room, the phone just missing Dale's head and it hit the wall behind him, making a noticeable dent.

Dale watched Kajal scream in his direction. All the frustration she felt from this year she threw at him in one hoarse whisper. She opened her mouth wide towards him. No words had come out, just a silent growl. The veins in her neck swelled and her eyes grew wide in her sockets, just barely staying in. He watched her and stared at her teeth in a perfect line all the way to the back of her infected throat. If he could, he'd step right into her mouth, and solve both of their problems by allowing her to swallow him whole and eat him up.

Dale kept his distance and waited for her to calm down.

Finally, when her words were allowed to come through, she said, It's not fair! It's not fair! It's not fair! She screamed.

Kajal, what are you doing? You're acting insane.

It's not fair! It's not fair, she cried, pouting and stomping her legs on the floor like a child.

What's not fair? Dale asked her.

All of it. You hear me? All of it. I want to die! I just want to fucking die, she said, crying.

Dale said nothing and just looked at her, not knowing how to respond. He did not recognize her then. There was nothing he could think to do or say. He didn't know how to help her.

All of this was a waste. All of this was for nothing.

All of what? Asked Dale frustrated.

Papa...

Dale just looked at her quietly and then said: Why don't we go outside? We can go for a walk?

Kajal said nothing for a long time, staying still in her position, hyperventilating on the couch until her breathing normalized and she hunched over, weeping. She waited so long to respond that Dale thought she might not have heard his offer.

Kajal?

I don't...want...to go out...right now.

I think it could be good for you, Dale explained, softly.

I'm sick! Don't you hear me? I don't feel good! I don't feel good!

The conversation went on for some time. Kajal finally calmed down enough to call her mother and tell her about it. Her mother was the only person who could consistently make Kajal feel better. Ruksaana and Ayad heard about the virus on a Pakistani news channel and thought it was only happening there. They weren't aware that it was also in New York. Neither of them was worried, concerned, or felt that the virus could affect them. Kajal asked her mother how they were feeling, and neither of them felt ill or had any flu-like symptoms.

Ayad hadn't left his bedroom in over a week and, on hearing news of the virus, canceled any future attempt to do so. Instead of feeling dread about the virus or worried about the state of the world, Kajal's little brother started to feel like things had finally turned towards his favor since his father's passing. Now, there was no need to worry about getting a job, feeling pressured into achieving a respectable career, or going anywhere outside his bedroom. He could now, without guilt, smoke weed in his mother's house for eternity and look outside his bedroom window and not wonder what was going on or who had it better because the competition was over. Everybody's lives now would be the same for the foreseeable future.

Kajal and Ruksaana decided it was best for Kajal to stay at Kareena's until she felt better. In the meantime, Ruksaana would get in touch with Blanche. When Kajal told her mother that Dale was with her, she was relieved that her daughter was not alone. She recommended they stay together and not fight, and that Kajal cook him her best attempt at her chicken salan, so that they can eat properly.

While Kajal was on the phone, Dale sat in the armchair patiently, not too far away, listening to Kajal speak to her mother in Urdu. He knew they were speaking about him on the phone. Dale did not hint to Kajal that he knew this. Her tone felt like it did not hold the weight of the scene that came earlier. He did not know where the screaming woman went, that he had just encountered, a few moments ago. She seemed soft, now, caring almost. He continued to look down at his cell phone in the armchair, scrolling with his finger through Instagram while listening to their conversation, waiting to hear his name again, hoping that it would come up.

He assumed being mentioned was a good thing and thought she wouldn't have wanted him there if she had not mentioned him. He surmised her telling him to leave earlier, she did not mean, but rather, was a bid for connection through a self deprecating lens; a test maybe he had passed. But since he did not speak Urdu, there was no sure way of him knowing.

Kajal's conversation with her mother ended, and she thought next about calling Kareena. It had been weeks since Kajal reached out and now she wanted to know if she could stay at the apartment or if the virus had changed Kareena's plans. She had not told Kajal if she would be coming back. The last thing she wanted to find out now was that Kareena was returning to the States to stay at her apartment for good, leaving her and Dale stranded together with nowhere to go.

Where could they go? She thought. She wouldn't live with Dale and his parents in Long Island. If she did, it would have to be a last resort.

Kajal looked in Dale's direction and watched him, sitting in the armchair, with a contempt she knew to be unfair but blamed him anyway for the current state of things. He was the outlet for her anger. She didn't have the language to articulate her emotions properly without feeling a sense of shame or guilt to help suppress them, which turned those feelings into rage, helping her flee any sort of real or difficult conflict the two may have.

She didn't want to show Dale her rage but she couldn't help herself. She saw how unfair her feelings were towards him, but on the other hand she couldn't help but express her feelings how they manifested. She would rather coddle Dale, like a child, than hurt him. But that softness she sought for could not be found within her. So, she said nothing and knew the best thing for her to do was send Dale away.

Everything okay, asked Dale, turning around in his seat to look behind him to find Kajal staring back at him.

Yes. I have to make another phone call, said Kajal, moving her wide gaze now at the ground beneath him.

Okay. With who?

Kareena. I have to see if it's okay we're both staying here.

She doesn't know?

No.

Any news on her father?

No, I haven't heard anything. I'm gonna call her from the bedroom, okay?

Sure.

Okay.

Kajal turned to walk away and almost fell down; she had become lightheaded and caught herself by falling onto the backend of the couch.

I'm not feeling good, Dale.

Dale stood up from the chair and helped lift her up by keeping his hands on her waist.

You should lie down, Kajal. The call can wait.

Can you get me a glass of water, please?

Yes. Please sit, though.

She did, and Dale ran into the kitchen, grabbed a glass from the cabinet, and filled it with water from the tap. The whole time Dale was getting her water, Kajal held onto the arm of the couch as if she could slip off it and fall onto the floor.

Why don't you just rest, repeated Dale, handing her the glass.

I just want to call Kareena first.

I think we should take you to the hospital.

No. I'm okay. Let me just make the call.

What if it is the virus Kajal, asked Dale.

I don't know. I'll die then.

Don't say that.

Maybe I'm just sick.

You are sick.

I hate hospitals.

You can't stay like this, Kajal. We have to do something.

Can you get me medicine? Like, Nyquil? Can you go to the store and get it for me? I think I just need to sleep it off.

I can do that, said Dale, happy to be given a task.

Kajal gently pushed herself off the couch and shuffled towards the bedroom.

I just need to make this phone call, then I can rest. I want to make sure Kareena's not on her way back here.

How can she come back? There are no flights running out of New York. How would she get here? Why don't you just text her?

She doesn't respond to my messages. She hasn't since she left. I'd feel better if we spoke.

Okay, said Dale, giving up.

Kajal never turned her head back to say goodbye. She was afraid that if she did not concentrate fully on her footing, she would never make it to the bedroom. Dale watched her walk away from the living room. He feared her insincerity was a sign that she did not care whether he came back with her medicine or not.

Inside the bedroom, she closed the door behind her and lay on the bed, exhausted. She closed her eyes, wanting to sleep, but something inside her would not allow her to. She felt restless and exhausted simultaneously. She focused on all the individual parts of her body that hurt, and she wished the soreness in her throat to go away, the pain in her chest to go away, and the pain in her head to go away.

Why did this happen to me, she asked herself.

Kajal opened her WhatsApp messages. She texted a *Hey* into their conversation, and she dropped the phone onto the mattress beside her, closed her eyes, and finally fell asleep.

She woke up minutes later to the sensation of her phone vibrating beside her head. Kareena was trying to Facetime her. Kajal sat up quickly and checked her face in the mirror. She looked messy and sick. Her hair was tangled and disheveled and tied in knots. Furious at how she looked, Kajal quickly ran her fingers through her hair, attempting to fix it, and sat down onto the mattress. And when she went to open the call, it had dropped, and she panicked, realizing she had missed Kareena's call.

Fuck, she whispered under her breath.

Kajal quickly returned to the Facetime app and tried to call Kareena back, this time not caring what she looked like.

Heeeey, exclaimed Kareena, opening the call.

Hey, sorry about that. How are you? I've been trying to get in touch with you!

Sorry. I haven't looked at my phone much.

Kareena looked sad. She was not the girl Kajal knew in school. There was a lack of energy. A sadness she was trying to suppress. Kajal felt like she was looking into a mirror.

Kareena turned the camera lens on her phone to show Kajal her view. Through Kajal's phone's screen, she could see the railing of a balcony and, in the distance, a hilly pasture that spread for miles beyond her vantage point. There was a road alongside the house where a car had been driving slowly past it until it disappeared, passing a slew of cypress trees trimmed perfectly and that which trailed alongside the road until its end.

There was a glare on Kajal's phone, and she had the impulse to divert her eyes away from the mosaic of light that shone down above the hills in the background. But she squinted her eyes and waited patiently for it to pass.

Wow, it's beautiful wherever you.

We're in France, said Kareena. A friend of my families invited us here. They thought it would be good for my father to be out of the city and into the country side. They've been very welcoming to us.

How is your father?

He's okay. It's scary because of the obvious but it's a lot less stressful than being in London. It's beautiful here and my father seems happy. There's a lot of space for my family and opportunity to walk around in the fresh country air.

That's amazing. I'm so happy to hear you all are doing well.

Yeah. For now. How are you? Asked Kareena

Kajal didn't know how to respond. She was afraid to come off as negative. She didn't want to make Kareena unhappy. She didn't want to tell her the truth.

I'm okay, said Kajal.

Yeah?

Yeah.

Good. Are you alone?

No, Dale's with me. Is that okay?

Of course. I can see your still at the apartment. It makes me happy to think of you there.

It's been really lovely to have the space, but I feel bad. I feel like I'm taking advantage.

No, you're not. We didn't know this was going to happen. Im happy you're there. Truly. My parent's are relieved.

Well, tell them I am forever grateful.

Is Dale upset with me?

No. Not at all.

You didn't tell him?

I told him some thing's. Not everything.

Okay. Is that okay? Are you mad at me?

No. Not any more. I was. But I don't care anymore. The world is too fucked up now for me to care about that. It's part of the past.

Well, I'm sorry anyway. I acted like a fool. I would never do some of the things I did in school again. It wasn't even that long ago but it feels like centuries.

Yeah, I know what you mean.

I think being around so much death and suffering changes you.

They have morgues on the street here. They have one just down the block. The hospitals are packed with people.

That's horrible. So scary.

I don't even want to go outside. I don't want to look at them.

Yeah, I can understand that.

Classes are virtual now. No one is allowed to go on campus.

Interesting. When did you hear that?

This morning. It came in an email.

Good thing I made the decision not to go back then.

Yeah, it's like not even worth it for me now. I didn't plan to spend this much money on a virtual program.

You should consider taking a leave of absence then.

Maybe. Im indecisive. Im too depressed to do anything to be honest.

Kajal turned to cough and used the inside of her elbow to cover her mouth, obscuring Kareena's view.

Are you sick, asked Kareena.

I, uh, yes, I am unfortunetly.

Are you okay?

I'll be fine. Dale is out getting me medicine.

Do you think it's…

I don't know, said Kajal cutting her off. I hope not. If it is that means Dale probably has it too.

Is he showing symptoms?

No, he slept on the couch. I told him to leave but he doesn't want to.

Good. I'm glad he's there. I'm glad you're not alone.

Sometimes I feel like I don't deserve company.

Why? Asked Kareena

I don't know. I think I hate myself sometimes and that makes me so sad to say, said Kajal feeling tears start to come down her face.

Oh, honey. You're an amazing person. Why do you hate yourself?

Because I have nothing, you know? I have nothing I value anymore. Anything I had, I lost.

So you have to find yourself again. And that's okay. That's a very human thing to feel. Especially now. But you have a lot to offer the world.

Thanks for saying that, said Kajal.

Finishing grad school isn't the most important thing Kajal. You're health is. You don't have to take on the world right now. You've had a tough year. You are allowed to go at your own speed. With the world changing as it is, the only thing we can do for ourselves is to protect ourselves. Dive into the person we always wanted to be. There's no more changing for other people or the world. We have to become the women we always wanted to.

You're right but how do we do that?

I don't know, said Kareena honestly. But we'll find out.

This virus, whatever it is, it can't last forever, right?

I hope not.

And what are we gonna do when it's over? Go back to the world as it was?

No way. I'm never going back there.

Me too.

I love you, said Kareena out of nowhere.

Kajal smiled and felt happy.

I love you too, said Kajal.

Kareena's mother walked in and asked her to help her with something in the kitchen. Kareena had to say goodbye, but she promised to keep Kajal up to date on her plans. When Kajal hung up the phone, she felt even more tired. There was relief in her conversation with Kareena that made her cry when the phone call was over. She sobbed until all of her tears fell out. Her eyes were closing without her permission. She got up from the bed and went into the hallway to check and see if Dale was back.

Dale? She said from the hallway, one foot lingering inside the room. Kajal's words echoed back to her like a boomerang. Dale had yet to come back.

Kajal went back inside the bedroom, closed the door behind her, fell on the mattress hard, closed her eyes, and finally allowed herself to fall asleep.

XVIX

Apex

Kajal dreamed Dale sitting in the middle of an empty 14th Street, in the plaza of Union Square Park. He sat up, observing the green letters of the Whole Foods sign across the street, waiting for the dizziness to end. His mouth was dry, his lips cracked. He hadn't eaten anything and thought incorrectly that it was relevant to the cause of the blurred image of the city landscape before him. He was bleeding on his forehead. He didn't remember getting off the train or even what got him out of the subway car, up the staircases, and out of the train station to the street.

He did not remember getting hit in the head but was aware of the droplets of blood that fell from his temple, making a breadcrumb trail from his feet to the edge of the steps he sat on.

Dale looked both ways down the block. It wasn't the lack of people that concerned him, but the absence of noise and traffic in what he knew to be one of the city's most congested areas. He hadn't been to this area since the new year. The usual sound of car and biker traffic and the Hare Krishna dancers were all absent. What was present was a silence that permeated between the buildings, which traveled for miles. He knew nothing would be different if he walked 10 blocks south from where he sat. He could hear the absence of noise from all around the city. The silence blanketed every crevice of the neighborhood.

Dale confused the city for an abandoned sound stage used in films. Staring down 14th Street, he thought about what sound stages used for film sets must look like after all the actors and crew left. He'd seen something similar years ago when his family took a trip to California, and they visited Universal Studios in Los Angeles and took a tour of the lot. The facades of fake buildings, streets, and neighborhoods all there waiting to be recycled for the sake of entertainment, to help create the worlds inside one's favorite TV shows, films, and commercials.

Dale moved his foot away from where the blood trail began and wiped the residue of a single droplet that stained the white part of his shoe off onto the curb lane. Observing the city landscape, Dale wondered if what he saw happening to the city he knew so well an example of life-mimicking art. Because the changes he saw happening in the city weren't a manifestation of some studio executive or some hungry writer trying to connect with a commercial audience. What Dale could only gauge at a distance was that whatever was occurring inside the city he was born into, he could only comprehend at the level he did because of the films and TV shows he watched throughout his life. He understood this new reality only from what he had learned from fiction.

Dale stood up too quickly and had to orient himself. His vision waned as he failed to remain standing. Walking two feet from the steps, he fell down onto his stomach. He stayed still for a moment, waiting for his vision to realign. The streets, buildings, and lampposts in front of him were all out of focus and moving in a wave-like motion as if the foundation of the ground he laid upon was of a cracked spinning record. Once his vision crystalized again, he stood up slowly, careful not to go too fast.

He headed west on 14th Street. A breeze reminded him of the cut he had on his forehead. The wound stung from the open air; he touched it, wincing from the pain. A slight drizzle of rain started to come down, the sky turned gray above him, and wind gusted dirt and leaves around him, indicating a storm was on its way. In the distance, he could see the heavy weather system approaching and silent threads of lightning thrashing above the mid-sized buildings towards the western sky.

The sudden appearance of a storm confused Dale. There was no sign of rain or stormy weather when he left the apartment. He didn't have an umbrella with him to protect himself from getting wet. It bothered him more than usual how unpredictable everything had seemed as of late. He couldn't tell if this is what the natural transition into adulthood felt like or if the world was ending. There was no sense of order or normalcy, which he now craved, more than safety.

Looking into the swirl of the clouds approaching, Dale felt a kind of psychosis take over. He no longer felt weighted down by gravity; nothing kept him anchored to the sidewalk. Inside his chest, a lightness appeared. Whether it was from the safety of being alone on the street or the approaching eye of the storm, Dale felt a sudden shift in energy, but he did not understand how to release it.

On impulse, he felt the energy exude from his diaphragm and push past his jaw. He screamed, looking up towards the sky. The sound of thunder crashed above him competing with the sound of Dale's voice, and he screamed as if to fight it. A cool wind breeze passed him.

When Dale's screaming subsided, his diaphragm settled into its lower frame, and as the storm approached him, the word *wow* escaped through him, like a ghost in a film fading from one world into the next.

In all its unpredictability and chaos, the storm and its changes to the city landscape Dale found exciting. He watched the show unfold before him as if he were a separate entity; the big popcorn epic climax approaching. Holding onto nothing now, Dale left the present, peaked into the future, and saw in his mind what the world would like right before it ended. After the affluent had left and migrated to Mars, the streets were emptied as they were now, and the rest of the world perished from fire, ice, or an unknown airborne disease.

If he was going to die, Kajal would be the person he'd want to be with in his final moments, even if he wasn't hers. Even if he knew she loved someone else or had never loved him, he would rather be standing next to her than not have her by his side.

Dale stopped at the corner and looked again at the gray folding clouds that formed above him, taking it all in. It was so quiet except for the noise from the storm and the pitter patter of rain falling on the sidewalk.

There was a chill in his lungs now. He tried to breathe in through the cold by taking in big, deep, conscious breaths, breathing in through his nose and out through his mouth. His irises turned into wide black holes that revealed nothing. Dale's mouth was slightly agape; no air was coming in or leaving. When he went to take a step forward, he could feel his feet not hit the ground when it dropped but fall straight through the air that sat above his ankles.

As he took another step, Dale lifted up from off the ground completely, both feet in the air now, and was projected forward into the sky, on an invisible conveyor belt he had no control of.

Maybe this was the remnants of his Catholic school upbringing, but he often felt somebody was watching him. An invisible audience. God. An angel that was a departed relative. It didn't really matter to Dale who it was, but in the time he spent alone in his parents' backyard growing up, he became aware of an invisible presence and always felt the need to entertain them. Acting like a buffoon when alone. Imitating specific nuances of his favorite comedic actors and characters from his favorite TV shows, films, or cartoons. Ending a bit, only happening in his head, with a punchline, then adding a beat by looking into a camera that was never there to acknowledge to his audience that he, too, was in on the joke.

This audience was who Dale thought about when his feet lifted off from the sidewalk and into the air. He took a moment to check himself. The weightlessness of his body floating midair, above the sidewalk, made him light-headed, and a wave of nausea passed through his stomach. With caution, Dale tried to keep his eyes open and take in his new surroundings. His mouth now caked in a dry coating and he would kill for a glass of water. In a disoriented moment, Dale looked down towards his feet and watched himself flying upwards, floating further away from the sidewalk, not knowing how he got here or how to navigate this new mode of transportation. If someone were to spot Dale now, he'd look like a child's balloon, lost from its holder, floating upwards towards the sky, running along the building's facade.

He stopped midair, worried someone might see him. He paused in an awkward position and tried to move again but had only made things worse, and he was now hanging upside down, with his two legs above him in a scissor-kick position. Dale made an attempt to swim upwards, to try and get himself back upright. But all that would happen with each attempt was that he'd fall back down into a 360 degree loop back into the upside-down position he started in.

Dale stayed stagnant in the air as the rain fell harder on him. He could feel a heaviness start to form in his head from all the blood that was rushing to his face. He could not figure out how to fly consistently in a straight line or get himself down back onto the sidewalk. He tried moving forward, reaching his arms west, hoping to pull himself in that direction, but each attempt was met with failure.

In a moment of psychical exhaustion, Dale rested his eyes and tried not to move. He thought about when he first learned to swim properly in a pool, holding his breath and keeping his arms by his side and legs out above the water.

His body sank closer to the ground when he released the air from his lungs. But with each new deep inhale, his body would return to where he started. He paid attention to his body's ebb and flow based on the types of breaths he would take. He started to take faster breaths and move his arms and legs in a swimming pattern, and only then could he navigate in the direction he wanted to go towards.

Dale found himself right side up finally, again, moving west as he intended, finding it better to relax his body and breathe in these quick, deep breaths while moving his arms and legs simultaneously and give in to any thought or effort that felt forced and have whatever that was allowing him to do this guide him to wherever it was he wanted to go.

In the corner of his left eye, he saw another body fly past him. For a moment he thought it was Kajal and almost screamed her name. But it was a different woman, flying at a similar speed. She was flat on her stomach, not yet fully equipped on the mechanics of using her body to do whatever it was they were doing.

Help! The woman cried, calling out to Dale.

This was the first person he'd seen since waking up on the steps outside the train station.

I don't know how to help you, screamed Dale.

What is going on? The woman cried. How do we get back down? What is going on with the world?

You have to breathe…I think, said Dale.

Breathe! What does that mean? Asked the woman.

A strong wind came and blew the lady off in another direction. Dale felt helpless but could do nothing but watch her float away, going rogue towards its own random destination, like a deflated balloon.

Dale paused from flying for a moment and watched her fade in the distance, feeling helpless. He contemplated whether or not he should go after her, but the rain was too strong, and she'd been taken so far fast from where he was that she'd become impossible to reach. What he saw of her now was only a black dot that he knew to be her.

He started to hear other voices above him. Dale looked up and saw the soles of other people's shoes floating above his head, having conversations.

Dale lifted himself higher, flying above the rain toward the groups of people flying above him. This was where everyone had gone. Dale looked down, and the view reminded him of his experiences on airplanes, just at the beginning of take off. He could still differentiate the buildings from one another. He was never afraid of heights, but this was an exception. He felt a rush of adrenaline throughout his body. There was no sense of danger or fear that he'd fall and break every bone in his body and die. He didn't question it anymore. Whatever was happening to him, it wasn't happening to just him but to everyone in the city.

He flew through the groups of people, some of whom seemed so relaxed in their faces it was like they'd been living at this altitude their entire lives. There were thousands of them, separated into different social groups divided by those who have come quickly to understand this new way of living and those hanging upside down, alone, in fear, trying to understand the tempo of their breath. He asked someone for directions to the pharmacy, and they pointed in a direction. The man's face seemed bothered by Dale's question, as he was one of the people who quickly adapted to this new environment. And after he answered, the man turned back and continued on with his conversation.

Holding his breath, Dale descended onto the sidewalk before the pharmacy safely. It was open, next to a café that was closed. The café had an outdoor patio with its tables uncovered, and chairs flipped and stacked on top of one another. The patio was under a stained hunter-green awning, and due to the forecasted sky, the tables and chairs were covered in a dark shadow, making it look more bleak and miserable than it usually would have.

Before heading inside, he turned around, looked upward toward the sky where he came from, and noticed the horizontal bodies flying above him. That was all he could see of them now. Little black shadows flying in various directions.

The store was empty, as expected. There wasn't a soul walking the aisles or anybody waiting behind the cash register to take the next customer's turn. The ceiling lights flickered fluorescent beams down onto the store's merchandise for no one to buy. As he walked in, Dale had to squint his eyes to adjust to the store's horrible light fixture. He walked through the aisles, searching for the cold and flu section. He hoped this was all Kajal would need. He prayed she would not die from the virus that was spreading. Though, based on his commute to the pharmacy, he believed they may have more significant problems than the virus to deal with; afraid when he went back to the apartment he'd find Kajal stuck to the ceiling, not knowing how to get herself down.

Looking through the options on the shelf, he picked up a bottle of Nyquil and a saltine spray with some throat lozenges, grabbed a mint tea box from another aisle, and walked to the back of the store where the pharmacy was located. At first, he didn't see anyone but heard rummaging in the back past where his eyes could see.

Hello, questioned Dale.

Be out in a second, yelled a polite-sounding voice from behind the counter.

Dale was hoping, due to the circumstances, that he would not have to pay. He thought about running out of the pharmacy with the Nyquil and saltine spray. But nonetheless he waited and before long, a short, balding, gray-haired man wearing a long white doctor's coat and a face mask came up to the counter and smiled.

How can I help you, asked the older man in a gentle voice.

I just wanted to buy these, said Dale, laying the items he had chosen onto the counter in front of the man.

Do you have a thermometer, asked the older gentleman, looking at the products Dale had placed before him. You'll be needing one of those.

I'm not sure.

Let me grab one for you. They're pretty inexpensive. Are these items just for you?

No, for my girlfriend.

Does she have a fever?

I don't know.

Here.

The old man disappeared from behind the counter again and returned with a perfectly new packaged digital thermometer.

Just 20 dollars more, he said.

For a thermometer?

You'll be needing it! We don't have any more left. This one's for you.

You don't have any of the cheaper thermometers? The ones you put under your tongue or something like that?

I'm all out, I'm afraid.

Where do you put this one?

In your ear for two seconds, and then it beeps.

Okay, said Dale, annoyed.

The older man typed something into his computer.

Are you the only one working here?

Yup. As of now. They had to let everyone else go. I was the manager. Now I'm everything else.

Even the pharmacist?

It's not like I'm writing prescriptions. I'm just handing out to those who have come to pick up their medications.

Have many people been coming in?

Not many, actually, the old man said with a smile.

Dale gave the man his credit card. The total came out to be $53.25.

Will you need a receipt?

No, I don't think so.

Dale watched the man type something again into his computer.

Have you been outside, by any chance?

No, I haven't stepped out yet. Not since I started my shift this morning. But I've seen them. Were you up there?

Yeah. I was.

How was it?

Hard to say, really. It hasn't happened to you?

Not yet! Maybe it won't happen to everyone. I wouldn't mind, personally, finding out what it would be like to fly. It must be wonderful. I always wanted to. Maybe soon I'll get my chance. A few people have come in here spooked, saying one of their friends just elevated off the ground mid-conversation, and they couldn't do anything about it! Kind of funny if you ask me! They just watched their friend float away. HaHa! It happened to somebody's mother! You should have seen the look on their faces. They were so scared!

Funny, huh, said Dale with a sigh.

Imagine that. The day we find out humans can fly, the only thing we can talk about is this damn virus going around!

The older man gave a soft laugh.

Yeah. That's true, said Dale, confused overall by the man's joyful demeanor.

Be careful out there. Don't die. It's the end of the world, said the man laughing, gleaming at the pharmacy's ceiling.

Is it?

Sure. How else can you explain everything that's going on?

I didn't know the end of the world would happen so soon.

Well, it's the end of the world as we know it! That's for sure. Everything's going to change now.

Change how?

I don't know. Have to find out, I guess. Hope I stay alive long enough to see it! Do you need a face mask, by any chance? It might help with the flying? I think that's why it hasn't happened yet for me. I've had mine on all morning!

How long do I have to wear it for?

I would recommend not taking it off.

Forever?

Yes. Unless you're showering, maybe. I keep mine on then, too. I like it, though. I find it kind of cozy, to be honest. There are waterproof ones on aisle seven.

Thank you. But I think I'm okay. I kind of like flying.

I bet you do. But here, take this one. It's free. Might as well.

Sure. Thank you, said Dale, taking the facemask off the counter.

Stay safe. Don't die! I think that's gonna be the new *Have a good day!* Tell all your friends from now on, *Don't die! Get home safe! Hope to see you next time!* Remember to wear your face mask. I think those will come in handy, eventually.

Dale smiled at the man and took what he bought from off the counter. He waved goodbye and once outside the pharmacy flew north towards Kareena's apartment.

From just above the fire escape, Dale opened the window and flew into the living room, landing softly on the rug in Kareena's apartment. Once inside, he closed and locked the window behind him. He checked to see if it was locked securely, and when he turned away, it would not open again.

He went to take off his face mask but decided to leave it on.

There was no sign of Kajal. The apartment was dark, messy, and quiet, but Dale felt relaxed being in its space. Happy to be home, that being wherever Kajal was. He went inside the kitchen to wash his hands from the sink and dried them with a towel used mostly for drying dirty dishes. Dale put a pot on the stove with some water to boil. He turned on the gas, and a flame puffed under the pot. Dale turned the nozzle down and lowered the flame to a comfortable light. He poured a serving of the Nyquil into the little plastic cup at the top. Then poured the hot water he boiled into a mug for tea and made his way down the hallway towards the bedroom where Kajal was sleeping.

He opened the door with his shoulder and peeked inside before heading in. All he could see was the shape of her from under the comforter, the comforter acting like a cocoon wrapped around her body.

Kajal, Dale whispered. And then he walked into the bedroom further, pushing the door open to pass through its threshold, and softly let the door close shut from behind him.

He placed the tea and medicine on the bedside table and pulled down the comforter to reveal the left side of Kajal's sleeping face.

He sat beside her on the bed for a moment, and with the back of his hand, he pressed it up against the middle part of her forehead to check and see if she was warm. She was.

Dale stood up from the bed and left the room, not wanting to disturb her further. He closed the door quietly behind him. To his knowledge, Kajal had not moved or noticed that he was in the room with her.

Dale went into the living room, suddenly exhausted. He sat down on the couch. From inside the apartment, he could hear no sounds, just the wind he heard from outside the building. It felt as if the world had paused momentarily, and Kajal and Dale were frozen still in time.

He could hear the sound of train tracks rumbling in the distance beneath him. He laid down on his side, his legs bent like he was kneeling, and he rested his head on the flat rigged cushion and looked outside the window at the evening's blue light.

A man he did not recognize was standing over him, taking his temperature. And with each heavy breath,

Dale's eyelids moved closer and closer together, a white light shining above them, moving back and forth between each eye, until they were shut by a gloved hand, and then the light was gone, and Dale saw nothing but darkness.

XX

Forever

Kajal woke up in Kareena's bedroom drenched in a puddle of her own sweat. Her fever was gone, but her throat was still sore, and she fell into a coughing fit. When more mucus came to the surface, she spit the mucus out into an already folded napkin, threw her legs off the edge of the bed, and rested them softly on the floor. She had felt like she had been hit by a truck.

There was no tea or medicine on the bedside table. She must have dreamt that. She wondered if Dale had come back from the pharmacy with her medicine, desperate for its sleep-inducing liquid to force sleep on her and to wake up better and past this illness. All she wanted was to get past whatever disease had infected her body. She wanted it gone. She wanted to feel better.

She forced herself to the door and entered the hallway. It was quiet in the apartment. Kajal went into the bathroom and turned on the hot shower. The steam filled the bathroom walls quickly. She stepped in and stood hunched over under the hot water, still. She stayed like this until she grew restless, turned the shower head off, and stepped out of the bathroom. She returned to Kareena's bedroom with just a towel on and found her phone to look at the time. A few hours had past since her call with Kareena.

Worried, she went into the living room to look out the window, her energy and strength coming back to her with each step she took forward. Outside, the street was barren of people. All the trees now dead on the block from the winter's chill. A light bed of snow rested on the sidewalk. Why had Dale not come back? Remembering her dream, she feared she had peaked into the future. She didn't want Dale to be hurt. She didn't want to live in the apartment alone. She rushed and put on warm clothes, ran down the apartment's stairwell and exited the building. She saw him in the hospital with a minor concussion; the emergency room packed with people. But when she stepped onto the sidewalk, and saw him coming from the distance, wrapped warmly in his jacket, holding a plastic bag from the pharmacy she felt relief.

When they entered the apartment the heat was intense and had pleased them for a little while, but it had become hard to breathe, and Dale opened a window. Kajal was so happy he had come home. He made each of them chai with the spices Kajal taught him to use, and they sat in the living room watching a movie on the television. They fell asleep and woke up. It was now dark outside. Dale followed Kajal into the bedroom, and he lay down beside her, finally. They were too tired to move. Dale and Kajal looked up at the ceiling, in their mind ruminating thoughts lay still, quiet, they tried to ignore them and force sleep. It was so quiet outside that it made the insides of homes and the hallways and buildings feel like a television on mute; light and movement occurred, but sound failed to manifest itself.

His ghost would remain with them for a few years more. Hussein watched Dale and Kajal from the corner of the bedroom. They could feel his presence lingering, but neither of them would say. Like his mother, he would give them space to heal and grow new roots and leaves and blossom into their new selves; in their own time. And only when that time came would he leave them. To where? Not even he knew. Only the memory of her father would last. And Kajal would remember the best of him.

Dale turned on his side and closed his eyes. Kajal watched him. She would have to tell him everything, but in her own way, on her own time, when she understood it all herself; what this year was for her. And his heart will break. She knew that and was afraid to be the one to break it, but she knew in her heart he would stay. She trusted him more than anyone; that's why she could abuse him. Take advantage of him. Break his heart. Treat him like she felt inside. She could be her true self with no one else, and she was angry, tired, and fed up. She hated the world and, therefore, hated herself. Hated to have been born a woman in this world. A brown woman set up for failure. Dale had everything she wanted, including love for her, and he could endure the toxic elements of their relationship, simply because of the tumultuous home he grew up in. Because of his father's rage, he could take on hers. It was familiar to him.

It was not an excuse. Kajal did not want to be this way forever but did not know how to change, move past her own ego, and not see herself as a victim. She was a victim. A victim of poverty. A victim of grief. A victim to her father's rage, ego, and pain. And yet she loved him. She would have to do the work he did not. They both would have to do the work their father's did not know how to, having been born at the time they were. In the new world, there was no room for these types of mistakes. They knew better. Their life would have to be dedicated to change, and its constant presence.

Dale would have to break his own heart to let hers grow, and the pain would feel like fire burning from under his skin; he would feel like compost for her garden and she fodder for his stories. They would have to move on from the people they were in their previous life and step into their new roles together. If he still wanted to be with Kajal, he would have to ask himself questions that felt impossible to answer and then decide with a conscious mind to walk with her into this new phase of their life. But he would take on this burden. She would watch him educate himself. He could do hard things and she knew that. He had the strength to see things through, till their end. It was his own form of self-torture to take action and live by his own morals, and vision. He'd do it to have her, and then for himself, and learn self love and self compassion through the process. And she will love him for that. Once he learned to love himself, she would love him more than she ever had. He'd have her in the palm of his hand and he in her's, and they, no matter what happens, whatever life brings them, would not lose each other. Even when the world falls apart, they'd have each other; and at least that was something. Some people have nothing. Some people choose nothing and other's the world gives nothing. But nothing would separate the couple after the work they'd put into their relationship, starting from this moment, in this bed, in this time. The decision to stay together would be the light that would stay lit at the end of a long, dark tunnel. The past year remnants of a dream, residue of the life they committed to, however long ago. They would break each other to keep each other, and grow again from that. And for that they would learn, was worth it.

Acknowledgments

I'd like to thank Lee Williams, who was my first audience for this book. He saw it in its rawest form and continued to encourage me. We workshopped his screenplay and my novel during Covid, on Zoom, to help keep both our heads out from the dark, and now that screenplay has been filmed and this book published. I want to thank the following readers: Joseph Tuzzolino, Steve Lazickas, Christine Nassar, and Maureen Linker. Few people will read your unfinished 300-page novel, but these people did or tried. Gilbert Girion, who taught me everything I know about writing. It's just too bad he doesn't like my writing (if you're not laughing, he is). To the Churchhill Tavern New York Story Night group. Daniel Sullivan, for listening to ten-minute audio messages of me reading the chapters to him as if I was Ian Mckellen doing Shakespeare. Cathy Gigante-Brown for years of advice and support. To Vinnie Corbo, without whom this book would literally not exist. I want to thank the music by The National and The Swell Season whose music, like a friend, lifts me when I'm down. Their music never helps me forget but rather reminds me I am not alone. I'd like to thank the work of the following writers: Haruki Murakami, Sally Rooney, Jonathan Lethem, Lauren Groff, Cormac McCarthy, and Kurt Vonnegut. I have each one of their phone numbers. The Wasti family: Samina Wasti, Madiha Wasti, Aatir Wasti, and Hussain Wasti for allowing me to be a part of their family. To my Mom, Dad, and Brother, whose constant love and support guide me. They are my strength and the foundation I stand on. I love you all. I hope this book makes you proud. Also, to my mother for stealing paper from her bank job to print out copious copies of this book for me to edit. Nothing more punk rock than that. And to my wife, Fariha, who shared her life with me these past fifteen years. Without her, there would be no life to fill these characters with. She is my muse and inspiration. And to our cat Ada, who helped me kill my darlings.

www.ingramcontent.com/pod-product-compliance
Lightning Source LLC
Chambersburg PA
CBHW030246030726
47493CB00023B/614

* 9 7 8 1 9 6 3 3 5 9 2 3 7 *